DEATH IN THE
BACK SEAT

DEATH IN THE BACK SEAT

DOROTHY CAMERON DISNEY

WILDSIDE PRESS

DEDICATION

For Mac

Published by Wildside Press LLC.
www.wildsidebooks.com

CHAPTER ONE

Hilltop House

Jack and I returned to New York a month ago. It is dull but we like it. Our friends come to see us, crowd our small apartment, drink our liquor and talk endlessly of books and plays and life and generalities. No one ever mentions our stay in the country. So far as the crowd is concerned, the entire State of Connecticut has fallen under a conversational ban.

But, as is natural, everyone thinks and wonders about those confused and dreadful events which occurred so long ago and yet so recently. I think, too. Memories get in my way and spoil my sleep. I pound my pillow and close my eyes, and there rises before me in the darkness a big white house, gaunt and stark against a barren hill; there comes to my ears the ghostly echo of a dog's wild barking: and I fancy that I can smell once more the peculiar, unmistakable odor of earth, freshly dug.

Small things bother me: the unexpected rustle of a newspaper, the stir of a curtain at the window, the sound of a footfall in the hall outside our living room. I find it hard to sit quietly when the doorbell rings, and I've developed a passion for buying lamps and keeping them brightly lighted.

My nervous system isn't what it was, Jack, my husband, who is sensitive, imaginative and, in addition, a grand guy, knows that. It was he who suggested I write this story. We talked the matter out, and borrowing from the psychologists, finally decided that for me perhaps the best way to forget would be first to remember. Once I set down on paper a record of everything which occurred between the 20th of last March and the 9th of April. I trust and believe my mind will be free at last.

On the second day of January, exactly six months ago, Jack and I changed our post-office address from New York City to Crockford, Connecticut. Our plan, and a good plan it seemed, was that Jack should paint, that I should write, that we should live simply and save large sums of money. We knew very little about Connecticut, and our first information concerning Crockford was gathered from the following dignified advertisement in *The Nation*:

> Colonial cottage, dating back to 1760, charmingly furnished, modern conveniences, 35 acres of beautiful hilly country, advantages of Long Island Sound, $30 a month—Luella Coatesnash, Hilltop House, Crockford, Conn.

In print the proposition sounded perfect. We favored both price and location. Our budget wouldn't cover guests, and we hoped to avoid expensive and riotous weekends. At the tag end of two city years, we had wearied of liquor bills, hangover mornings and Bohemia's doubtful pleasures, and longed for the reputed peace and quiet of country life.

Crockford, Connecticut, 27 miles beyond New Haven, is more than 100 miles from New York and is difficult to reach except by motor car, although buses do leave New Haven twice daily. The cottage described in the advertisement was six miles from Crockford, long, country miles along a rutted country road. On a December afternoon, accompanied by a dyspeptic, melancholy real-estate agent, we inspected the cottage. It was a small square house of the salt-box type; it sat primly at the foot of a steeply climbing hill; it looked very clean, sedate and beautiful against the snow-white landscape. Enchanted by our first glimpse of an unspoiled New England, Jack and I caught each other's hands and stared open-mouthed. Yellow pines encircled the cottage; a flagged path led to its lovely fan-light door; a stone fence neatly framed the cottage, the pines and a minute patch of land. In recollection the whole day stands forth as singularly gay and foolish.

"What's the fence for?" Jack asked.

"Maybe it's to keep out wolves."

"What if there aren't any wolves?"

"Never mind. We'll have each other."

Ten days later we moved in. The loneliness and isolation were pleasant in the beginning. We enjoyed owning a telephone which seldom rang and looking out upon a road where the simultaneous passage of two cars constituted a traffic jam. We delighted in undressing shamelessly, with no thought of lowering the window shades. Everything was different, fresh, exciting—the sweeping distances of hills and trees, the sparkling air, the deep cathedral quiet, the early darkness which fell swiftly like a curtain.

The modern conveniences turned out to be a small, undependable bathroom and electric lights. Floor plugs were entirely absent and the fixtures were horrible, bulbous affairs hung from ceilings so low that for a time Jack, who is tall, threatened to make immediate alterations with an ax. "If I crack my head once more, Lola, that living-room dingus goes. You needn't laugh. I mean it."

"You'll learn to duck."

He did learn. Also, later on, we learned something about the erratic quality of rural electric power. City born and bred, serenely unaware of the complexities of country existence, we didn't dream that our power would fail with every heavy rain and that we would spend many a stormy night in the dark. Nor could we anticipate the havoc which thunderstorms would play with telephone wires.

While I mastered oil-stove cookery, quite a trick in itself, and while

Jack cautiously investigated wood chopping, the first month slipped past. Various unexpected irritations developed. We ran out of cigarettes at odd hours and missed the corner delicatessen. Also we discovered that our budget had been exceedingly optimistic. The Crockford tradespeople, to the last man labored under the misapprehension that New Yorkers could and would pay double for everything.

Then there was the pipeless furnace which Jack, softened by years of apartment dwelling, found an insoluble mystery. After two weeks, when we alternately burned and froze, he threw up his hands and we hired Silas Elkins, local talent recommended by our landlady. Silas was a thin, gangling individual, habitually dressed in overalls, usually accompanied by a small, timid, sand-colored dog. One look at Silas convinced me that he was incompetent, and further acquaintanceship failed to change my mind. In addition, he had bad manners, arrogance and an astounding conceit. Except for himself, so far as I know, he admired only one person in the world—and that person was Luella Coatesnash. Long before I first laid eyes on him, he had adopted all her ways and notions as his own. He quoted her almost daily and did everything in his power to force our regime to duplicate hers. Nearly every day I would hear him and Jack engaged in battle.

"You're using too much coal," Jack would begin mildly.

"If you folks would go to bed at nine o'clock when other folks do and not want heat till twelve…"

"But we do want heat till twelve, and we aren't up at six when you fire the furnace."

"Mrs. Coatesnash has her furnace fired at six sharp. She's had it done at six o'clock for twenty years."

Silas continued to adjust our heat and, consequently, our habits, in the manner he considered fitting. We retired earlier and rose earlier. We hadn't the money to import labor, and it was, for all practical purposes anyway, impossible to replace Silas; poor as they were, the families living in and around Crockford did not work out. They would sell us fresh eggs, chickens, home-made jellies at prodigious prices, but they declined to clear the snow from our driveway or wash our windows. All such chores fell to Silas. He was the handy man—if the term is loosely applied—for the vicinity. Perched atop a battered bicycle, he pedaled about on neighborhood errands, doing each task arrogantly, stupidly, inefficiently.

His total unawareness of his own limitations was perhaps his most exasperating quality. In some mysterious fashion he had convinced himself he was an instinctive, untaught master of all trades. He told Jack how to paint, he told me how to write. I caught him one morning telling a county road surveyor how to straighten out a curve in the road. On another occasion after assuring me he was an expert plumber, he spent four solid hours in a fruitless attempt to repair a leaky water tap.

I find myself painting an unpleasant picture, and that first month, colored in recollection with the glitter of frosty stars, the smell of wood smoke and the soft constant flutter of snow at the windows was, in many respects, perfect. Jack and I got a great deal done. From nine until twelve we worked, calling encouragement back and forth. Lunch over, we hurried into coats and galoshes and explored the countryside. Sometimes we took the car, mostly we walked, since Jack liked to carry his pad and sketch a clump of bright red berries, or a stone wall tangled in leafless briars, or a tattered scarecrow, forlorn and desolate in the midst of winter. In the evenings we amused ourselves with the radio and spirited games of double Canfield.

From Silas and a Mr. Brown who delivered our coal we heard rumors of the gay whirl in Crockford—box suppers held monthly at Town Hall, bi-weekly basketball games in the high-school gymnasium, an occasional old-fashioned dance. A town band practiced discordantly once a week, and Silas, who played the cornet, was a regular attendant at these musical festivals. There was even a Wednesday-night and a Saturday-night movie. No one suggested that we take any part in the village activities, and it didn't occur to us to do so. Thus, quite innocently and unknowingly, we gained for ourselves the reputation of being a stand-offish city pair, stuck-up and queer.

If there had been near neighbors, I might have taken the trouble to call. But the cottage was peculiarly isolated. The next house on the road, visible in daylight through a band of separating trees, belonged to Henry Olmstead a New Haven architect, and was occupied by him and his family only during the summer months. On the other side, the west side, sprawled a tumble down windowless ruin part of an estate tied up in family litigation.

That left as neighbors Mrs. Coatesnash our landlady, and Laura Twining, officially her companion but actually maid, cook, masseuse and overworked slavey. Three-quarters of a mile to the north of the cottage, in solitary grandeur, the two women lived in the thirty-room dwelling designated formally as Hilltop House.

Famous locally and built by the first Coatesnash who had emigrated from England to the colonies, Hilltop House clung to the opposite side of the hill which our home faced It was decidedly more impressive for sheer size than for beauty; generations of additions had destroyed any original grace or dignity. In June the dwelling would be mercifully hidden in a thicket of box and oak. In January, looking up and across the rocky, ascending pasture land we could see the upper story of the mansion's three stories, a row of shuttered windows, a towering chimney shaft and a gingerbread cupola adorned by scroll work which somewhat resembled the crocheted edging my mother used to sew on underwear.

Except for the day we signed our lease, we viewed Hilltop House from a distance. Mrs. Coatesnash was an unsocial woman who made it plain that she desired no traffic with impecunious young tenants.

Laura Twining, the companion, was another matter. She had lived ten long years in the country and she loved an audience. We became the audience, more often than we chose. I liked Laura, or perhaps I only pitied her, and I willingly admitted that a little of her company went a long way. Jack frankly detested her. He likes good-looking women. Laura had a kind of peasant stoutness, pale, watering eyes, a prominent shiny nose, and a general air of having slept in her clothes. Her mannerisms were those of the socially insecure. She batted her eyes, she smoothed her hair, she patted her skirts, she straightened her stocking seams, and never got comfortably seated in a chair.

Almost every afternoon one of us would spy Laura striding down the pasture footpath, her thick body bulging in a coon coat, her untidy gray hair straggling from beneath a shapeless hat, her homely face wreathed in the happy smile of a lady about to pay a call. Jack would groan, and I would feel an inward sinking. Neither of us had the heart to be unkind; and when you live in the country, people know you are at home. They look in your yard and see your car.

Consequently we were often bored. Laura's mind had a remarkably tenacious grasp of the obvious, the trivial, the dull. And she was extravagantly loquacious. Commonplace tales of her poverty-stricken childhood in the Middle West and later struggles in New York poured forth in an endless stream; she dwelt tirelessly upon the ten good years spent with Luella Coatesnash.

"It's been a quiet life perhaps, but my future is provided for. I don't have to worry about my old age, and that's something in times like these, isn't it?"

Jack sighed. "You're fortunate."

"Indeed I am. If Luelia were only a bit more sociable I'd be perfectly satisfied, perfectly. Not that one can blame Luelia. She lost her only child you know, a lovely girl, and since then she's never really been the same. In the old days, I'm told, she entertained on a grand scale, caterers from New York, flowers from Bromley's in New Haven, solid gold plate…"

Laura's eyes glowed, a little color tinted her cheeks. She possessed the curbed, thwarted instincts of hospitality, and a rather pitiful groping toward a full and gracious existence. She read family magazines and clipped out recipes, poems, bits of homely philosophy. Her purse and conversation bulged with such items.

Absorbed in our own concerns, Jack and I gave her the dry crumbs of companionship and listened to all she had to say with scarcely half an ear. For two months she sat at our fire, drank our tea, told us about herself, and at the end of the relationship we were to discover that we knew virtually nothing of the real Laura Twining. She struck us as anything but an interesting or a mysterious figure.

I think now a part of our blindness may have lain in the fact that we never saw her in her own setting. It was impossible for her to invite us to

Hilltop House—no one set foot upon the sacred grounds without a definite invitation from the *grande dame* herself—and Laura keenly felt this unhappy situation.

I remember the day when Jack offered to accompany her home.

Instantly she became distressed and agitated. "It isn't at all necessary. It's just a step."

"I'd like to stretch my legs."

Her protests redoubled; eventually Jack woke up, said dryly, "Suppose I take you as far as the bend in the road."

"That will be lovely." She couldn't let the matter drop so easily, but must add the explanation, the painful apology. "I do wish I were differently situated. I'd love to have you visit me, but people upset Luelia. She sees almost no one."

"I understand."

I have said we entered Hilltop House on the day we signed our lease. We didn't realize then how unusual was the occasion, nor were we particularly impressed. Although Mrs. Coatesnash was the wealthiest woman in the county, most of the mansion year in and year out was kept thriftily closed. I daresay the two women habitually used no more than three of the thirty-odd rooms.

On the occasion of our call the drawing-room was opened—a lofty room paneled in oak, hung with fading tapestries, a somber and pathetic reminder of a magnificent past. The furniture which crowded the place was a history of American and English cabinet-making, but it was also shabby, worn, in need of repair. A long-silenced grand piano displayed the depredations of mice; a Chippendale sofa lacked a leg and was propped up with books; a Duncan Phyfe table was cracked down the middle. Dust lay thick in corners, powdered the velvet draperies and blurred a lovely gilt mirror which reflected the room. The crystal chandeliers—there were three—had no more sparkle than unwashed windows. I should add that I kept on my coat. The house was bitterly cold.

Luella Coatesnash did not rise. She sat before an enormous fireplace where two sticks of wood sizzled and sputtered, a stout woman past sixty, dressed in ancient taffeta, hair piled high in the style of a bygone day. Diamonds glittered on her fingers and encircled her throat. At her feet crouched an English mastiff, motionless as an animal carved in bronze. Behind her chair, pleased, eager and uneasy, fluttered Laura. She made the introductions. Mrs. Coatesnash inclined her head like an empress, served us weak tea and demanded three months' rent in advance.

"You're getting the cottage very cheaply, Mr. Storm. Three months in advance is the usual arrangement."

"I've never paid more than two in New York."

"This is Connecticut."

Jack wanted to argue, but I frowned, and reluctantly he parted with the ninety dollars. Our hostess softened. A slippered foot prodded the mastiff.

"Ivan, these are friends."

The dog oozed to thin, gray legs. This unpleasant animal was the darling of his mistress's heart. He was also, I thought privately, probably better fed than Laura. I shrank as he advanced, and Mrs. Coatesnash smiled.

"You don't like dogs, Mrs. Storm?"

"His size is a little alarming." Mrs. Coatesnash stroked the dog's huge head. "Ivan is the finest mastiff in this country. As he should be. Our family has been breeding mastiffs since the confederation of the states." Jack took on the wary look common to males whenever a genealogical discussion looms. It didn't save him, or me. Mrs. Coatesnash was a New Englander. She went firmly into both our families, and quickly satisfied herself that we were nobodies sprung from nowhere. Ohio, indeed! She seemed doubtful about the future of her cottage, and warned us to cherish the furniture, to watch out for cigarettes and to take care not to set down wet glasses.

"I'm holding you responsible, Mr. Storm."

I got a little red, and Jack didn't trouble to conceal his irritation. Laura was determined that the occasion go off well. She said breathlessly:

"Mr. Storm will love your things, Luella. He's an artist, you know. You remember my saying so. He paints."

"I collect," said Mrs. Coatesnash.

"How interesting," said Jack in his blandest tones.

Mrs. Coatesnash gave him a suspicious look, and then proposed a tour of her private gallery. As we assented, an interruption occurred. The doorbell rang with rusty violence, and Mrs. Coatesnash glanced hurriedly toward the corner clock.

"If you'll forgive me, we can see the pictures some other day. I'm expecting another caller."

This was cool enough, and I rose at once. A crisp, amused voice called from the foyer, "Nonsense, Luella, I won't be treated as company. If you're doing the gallery, I'll trail along." A moment later I had my first glimpse of Annabelle Bayne, and a surprising figure she presented in that somber room. She was slim, dark, vivid, around thirty. Her strange white face, her brilliant painted mouth, the restless peculiar manner which was so much a part of her, seemed startlingly out of place. Even the clothes she wore— the smart Harris Tweed suit, the modish but unbecoming hat, the green gloves which matched green shoes—seemed designed not for the village of Crockford but for the city of New York.

As a matter of fact, the name of Annabelle Bayne *was* known in New York. I placed her immediately. Annabelle Bayne was a writer of a very specialized type. Her writing was drawn from life, yet was smartly, cruelly out of focus, and I've heard it said that her friends could not sleep easily until they had read her latest clever little piece and discovered whether or not they had escaped the acid bath. She was always poking fun at small towns and small-town people. She was heartily disliked in Crockford.

I couldn't imagine how it happened that she and Luella Coatesnash were on friendly terms. Yet friends they were. They embraced, and the old woman seemed honestly pleased with her visitor. Annabelle greeted us vivaciously enough, and even spoke vaguely of a future meeting. To Laura she was less pleasant.

"Hurry my tea, please," she said crisply. "I'll need nourishment before I can look at pictures."

Laura said nothing, but her lips trembled, and I decided that I didn't particularly like Annabelle Bayne. The tour through the gallery, which by this time neither Jack nor I wanted to make, was hardly a success. For one of Mrs. Coatesnash's bulk, the walk along the drafty corridor beyond the drawing-room was a definite effort. She leaned heavily on a gold-headed cane, and on the other side Annabelle supported her. Beside the two women padded Ivan, silent and ghostly, eyes lambent in the gloom.

Most of the pictures—Mrs. Coatesnash considered them all worthy of the Metropolitan—were frankly terrible, although the collection did include a Stuart of an early bewigged Coatesnash and a small very good Trumbull. As I paused before the Trumbull and stepped back to obtain a better perspective, Mrs. Coatesnash surprised me by saving sharply:

"Stand still. Mrs. Storm. Just as you are."

I moved instinctively, and she tapped her cane against the floor in exasperation. "You've spoiled it. It's gone now."

"What's gone?"

"For a moment I thought you resembled my daughter. I see it was only the way you were standing. Jane was much younger." I am twenty-two, and even so I wasn't pleased. Annabelle Bayne said then, quickly and in a voice queerly emphatic, "You've forgotten, Luella. Jane would be older now. By many years."

A look passed between the women, a look I could not comprehend, a look which made me uncomfortable in some dim way. Mrs. Coatesnash turned, limped back into the drawingroom. We were done with the gallery.

Mrs. Coatesnash bade us a contained good-bye, and, in parting, observed that if anything went wrong with the cottage we must expect to shoulder the expense. She had done her share in turning it over in good condition.

"What an afternoon!" said Jack, after we had escaped and started the car around the hill road home. "Thank God, my dear, I didn't marry you for your ancestors. Thank God my own were honest shoe clerks."

"You didn't like Mrs. Coatesnash?" I said innocently.

"'Didn't like' is much too mild! Of all the snobbish, disagreeable, money-hungry old harridans I've ever met, she's undisputed tops. Did you notice how she grabbed the rent? I'll bet that money never sees the light of day again."

"What do you think of Annabelle Bayne?"

"She," said Jack with a sly grin at me, "was better looking. And she's a very smart girl—if you like that type. But Annabelle's no problem of ours, and Mrs. Coatesnash is. That woman—mark my words—is going to be a sweetheart as a landlady."

"How can she bother us if we never see her?"

I soon discovered. Luella Coatesnash seemed to be one of those women who never do anything for themselves which they can persuade, bully or coerce others into doing for them. Within a week and without our catching a glimpse of her, she managed to become a pretty definite part of the Storm regimen. We had hardly installed ourselves in the cottage before she began to entrust us with the commission of various small, profitless, troublesome chores. When we drove into the village to do our daily shopping, we were requested to buy for Hilltop House ten pounds of sugar or five gallons of oil—thus saving our land-lady the slight expense of getting out her own car. If we planned a day in New Haven there was invariably a letter to be posted for Mrs. Coatesnash—a letter which must make a particular train. Twice, when the old lady went to New York to consult with her lawyers. Laura Twining appeared to ask that we feed and exercise Ivan.

"Luella thought you wouldn't mind for a couple of days. We'll be back Wednesday noon."

We did mind At best. Ivan and I regarded each other with a sort of armed neutrality, and I never quite persuaded myself that he remembered his mistress's injunction to treat us as friends. Moreover, the dog required a special type of food, which we bought. Nothing was ever said about repayment.

Recalling those days. I find myself wondering how it happened that Jack and I never rebelled. Probably because it is usually easier to say yes than to say no. Anyway, we never got around to refusing.

This situation is recorded in detail because it became highly important later on. It explains why we were not surprised by the telephone call, a point on which we found it difficult to convince the police.

In February we heard from Silas that our neighbors were going abroad. He had been hired to care for Mrs. Coatesnash's three blooded cows, to do the gardening during her absence and to keep an eye on Hilltop House. He was to occupy a dingy servant's lodge in the rear of the main dwelling, which had been opened, swept and sketchily furnished for his use.

"Then you won't be working for us," Jack said.

Silas shuffled his feet. "If it's all the same. I figure on keeping my job with you."

"Won't the work be too heavy?"

"There's only the cows and the gardening at the other place. I can get done by noon."

Jack had a sudden flicker of insight. "Silas, how much is Mrs.

Coatesnash paying you?"

Plainly the hired man didn't wish to answer, but after the question was repeated, he said reluctantly, "Free use of the lodge and half the profits from the milk."

Jack was indignant.

"Mrs. Coatesnash may be a little close," Silas said defensively, "but she's fair. She's got too much sense to throw her money to the birds, which is more than you can say for some. In lots of ways she's been awful good to me."

Since the matter wasn't our concern, Jack shrugged and said nothing further.

The day before Hilltop House was closed, Laura Twining dropped in to drink a final cup of tea. She wore a new dress, gray poplin trimmed with lace. It was chosen with her instinctive bad taste and she wanted reassurance as to its appropriateness for shipboard. Though talkative as ever, I thought she seemed depressed.

"The packing has been a trial." She aimlessly smoothed her lace. "I'm going to miss you two young people."

Somewhat conscience-stricken, we tried to cheer her up. Jack offered her a cigarette. She always declined, but she liked the gesture. I poured fresh tea and passed a homemade cake.

"Aren't you excited by your trip?"

"I don't care for Paris."

"Then you've been there before?"

"Nine times." Naturally we were surprised. Laura explained. It appeared that Mrs. Coatesnash's long-dead daughter had been born in Paris in the month of February. Every February the bereft mother traveled across the ocean to spend a few sad weeks in the now unfashionable neighborhood where her only child had come into the world. "The neighborhood's run down terribly, but Luella doesn't seem to notice. I guess she thinks of the place as it used to be."

Jack disliked Mrs. Coatesnash too heartily to be sentimentally impressed. "Anyhow it's a swell break for you," he said. "You must know Paris like a book."

"The Paris I see is pretty much like Crockford. Luella hates sightseeing, so we never take in the museums or galleries. We go almost nowhere. We eat in the same restaurants every year, walk the same streets, play the same games of solitaire. It's funny how I used to hope to get to a Paris theater."

This was Laura's first admission that her life with Mrs. Coatesnash was not perfection. She was abashed by the little confidence and earnestly sought to temper her words. "There's no denying Luella is difficult at times, but then I'm difficult too. Luella tells me I'm a dreadful bore. I've probably often been a trial to you." Our denials weren't quite quick enough. A small horrid pause occurred. Laura's eyes filled. "I'm sorry if I've bothered you. I seem to bother everybody. Never mind—please don't get up. It's time for me to leave."

That was Tuesday. On Wednesday, as we set forth on our daily walk the Coatesnash car, a decrepit limousine, laden with baggage, swept upward at the bend and passed us on the road. A stern-faced important Silas sat behind the wheel. Luella Coatesnash, Ivan, Laura Twining and assorted suitcases crowded the tonneau. We waved: Mrs. Coatesnash nodded formally; Ivan barked, and the car sped off toward New Haven. I have never been certain whether or not Laura Twining actually saw us. She made no sign of recognition. At eight that evening the *S. S. Burgoyne* left New York for Cherbourg.

"Shall we wire flowers?" I asked.

"Flowers! Over my dead body we send flowers. Now if you suggested arsenic…"

"I thought for Laura."

"I would rather," Jack said, "buy myself a bottle of brandy." I smiled and agreed with him. The two women had meant nothing to us. I was glad that they were gone. I had no way of knowing that the time was soon to come when I would vainly wish them back in the big white house on the hill.

CHAPTER TWO

Tall, Thin, And Ungracious

Within a fortnight we were happily adjusted to the absence of our neighbors. It was pleasant to have no errands to run for Mrs. Coatesnash delightful to anticipate no little visits from Laura. Jack sang at his easel and I worked with a carefree mind. Silas proved to be the single flaw. Burdened with milking, planting, gardening, he became more inefficient than ever and harder to locate in times of domestic stress. However, as Jack put it, the gain undoubtedly offset the loss.

We had not expected to hear from the travelers, nor did we, although some of the especially favored villagers had postcards to show. In the Crockford grocery store one afternoon we saw Elsie Crampton, a bustling village social light, displaying a trophy received from Luella. A hand-painted snapshot of the Tuileries, if you please! An admiring ring of female shoppers thought it wonderfully artistic, and from the high-pitched gabble we gathered that Elsie Crampton planned to have the postcard framed. She needed a spot of color to "brighten" her foyer.

The incident at once amused and annoyed us. We never understood or quite appreciated the veneration in which the village held the Coatesnash family of Connecticut. The popular interest devoted to Luella's foreign travels struck us as stupid and disgusting. We took care not to encroach on our landlady's grounds, although we sometimes turned at the bend and scrambled along the hill road past Hilltop House, shuttered and silent in the twilight, white and forlorn against the gray skies of March. It rained a great deal that month.

It was raining the day we received the telephone call. It was the 20th of March, about five weeks after Luella Coatesnash and Laura Twining left Crockford, and Jack and I had finished our stints in the morning. We were lingering over a late luncheon, plotting my next short story, when the telephone rang. Persons on a party wire soon accustom themselves to listening for a particular ring. Instinctively we halted the conversation.

"That's ours," said Jack.

"I thought it was only three rings."

Again we listened. The telephone emitted four short rings—our signal—and I rose, answered. For an instant a dull buzz sounded on the wire and then came an unfamiliar male voice, blurred and indistinct.

"New York calling."

A long pause followed. I moved the hook up and down.

"Hello. Who is it?"

The pause spun out ended. A second time the deep breathy voice spoke, close to the mouthpiece now, imperative, "Let me speak to Jack Storm immediately."

Lifting an eyebrow, I handed over the instrument. Jack engaged in a short conversation which I reproduce as clearly as I remember it.

"What?... Why?... But she is in Europe... What did you say your name was? Oh, I understand... All right then, I'll be there."

Looking baffled, Jack replaced the telephone receiver, sat down. I was full of curiosity.

"Who was it?"

"A man named Elmer Lewis. I just promised to drive to New Haven to pick him up."

"Who in the world is Elmer Lewis?"

"Apparently a friend of Mrs. Coatesnash's. He's leaving New York on the three o'clock express and has to be in Crockford by six."

"Suppose he does! Why should you drive to New Haven for him?"

Jack shrugged philosophically. "Just what I've been wondering myself. Unfortunately, I didn't think quickly enough to refuse. As nearly as I can make out, Mr. Lewis wants to save taxi fare. Mrs. Coatesnash probably told him that we run a free jitney service."

"Why is he coming to Crockford anyhow?"

"He said he had some business to transact for the old lady."

"She's in Europe."

"So I remarked. He said he had a letter from her this morning. No doubt she suggested in the letter that he get in touch with us. She knows we're suckers."

I glanced toward the streaming windows. Rain gushed from the skies. I felt no premonition of danger, but I hadn't liked the voice on the telephone and I was thoroughly irritated by this imposition upon our good nature.

"Well, you aren't going. Jack. Let Mr. Lewis whoever he is, hire a taxi if he needs transportation. It's insane for you to drive fifty miles through this rain."

"I promised."

"I don't care what you promised!"

"Be reasonable, darling It I knew how to reach Lewis I might be able to call it off. But he is probably on his way to the train now. He might wait hours in the New Haven station."

"Let him!"

Jack firmly declined, and at four o'clock, when he splashed out to the garage, I followed, still indignant but unwilling to be left at home. The trip was nerve-racking even at the start. The heavy downpour had washed out a section of the Boston Post Road and, as a consequence, our ordinarily peaceful back lane teemed with through traffic, bad drivers and confusion. Rain pounded down, brakes shrieked, horns blew, cars skidded at the curves. A high wind blew unceasingly. In wifely satisfaction I ventured a few false words of commiseration.

Jack said in a kindly tone, "How would you like a sock on the jaw, my love?"

"I suppose you personally think this is dandy. It's just the day for a drive, isn't it? Nice and wet." Jack laughed, I giggled and we were friends again. The rain diminished slightly, and by dint of various hair-raising maneuvers we succeeded in making up lost time. Jack disliked, he remarked with a sidewise grin, to keep Lewis waiting. Something occurred to me.

"How are you going to recognize Lewis?"

"He said he would know us by the car."

"But he hasn't ever seen the car."

"That's funny." A tiny crinkle showed between Jack's eyes. "That's darn funny. He described the make, color, model, spoke of the rumble seat."

I was blankly incredulous. "Surely Mrs. Coatesnash didn't write him a detailed description!"

"She must have." The crinkle disappeared. "If that lady is anything she's thorough. Only, for a minute it struck me as being queer."

It continued to strike me as queer. I was not alarmed—exactly. Indeed I vaguely scented a practical joke, and as I strove to remember that phone call in detail, it began to seem to me that the masculine voice might well have been disguised. I ran over the practical jokers among our acquaintances and arrived at no conclusions. Nevertheless, I retained a misty, teasing impression that I had heard the voice before and that it had been disguised.

We entered the outskirts of New Haven at a fast clip. The rain had lightened to a dreary drizzle but evidences of the storm lingered. Gutters rushed in miniature torrents, inch-deep puddles glistened in the streets, umbrellas bloomed at the crossings. Not yet five o'clock, it was already quite dark, and in the shadowy dusk ahead shone the railroad station, a brilliant spot of light. Laughing and talking, tweedy and gay, week-end people poured into the raw damp evening. At the end of a line of cars we parked while Jack got out to reconnoiter.

Several minutes passed before I observed a middle-aged man who had emerged from the station and who was slowly making his way along the curbing. Something arresting about his appearance caught my eye. He was extremely tall, extremely thin, and his walk and bearing suggested authority. His skin was an unpleasant gray-white, pallid with indoor living. His jaw was narrow, slashed by deep vertical lines, and his thin, taut lips bore the curve of arrogance. Even the manner in which he progressed along the crowded sidewalk, brushing others aside, affirmed that he was accustomed to demanding and getting his own way.

There remained his clothes. They were fantastically unsuitable. A long ill-fitting overcoat, very shabby, flapped at his heels, revealing a shiny blue-serge suit and a shirt with a celluloid collar. The collar was soiled. His hands, burdened with traveling bags, were gloveless; a battered derby hat rode uneasily on the back of his head.

This man moved along the curb, pausing to peer into every car in the long line. At length he reached our car. He stopped on the sidewalk directly opposite, stared, frowned, stared again. His eyes, an intense blue, glittered behind thick glasses. He set down his two traveling bags.

I realized at once that this must be Elmer Lewis and that he was puzzled by Jack's absence. There was no reason why I should not have spoken to him. Still I did not. For one thing I disliked him instantly. Possibly I was prejudiced in advance, but Lewis's appearance and manner, his strange apparel, did nothing to minimize the prejudice. For what seemed a long time he remained motionless outside the lowered window of our car, staring in.

My antipathy increased. I glimpsed Jack swinging from the station and checked an absurd impulse to cry out, to stop him, to prevent the meeting. Jack set foot on the running board. Immediately the other man stepped forward.

"Here I am," he said.

Perhaps because he had resented the trip Jack pretended a greater cordiality than he actually felt. He grasped the other's hand in a hearty fashion. "You're Mr. Lewis?"

The stranger submitted to a limp handshake. "I'm Lewis. You have kept me waiting at least ten minutes."

Jack was a little dashed, but politely apologetic. "Sorry. I was looking through the station. This is my wife, Mr. Lewis."

"So I guessed. I've stood here watching her."

"I was almost on the point of speaking," said I.

"Well," said Lewis in a flat, nasal voice, "you took your time about it."

This ungracious speech resulted in an awkward pause. Jack broke it by opening the rumble seat and attempting to relieve our guest of his baggage. Lewis drew back sharply.

"Never mind! I prefer to place my own bags."

Whereupon he dropped one bag into the rumble seat and shoved the other into the seat with me. After settling his luggage, he climbed nimbly into the rumble seat. The drizzle was still intrusive; the evening air moist and dank. Jack's instincts toward hospitality, sinking fast, were not yet entirely dead. He entered a mild protest.

"You had better get in front. You will find it wet riding in the open."

"I don't mind wet weather."

"There's plenty of room up here for three," I interposed. "You can ride with us and we can put both bags behind."

"I'm staying where I am."

Jack, still standing on the curb, was thoroughly annoyed by now. I glanced through the window at him and shook my head. He shrugged his shoulders resignedly. When he spoke to Lewis again it was with an emotionless civility.

"Just where do you want me to take you?"

"Crockford."

"Where in Crockford?"

The thin lips parted to disclose a row of white teeth, very square and even. "Don't you know where I want to be dropped?"

"How should I?"

For the first time Lewis seemed uncertain. Then he recovered himself and his glance was hard and level. "I will make the arrangements after we reach your cottage."

"Our cottage is six miles on the other side of Crockford."

"Then I'll go that far with you. I want to see the cottage. Mrs. Coatesnash requested it."

At a complete loss, too astonished to voice the obvious objections, Jack put an end to the conversation by getting into the car and starting it with a terrific jerk. I lurched backward.

"Sorry, Lola. That was meant for Lewis, and I rather hope he breaks his neck."

We flowed into traffic, crossed the bridge beyond the lighted railroad offices, debouched into the Post Road, quit the Post Road for our own. The night was desolate. Wind sighed and moaned and blew the light little car along. A few drops of rain hissed at the windows. For awhile we didn't speak.

Then, "I think he's crazy," said I, low.

"Why should Mrs. Coatesnash ask him to go to the cottage?" growled Jack. "We've paid our rent; he's got no right there."

"It's beyond me. Do you suppose he came up from New York simply to look at our place?"

Jack irritably sought to fathom the puzzle. "Mrs. Coatesnash may be planning to sell. That might explain why she didn't condescend to write us. She wouldn't risk losing rent till she was sure of a sale. Not that dame!"

"Then you think Lewis is a real-estate agent?"

"A real-estate agent with the winning attractiveness of a surly baboon!"

The peak of traffic was over. Occasionally, not often, another car shot by. We sped into darkness intensified by empty fields and the ghostly arms of telegraph poles. Like a twisted ribbon ahead, lost in an endless perspective, stretched the lonely country road. The bag on the seat—Lewis's bag—jostled continually against me. Once as I caught the braided leather handle to shift position, I happened to glance back into the rumble. Lewis was watching. He had half risen, one hand gripped the side of the car,, his spectacled eyes peered at his bag and at me. I expelled a sharp breath.

"What's wrong, Lola?"

"Nothing."

I was ashamed to admit I had been startled by a pair of staring eyes. Then, glancing at the windshield mirror, I perceived that Lewis remained in the odd, half-erect position. It seemed impossible that he could maintain it, yet he did. He kept one hand in his overcoat pocket. The other supported his weight. His dense blue eyes were glued upon the bag with the braided handle. Snatching at the curtain which covered the back window, I pulled it down Jack roused from the reverie that overtakes good drivers on a clear highway.

"What is it, sweetheart? You're trembling."

"Mr. Whozis makes me nervous. He keeps staring in. Please let's hurry."

Jack grinned, undisturbed. He had hunted too many nonexistent burglars during our life together to take seriously any intuitive fears.

"Please hurry, Jack."

Usually I am a great girl for caution, Jack cocked an eyebrow. "Forty miles an hour is fast enough with the roads in this condition."

"Drive faster, please. The stores will be closed. We need eggs for breakfast."

"I'll get them in the morning."

"Please, Jack."

"Have it your own way!"

He made a vigorous surrender. The car shot forward as if pushed by a giant hand; the speedometer needle leaped from 40 to 45, danced a jig at 55. A few miles outside Crockford, over the banshee howl of the wind we heard the pop-pop of a pursuing motorcycle. A State policeman whizzed abreast of us. Jack gave me one look.

"Your party, Lola."

We pulled dismally to the side of the road. Coughing and snorting the motorcycle stopped and a dark slim man in shiny boots alighted and approached us from the rear. I recognized the policeman, and instantly rallied my feminine charms. Lester Harkway, if not a friend, was at least an acquaintance, the first person we had met in Crockford. He had directed us to the cottage, and afterward, when we passed him patrolling the roads, he always touched his cap. He regarded us now with frank disfavor.

"You kids were hitting fifty-five. This is a public road not a merry-go-round."

"It's late," I said appealingly. "I was in a hurry to get home and talked Jack into it."

"I should say you were in a hurry. I've got a good notion to give you a ticket."

Harkway, pretending a greater anger than he felt, intended, I was sure, to let us go with a warning. At this point Elmer Lewis projected himself into the affair with a lack of tact and in a manner which I had begun to believe was typical. Leaning from the rumble seat, speaking in brisk, insulting tones, he informed Harkway that he personally had no time to waste on "hick policemen." Jack's jaw dropped and my eyes popped out. Harkway was Irish. He made up his mind at once, scribbled a ticket, ripped it off the pad. His face was bright red.

"It's tough on you," he said to Jack, "but damned if I'll swallow your friend's lip. By rights he ought to pay the fine."

Again Lewis interrupted. "That suits me. Hand it here." He reached for the slip of paper.

Half out of the car by now and furious, Jack seized the ticket. "Suppose you let me manage my own business!"

"As you choose! Only I wish you'd remember I'm in a hurry. I don't propose to sit here the rest of the night."

"By God…"

Harkway stepped hastily between the two angry men, but fortunately didn't need to interfere. The emotional storm blew up and over. I caught Jack's coat, and he got back into the car. He slammed the door himself. However much a nasty brawl might have lightened his spirits, he perceived it wouldn't really clear the air, and also, on second thought, he disliked letting me in for it. He heaved a long, relinquishing sigh. Harkway flashed me a friendly grin, remounted his motorcycle, waved us on. Jack gripped the wheel, stamped on the starter and, until we reached Crockford, said nothing.

Every inch of space before our favorite grocery store was jammed. Jack pulled up abruptly on the other, darker side of Main Street beneath an enormous elm which shaded the Episcopal Church. He turned to me.

"Give me tomorrow's grocery list, Lola."

"What are you going to do?"

"A little shopping, and something else that badly needs doing. Give me the list, Lola."

"What else?"

"You needn't worry. Nothing is going to happen. Nothing serious. My passions have cooled somewhat." Jack grinned. "However, I'm going to get rid of that oaf. In about five minutes I'm coming back with a double-armload of groceries; at which time I will tell Elmer Lewis that I can use the rumble seat for onions. He has arrived at the end of the line."

Jack strode across the street. I, also, immediately departed. I wasn't frightened any more, just relieved at the knowledge that soon we would see the last of Lewis. As I scrambled over his bag and under the wheel. I turned and hurriedly announced that I would wait in the drug store. I allowed him no chance for protest or questioning. My idea was that a scene was brewing and I desired no part in it.

The drug store was at the end of the block. Seated at a marble-topped table I consumed a chocolate sundae and watched the door, anxious to receive the welcome news that the incubus had been lifted. Five minutes dragged by. Like a tediously turning wheel my mind retraced the events of the evening. I recalled my earlier conviction that the voice which demanded our appearance in New Haven had been disguised.

Something about the voice troubled me—something elusive as a shadow. What was it? Suddenly I grasped the shadow. Lewis's voice and the voice of the telephone were not the same!

It was not Lewis who had telephoned Jack, but someone else, someone who had said that he was Lewis.

Check unpaid, gloves left behind, in flying haste I quit the drug store. Nearly a block distant on the opposite side of the street was Hahneman's Fancy Grocery, an old-fashioned emporium with a wide porch elevated from the sidewalk. Laden with packages Jack was descending the steps, trailed by a grocery boy with additional packages. Risking traffic, I darted into the middle of the street. Jack spied me and paused at the curb until, gasping, I reached him. "Lola, for heaven's sake…"

"Lewis didn't phone you! I know he didn't. It was someone else—a different voice."

Jack shook his head in a pitying way. "Your imagination may bring in an occasional check, but it's hell on a husband's nervous system. Suppose Lewis didn't phone. Couldn't he have a secretary and couldn't he ask his secretary to make the call?"

I was flattened. The natural explanation had quite escaped me; it had remained for Jack to point it out. The three of us. Jack, Dennis Cark, the grocery boy, and I, crossed to the parked car. Lewis sat stiffly in the rumble seat—stiffly, motionlessly, in the gloom of the great elm—and then the beams of passing headlights illuminated seat and passenger. There was a dark wet patch on the upholstery; there was a dark wet patch on Lewis's coat.

"That's blood," said Dennis Cark, and stopped beside me.

Jack sprang forward and leaped to the running board. The groceries spilled from his arms to the street. He bent over. His voice seemed queer and high.

"Stay back, Lola. This man is dead."

"Dead."

"He's been shot." Jack straightened. "I—I can't find a gun. It looks like murder."

CHAPTER THREE

Discovered in the Rumble Seat

I don't remember a great deal about the next few minutes. There was a roaring in my ears, and I had a hazy impression that if I didn't snap out of it, I was going to disgrace myself and faint. A crowd—one of those crowds which seems to materialize from nowhere—instantly collected, and Jack, to be counted on always in emergency, clung to the running board and shouted at them to stand back from the car.

To me he said, "Get the police."

Something—his tone perhaps, the knowledge of what he expected of me—carried me down the block to the house where the village police chief lived. John Standish was sitting down to his evening meal when I burst in on him. He was a bulky, middle-aged man, and though he rose at once from the table, he seemed, in my excited state, intolerably slow. I know he made me wait while he went upstairs for his hat and coat.

Not until we were on the street did I appreciate how his calmness had steadied me. His manner, as I was to discover, was all a trick. But I was prepared to like John Standish. Curiously, it did not occur to me to consider him as a possible source of danger to me and mine.

The crowd had thickened around the car, and traffic was snarled in the street beyond. Two constables—whom Standish had phoned from the house—were attempting to rope off the place. The police chief pushed through. He explored the car, the rumble seat, the adjacent pavement and studied the body before he turned to Jack.

"It's murder, all right," he said. "Suppose you tell me all about it."

"I hardly know where to begin."

"Begin," suggested Standish, "by telling me who shot this man."

"I wish," said Jack in a thin, tired voice, "I could. Unfortunately I wasn't present when the murder occurred."

Standish frowned. "Where were you?"

"In the grocery store across the street, shopping. My wife was at the drug store. Lewis was alone in the car."

"How long was he alone?"

"Ten minutes at the most. Immediately I got back and discovered what had happened, my wife went for you."

"Lewis? You say his name was Lewis?"

"Elmer Lewis. He was a friend of my landlady's—Mrs. Luella Coatesnash. I picked him up in the New Haven station this afternoon."

"Where did he come from? What's his home address? Who's his nearest relative?"

For the first time and with a certain inward shock, I realized the paucity of our knowledge concerning Elmer Lewis. I saw Jack hesitate. Then he plunged into a lengthy account of the phone-call episode. As if suddenly aware of the many eager listeners, Standish broke into the story and looked around. Umbrellas filled the sidewalk and the street, overflowed into the Episcopal churchyard and bobbed on the church steps like tiny tents in a mushroom city.

Turning from Jack, the police chief put a few general questions. Had anyone noticed the car during the interval when Jack and I were gone? No one had. Had anyone heard a shot? Again no one had. This was not surprising. The physical conditions, the weather, even the deserted spot where we had parked the car, presented an almost perfect set of circumstances for tragedy. The din of Friday-night traffic, the honking and the backfiring, would screen the sound of a shot, and stragglers hurrying through the rain would be too intent on keeping dry to observe with any interest a little gray car lost in the broad, thick shadows of the great elm.

It next occurred to Standish that someone in the crowd might be acquainted with the victim. A line formed and one by one the bolder villagers stepped to the running board and peered into the rumble seat. Each, as he stepped down, shook his head. The crowd was fairly representative, and thus it appeared that Elmer Lewis was a comparative stranger to Crockford.

As this examination terminated. Dr. Rand arrived to authorize the removal of the body. The village coroner was a gray-haired man of sixty who had secret leanings toward the stage. He had white, delicate hands and moved them constantly as he talked. It was reliably reported that he had studied Delsarte. A small-town physician all his life, a hundred miles from Broadway, he was long accustomed to death, but, as he was to tell us later, he never got to like it. Climbing to the fender of the car, deftly balancing himself, Dr. Rand turned his flashlight into the rumble seat.

Seen in the bright illumination, Elmer Lewis looked startlingly alive. The eyes behind the steel-bowed spectacles stared forth wide open; the face, a little more pallid than in life, shone in the damp; the thin lips were slightly parted. The dead man slouched loosely in his seat; one hand was in his pocket, the other drooped across his lap. But except for the stain on his coat he might have been waiting for us to drive him to the cottage, arrogantly determined that we take him there. The nearest onlookers gasped and retreated.

The coroner went grimly to work. He touched the dead man's eyelids and throat, clasped the pulseless wrist. As he attempted to pull Lewis's hand from the overcoat pocket, he accidentally struck the steel-bowed

spectacles. With a macabre alacrity they began to slide. A woman specta-
tor screamed. The coroner snorted, caught the spectacles, pocketed them.
Turning, he made an acid speech to the curious throng.

"No one is holding you people here. You'd be better off at home and
more profitably employed. I wager half you women haven't washed your
dinner dishes."

The crowd broke ranks. Dr. Rand returned to his labors, unbuttoned
the overcoat, stripped open waistcoat, vest and shirt. Following the course
of the wound he located the bullet. It had penetrated the body and dropped
to the floor of the car. Dr. Rand picked up the bit of bloodstained lead and
handed it to Standish.

"There's Exhibit A. The poor fellow died instantly, never knew what
hit him, no sign of struggle. Happened some time during the last half hour.
That's all for now. You can take him to the morgue." Removing a lap robe
from the car, the physician covered the body, interrupted himself to say
testily, "Where in hell is the ambulance? Are those drivers always at the
movies?"

Just as he spoke, the local ambulance clanged magnificently through
Main Street and stopped, sputtering, at the curb. After the ambulance and
its burden had gone away, John Standish casually hoisted himself into the
now-vacant rumbleseat and said:

"Mind driving me to the station?"

Although the police station was immediately across the square, that
ride was the longest I ever took. Of the three of us, John Standish alone
bore it well. As we alighted, he noticed the bag between Jack and me—
Lewis's traveling bag, which we had quite forgotten. Standish carried the
bag inside.

The police station occupied the basement of the village court house,
and had a separate, neatly labeled entrance. On either side of the entrance
grew potted cedars, provided by the Garden Club and watered in rotation
by designated members. Passing these civic tributes, we entered a large un-
carpeted reception room with a door at each end opening into two smaller
rooms. One of these was used by officers of the State police as a dressing
room. The other served as the village police station.

In towns the size of Crockford, police stations close at six o'clock and
police protection virtually ceases. Standish unlocked the second door, and
we followed him into his poorly furnished office. Carelessly dropping the
bag, the officer knelt, touched a match to a fire laid in an unsightly grate.
Jack pulled out a chair for me—there were half a dozen ranged around a
scarred pine table—selected another for himself. The previous excitement,
the bracing need of decision was gone and reaction had set in; I thought
Jack looked depressed and very tired.

The fire refused to start, Standish struck another match, and I achieved
an initial unpopularity. Studying my surroundings, I saw built across the

back of the small room what appeared to be a barred iron cage, like a cage in a zoo. The contraption, open at the top, boasted a heavy iron, double-padlocked door. There was a cot inside.

"What is it?" I asked.

Jack turned. "It must be the jail."

Now, I am a New Yorker, and at the moment I remembered the towering, somber mass of the Tombs. The contrast was too much. I laughed, partially from nerves, to be sure, but I laughed. Standish turned around.

"It's small, Mrs. Storm, but Crockford is a law-abiding town. Always was, till a couple years ago when you town folks started coming, bringing your liquor and big-town ideas."

After that I kept still. At length the tardy fire blazed up and Standish, lighting a smelly briar pipe, settled himself at the table, Jack spoke in a fagged voice.

"My wife has suffered a severe shock. She's dead tired. So am I. We've had no dinner. Can't we let any further questioning go till tomorrow?"

Standish eyed me particularly. "This is murder, Mr. Storm."

"Very well then. Only please be as quick as you can."

The other took his time. He was the official embodiment of the law and he permitted that important fact to sink in. He sharpened a pencil, laid out a notebook, telephoned for Minnie Gray, wife of one of the deputies and public stenographer, and finally gave us his attention.

"There are several things I want to clear up immediately. For instance, the phone call. You say it came from New York?"

"The call was made in New York about three o'clock," Jack said. "I can't tell you the exact time; I didn't look at a clock. But Lewis left there on the three-fifteen."

"Did you see him get off the train in New Haven?"

"No." Jack smiled faintly. "However, I was told he would be on the three-fifteen; when f arrived at the station the train had just pulled in, and Lewis was waiting with his bags. So I assume…"

The first hint of what Standish's attitude was to be leaked out "In this case I'm beginning to think it isn't safe to assume anything. I want facts, a lot of facts. In the first place, who is Lewis? What was he doing here in Crockford: What was his business?"

"He didn't say. I understood it concerned Luella Coatesnash; apparently she had asked him to go to my cottage. That's all I know about it. I spoke to him for only a few minutes outside the station."

"Then you didn't hold any conversation on the way over from New Haven?"

"Lewis rode in the rumble seat. Lola and I were in front with the windows closed."

"Isn't there room enough in front for three?"

"Lewis chose the rumble seat. Indeed he insisted upon riding there."

"In the rain!"

"Yes, in the rain. I thought it peculiar. I did my best to dissuade him. I failed."

Standish's pipe went out. He re-lighted it. He looked skeptical. I put in a quick suggestion. "Maybe Lewis didn't *want* to talk to us. There was something queer, secretive about him. Perhaps that is the reason he chose the rumble seat."

"Possibly." Standish turned politely to Jack. "Suppose we go back to the phone call. That call must be traced."

"Don't the local operators keep track of long-distance calls? "I'll check with them later. At the moment I am interested in your help."

"Then it might be better to talk to Lola. She answered the phone. Lewis was on the line when I got there. Or rather his secretary was."

"His secretary!" The stiff, gray brows climbed. "Didn't you talk to Lewis himself on the phone? Certainly you gave me that impression."

"I didn't mean to."

"Then you didn't talk to Lewis on the phone?"

"I don't think so."

"Think! Don't you know?"

Jack made an impatient gesture. "You're rushing me and I want to get the story straight. The man I talked to on the phone said he was Lewis, but later on when I met Lewis I decided he wasn't the person who phoned. Lewis's voice was different, higher, more nasal, much thinner."

"Why do you say you spoke to Lewis's secretary?"

"Simply because I imagined…"

"Let me provide the imagination; you stick to facts." The officer brusquely moved his chair toward mine. "Now, Mrs. Storm, please be exact. When you spoke to the New York operator this afternoon did you hear any mention of an exchange? Did you hear coins dropping—we might learn in that way whether a public phone was used—did you hear any scrap of conversation which might help us fix the locality where the call originated?"

"No," I said.

"Will you tell exactly what you did hear?"

I started bravely, came to an awful pause. At that unpropitious moment an appalling thought occurred to me. I realized that at no time had I heard a woman's voice. Yet telephone operators—and an operator would necessarily put through a long-distance call—are invariably feminine.

In the growing silence I re-checked my findings; the results remained the same; the phone call stood forth in sickening detail. The words, the accents, the voice, particularly the voice. The male voice which informed me that New York was calling, the male voice which requested Jack.

"Have you remembered something, Mrs. Storm?"

"I'm afraid I have." My heart knocked painfully. "Aren't telephone operators always women?"

"I suppose so…of course…I never knew of a male operator at a central exchange. Why do you ask?"

Standish's face grew cold. Jack's bewildered. Both stared. Except tor the crackle of the fire, the room was still.

"The phone call," I said, "might not have come from New York. I didn't hear a phone operator, so there's no proof it did. None at all."

"But. Lola, you told me…"

"Be quiet, please. I was mistaken—tricked. I believe now. I was *meant* to think it was a New York call; I did think it. Quit staring, you two. This is no fun for me."

I was on the point of hysterics, and both men perceived it. Standish harrumphed Jack moved closer to me; his eyes said, *Steady girl, steady.* He put his hand on my arm. Then I had to behave With a definite effort of will I gave a full account of the phone call, straightforward, coherent—and, at any rate to Standish, unconvincing He soon made that clear.

"Am I to understand that you didn't hear a long-distance operator?"

"That's right."

"Weren't you suspicious when a male voice said New York was calling? Didn't it occur to you that someone might be faking a long-distance call?"

"Not at the time. I had no reason to be suspicious. Can't you see I hadn't?"

The little try at extenuation fell flat. "Did you hear two voices, Mrs. Storm, or only one?"

"I can't be sure. At the time I supposed there were two. But now I'm inclined to think there was only one."

"Could you identify the voice you did hear?"

"I might identify it; I didn't recognize it." My next words were carefully chosen. "In fact, I had a definite impression that the voice was disguised."

I had expected a reaction. I got none. From the amount of interest Standish exhibited, he might have believed the latter part of my statement to be a deliberate embellishment. I had got off to a wrong start. I did not know whether he thought my story of the telephone message was untrue or whether he thought it was colored and confused by what had happened afterward.

Standish wound up that part of the inquiry. "Well, this is the matter in a nutshell. We don't know what time the call was made, who made it, whether it originated in New York or was only made to appear so. My guess is we will have difficulties tracing the telephone message."

His manner, courteous but cool, indicated that he considered the young Storms unsatisfactory witnesses. Gladly disposing of me, he resumed his interrogation of Jack.

"Pretty tough driving this afternoon, wasn't it, what with the rain?"

"Terrible."

The officer gloomily drew a lungful of smoke. "I'm not for a minute doubting your veracity, but I don't quite understand your making that long drive as a favor to a man you'd never seen or heard of. It looks curious."

"Curious or not," Jack said shortly, "I've explained how it came about. I was taken by surprise, and I had been called upon so often to do various unpleasant little jobs for Mrs. Coatesnash that I automatically agreed."

"What time did you leave your home?"

"At four o'clock."

"Can anyone corroborate you? Did you meet anyone who knows you on the road?"

"Not on the way over. On the way back, about five miles outside Crockford, we were stopped for speeding."

The officer's eyes brightened. "Who stopped you?"

Before Jack answered, Minnie Gray crept in. A small timid woman with enormous teeth and a perpetually worried air, she took an interminable time snapping a rubber on her notebook locating a soft lead pencil, adjusting her skirts.

"And please speak slowly, Mr. Storm. Sixty words a minute is my speed."

Neither Jack nor I understood that we could not be compelled to submit to a formal questioning. The scratch of the stenographer's pencil, the frequent admonitions to slow down, the consciousness that every spoken word went promptly into a neat little notebook, threw Jack off his stride, made him choose his phrases. An artist, not a business man, he was ignorant of his own legal rights and the police chief took advantage of this ignorance. He asked questions which no lawyer would have allowed, and Jack obliged with replies which in cold print conveyed a quite different impression than he meant to convey.

Standish returned to the examination with his customary thoroughness. "Let's start with your being stopped on the road."

Jack carefully told of Harkway's pursuit and of Lewis's interference in the subsequent colloquy. In reproducing the dead man's language and his own, it was impossible to avoid a revelation of the disagreeable scene. Jack didn't dodge the point but with Minnie's notebook staring him in the face, naturally didn't stress it.

Standish listened closely. "You were angry?"

Jack hesitated. "Angry isn't just the word. I would prefer to say that I was irritated. Lewis had an—an unfortunate manner. I've described how he behaved in the station. Then, later on, by butting in he got me loaded down with a ticket. Of course I didn't like it. Who would?"

"Did you and Lewis quarrel?"

"He said a few things; I said a few. It was more an argument than a quarrel."

"Why did you put up with him? As I picture it, Lewis acted badly from the first. It was your car. Why didn't you ask him to get out?"

"We were five miles from town; it was raining; I decided to wait till we got to Crockford. I meant to get rid of him then. I believe I told you so."

"Yet when you reached Crockford you went into the grocery store and still he was in your car. Still you hadn't spoken? Or had you?"

Jack grinned wryly. "My curse is a stupid sense of humor. I intended to come back from the grocery store and tell Lewis I needed the rumble seat for onions. It sounds absurd, but it's the truth."

Standish made no comment. Lifting his telephone, he put through a call to the New Haven police station and requested that Lester Harkway be located and sent to the Crockford station. His expressionless gaze returned to Jack.

"What time was the arrest made?"

"Here's my ticket." Jack drew the paper from his pocket, consulted it. "The time is given as 5:50 p m. The place is on the back road five miles outside Crockford."

"May I have it if you please!"

The tone was curt, the inference clear. If our story could be backed up by physical evidence, Standish desired to view such evidence for himself. He briefly studied the ticket, slipped it into an envelope, placed the envelope in a drawer, banged the drawer, and with vigor reverted to the fray.

The sleepy slowness vanished; his blue eyes crackled; his purpose became apparent He was determined to force an admission that Jack and Lewis had quarreled violently on the road. His efforts to gain his end were those of the typical policeman; ignoring Jack's replies he persistently repeated the same questions, over and over, until they had the tormenting monotony of water dripping on stone. A system which, I can attest, is calculated to play havoc with the nervous system. At last Jack lost his temper.

"What are you trying to do? Blow up an unimportant argument into a motive for murder? What are you looking for? A confession?"

"I am merely trying to get at the truth."

"You're taking a damned unpleasant way about it." Jack got up from his chair, and his face was white. "If you're inferring that I was angry enough to shoot Lewis—which I wasn't—if you're inferring that I was armed—which I wasn't—then you might go a step further. No person in his right mind would shoot a man to death, leave his body on a public street, and immediately afterward go shopping! Or do you take me for a fool as well as a murderer?"

Into the electric atmosphere, like a two-for-a-penny firecracker, broke Minnie's plaintive voice. "Mr. Storm, you simply must speak slowly. I didn't get half you said."

Jack glanced at her distressed face, at me, regained his equilibrium. He sat down. "I'm glad you missed it." Already realizing his outburst had been ill-advised, he looked at Standish and entered a resentful half-apology. "I shouldn't have blown up, but I've been chivied and harassed until I hardly knew what I was saying. I've done my best to cooperate. Won't you agree I haven't acted the part of a criminal?"

This elicited no reply. A quick knock sounded at the door. An excited voice called, "You there, Standish? May I come in? I've got something important for you."

CHAPTER FOUR

The Pigskin Bag

The door opened and anti-climax walked into the room in the person of Harold Blair. Standish's chief deputy was a plump, waspish little man who had adopted, and adapted to a Crockford career, the airs and graces of fictional detectives. The knowing expressions, the dramatic manner, the haste when no haste is necessary. Short rapid steps carried him to his superior. He glanced portentously at the group and announced in a highly audible whisper:

"I've found something—an important clue."

This clue, flung proudly upon the table, seemed to my inexperienced eyes merely a tiny cylinder of brass, somewhat scuffed and dented. Jack recognized it for what it was—the metal jacket of the bullet which had done for Elmer Lewis.

At that time I knew nothing of guns. I was to learn a great deal. Elmer Lewis had been shot with a .45 caliber automatic pistol—the type of weapon which fires, extracts and ejects the empty cartridge shell, and is ready to fire again. The hand touches the trigger, the complicated series of mechanical reactions instantly follow. Dr. Rand had recovered the bullet; now Blair produced the empty cartridge shell which had dropped to the ground a twinkling fraction of a second before Lewis died. Standish brought out the flattened bullet, lined it up beside the scarred metal jacket, and the little blood brothers were reunited. Blair preened himself. Standish moodily studied the two exhibits.

"Where did you find the shell?"

"On Main Street, to the left of where the car was parked. I marked the spot, told Gray to keep the crowd off. Thought maybe the murderer might have left footprints."

Jack ignored this absurd suggestion and with it Blair. He turned to Standish. "I'd like to know. Doesn't the spot where the shell dropped fix the place from which the gun was fired?"

"Approximately."

"The murderer stood underneath the big elm," Blair said promptly.

"Exactly," said Jack. "It was dark there; the street was noisy. A set-up which allowed someone to creep up to the car shoot Lewis, and escape unseen and unheard. Lola and I were gone a full ten minutes."

Standish listened in silence. Something about his expression frightened me and I guessed what he was thinking. Whatever we had established, we had by no means established our own absence from the car at the fatal moment.

I said. "What are the chances of locating the gun?"

The police chief smiled as one smiles at a child "Very slight, in my opinion A forty-five is a common type of weapon. Connecticut factories must turn out hundreds every month."

"I was thinking of ballistic experts. Can't they determine by markings on the bullet whether a particular gun was used?"

"First they've got to lay hands on the particular gun. Quite a poser, if you ask me. Directly one man kills another, as a usual thing, he can't get rid of his weapon fast enough."

I restrained a sharp impulse to point out that jack could hardly have discarded a weapon in the short trip from car to grocery store. At this moment Standish requested Jack to stand up. Beginning at Jack's knees he patted his body to the shoulders—a quick, expert procedure that left no doubt as to its meaning. He picked up my pocketbook and peered inside. He went through the pockets of my coat. He found no gun. The overhead light wore a green shade; Jack's face had a greenish cast.

"I suppose you will also search the grocery store and the drug store?"

"We have already," said Standish.

A long hush ensued. Water slid down the window-panes, the fire crackled and leaped up the chimney, throwing crimson shadows upon the floor. Jack said steadily:

"I would like to clarify my standing here. If I'm helping you, that's one thing. If I'm definitely under suspicion I want a lawyer."

"You don't need a lawyer—yet." The phraseology was disconcerting and was planned to be. Standish's tone, however, was gentle. He smiled in a fatherly fashion, and set out on a different and equally alarming tack. "See here, Storm, I'll be perfectly frank with you. I don't believe you're a cold-blooded killer, you aren't the type. Furthermore, being practical, you had no chance to get rid of a gun. On the other hand—" he paused "—I am convinced you haven't told the whole truth about tonight. For your own sake, I suggest you do."

Too tired to repeat useless protestations, Jack only shook his head. We had another interruption, this time a welcome one. Lester Harkway knocked from the reception room, strode inside, bringing with him the fresh smell and feel of rain. He had already heard garbled rumors on the street. A curious glance traveled from Jack to me, before he reported to Standish that he was detached from duty indefinitely.

"All night—if you need me."

Shouldering off a damp overcoat, he seated himself and prepared to listen. Standish commenced to piece together the long-drawn-out story of the evening. It seemed to me that every word pointed in our direction. *We* had received a mysterious phone call which it was apparently impossible to trace—*we* had driven to New Haven on a stormy afternoon to accommodate a man we didn't know—*we* had disliked that man and he had been found murdered in *our* car. Fair as the summation might have appeared in the speaker's view, to my ears it possessed the disturbing quality of an indictment. I watched Harkway throughout—he was seated opposite—but vainly. His face kept its own counsel.

"How can I help, Chief?"

"I want your version of the quarrel on the road."

After a little hesitation and with an obvious attempt to provide uncolored facts, Harkway furnished his account of the much-discussed incident. The account was substantially the same as Jack's, and I was duly grateful. Standish grew restless.

"This argument then—in your opinion—was just an argument? Nothing serious?"

"Exactly what do you mean by serious?"

"Was the argument serious enough so that it might have been resumed later on? Say, here in the village?"

Harkway's head bobbed negatively. "I have no way of judging how Storm felt, or Lewis either, for that matter. I mean after I left them. And you probably wouldn't be interested in an out-and-out guess."

"Certainly I don't want a guess," said Standish testily. "I'm simply interested in hearing what you observed and what conclusions you drew."

"You've got the story. Storm was mad; Lewis acted as if he was; and I was hot under the collar myself. It was pretty much three-cornered." Harkway shrugged. "There it is, and not much to write home about."

Gradually the argument between Jack and Lewis had been reduced to its proper status and now stood forth as no more than a squabble between two impatient men. I drew an easier breath. Harkway who had been on duty since early morning yawned, covered it quickly, apologized.

"Is that all?"

"Unless you have something more to say."

Here Harkway paused noticeably. "I hardly know how to say what I mean, but anyway it struck me there was something screwy about that argument. About Lewis's part in it. Of course I might be wrong. It's just a notion I *had.*"

"Please go on."

I don't remember precisely the manner in which the young policeman worded his next statement, but undoubtedly he phrased it badly. His vocabulary wasn't made for subtleties and the impression he had received during the argument on the road was a very subtle thing indeed. In effect it was this: Harkway was convinced that when Lewis thrust himself into the colloquy he had done so with the deliberate intention of making himself obnoxious.

"Lewis acted like he yearned to stir up trouble, Chief. Like a man spoiling for a fight. I thought he was trying to get Storm's goat. That don't sound sensible, but it's what I thought at the time."

This also was my opinion, although it seemed to deepen the mystery of our passenger and his behavior. Why should Lewis purposely have sought to antagonize his benefactors? Frowning, Standish addressed himself to Jack.

"Did you think Lewis was purposely attempting to pick a fight?"

"It didn't occur to me just that way. Certainly I considered his actions very strange. Abnormal. Unreasonable."

Harkway interrupted. "There was something phony about the guy. For all his loud talk he was nervous as a cat. My headlights fell on his face when he leaned out of the rumble seat and he jumped like he'd touched a hot stove. Pulled up his coat collar and jammed his hat over his eyes—like—like he was afraid I might get too good a look at him."

Jack eyed Standish challengingly. "Lewis had a similar effect on Lola and me. Phony is a good word to describe him; he wasn't the sort you think of in connection with Mrs. Coatesnash. Personally I wonder how and where and why she picked him up."

As if suddenly reminded, Standish reached for the telephone, stayed his hand. "Do you know Mrs. Coatesnash's Paris address?"

Jack shook his head. "Silas would know."

I said, "Friday is band-practice night. He won't be home."

Standish smiled, called several numbers, and finally got the address. After which he phoned the New Haven telegraph offices and dispatched the following cable:

LUELLA COATESNASH
HOTEL ST CLAIR
RUE MORTANCE, PARIS, FRANCE.

ADVISE IMMEDIATELY CROCKFORD POLICE ELMER
LEWIS'S HOME ADDRESS AND NATURE OF HIS BUSINESS
WITH YOU.

When he replaced the receiver, the telephone rang. He spoke briefly, hung up and informed us that the coroner was coming over with his report.

On the heels of the announcement Dr. Rand arrived. At the fag end of a crowded day divided between his private practice and his official duties, a day begun with a delivery and wound up with an autopsy, the man of sixty looked fatigued but well equipped for further activity. He dropped a bundle of damp, wrinkled clothing with some relief. Then, like the actor he was, he glanced around to get the feeling of the group. I felt he had something up his sleeve. He combed rapid fingers through his snowy hair.

"Quite a gloomy gathering. You're lucky you didn't have my job. I assume you haven't solved the murder yet."

He tossed over a written report which dealt in technical terms with Lewis's mortal wound, listing the time, manner and medical causes of his death Standish laid it aside. "Did you find any identifying papers on the body?"

Dr. Rand's eyes now disclosed a subdued sparkle. "There wasn't a sign of letters, cards, memos or any of the trash we men usually burden our pockets with. In itself, a fact worth noting."

"Any marks in the clothes?"

"No laundry marks, no label even. The labels had been cut with scissors from the overcoat and waistcoat. It might almost appear that Lewis anticipated this investigation and provided against it." The physician lifted his hand. "A minute, please. Allow me an opportunity to develop the theme. I promise you will find it worth your while to resume. I examined the body carefully and the farther I went, the more curious I became. Lewis has soft, white, manicured hands, a shade too manicured for my taste. His socks and underwear—look at them yourself—are the finest grade. Ditto his boots, which are London-made, unless I'm very much mistaken."

Recalling the shabby overcoat, the well-worn suit, I experienced a twinge of surprise. Standish began to poke among the clothing spread upon the table. The rest of us attended Dr. Rand, who paced slowly up and down before the fire.

"Now look at the hat, suit and overcoat—quite different, aren't they? Cheap, shoddy stuff! The suit was a wretched fit, yet the boots were custom made."

"Anything else?"

"An operation for appendicitis a few years back—an excellent surgeon did the work—I've never seen a more beautiful scar." Brought to himself by Standish's impatient snort, Dr. Rand repressed his professional enthusiasm. "Equally good dentistry—the man's teeth were…"

"Let's pass the teeth."

"Are you interested in learning that until a short time ago—two days at the most—Lewis sported a small, neat mustache? One of those broker decorations. There's a bare patch on the upper lip, lighter than the surrounding epidermis and recently shaved."

"Certain of that?"

"Positive. The condition of the skin indicates he wore a mustache for years, undoubtedly was handsomer with it on. He's got a bad mouth, if you noticed. If I had been Lewis, I would have kept the mustache. Curious he didn't choose to."

Dr. Rand smiled blandly and continued the performance. I liked him. He was a peculiarly vital man, who breathed excitement and gave it forth.

"Next," said the physician, "we come to the spectacles Lewis wore.

Here, take them. They're worth attention."

Standish accepted the spectacles. "They look o.k. to me."

"Then look again at the lenses."

Standish and I saw simultaneously what the physician meant. Convincing on casual scrutiny, the spectacles proved obvious counterfeits when examined carefully, and of no possible aid to vision. The thick clumsy lenses had been cut from ordinary window glass, the frames fashioned of a cheap lead composition. Such spectacles are often sold at toy counters. Standish lifted them to his eyes.

"Maybe he wore them as a protection from the wind."

"Lewis was wearing the glasses," I said, "when he came out of the station."

"No doubt he was," remarked Dr. Rand. "Amazing what a change a pair of spectacles will work in the appearance. These fit with the missing mustache, the suit, the hat, the overcoat. Taken in conjunction with the watch, they become even more significant."

He had expected a mild sensation; he got it. Standish abruptly dropped the eyeglasses. "What watch?"

"Lewis's watch, naturally! Or rather the watch he carried in his left-hand vest pocket."

With this cryptic statement. Dr. Rand drew from his own pocket a slim platinum watch, no wider than a silver dollar and circled in square-cut diamonds. An expensive, fragile, lovely bauble. Standish extended his hand. Dr. Rand himself forced open the case to reveal delicate, swiftly moving works and a smooth platinum back inscribed with two initials. These initials were H. D.

Standish stared hard. "H. D doesn't stand for Elmer Lewis!"

"My thought exactly."

"In other words he wasn't Elmer Lewis."

"Not unless he stole or borrowed the watch. Take your choice. I've taken mine."

So had we all. The fine underwear, the cheap outer apparel, the ridiculous eyeglasses, the shaved upper lip, the lack of labels and the pockets empty of personal memoranda, like tiny signposts pointed to an inescapable conclusion. Elmer Lewis had chosen to alight in the New Haven station as a man without a past. Two initials, forgotten or overlooked, had betrayed the plan, even though they did not elucidate its reason.

Standish placed the watch beside the spectacles, got heavily to his feet. Stooping, he lifted the brass-bound traveling bag, previously removed from our car. The bag was securely locked. He grunted, strove unsuccessfully to force the catches. A sudden question in his eyes, Jack leaned forward.

"Where's the other bag?"

Standish ceased his labors. "What other bag?"

"The bag in the rumble seat." As often when perturbed, Jack began to stutter. "Didn't I say there were two bags? One in front with us, one in back with Lewis."

Standish spun upon the coroner. "Doc, was there a bag in the rumble seat when you examined the body?"

"No—no. There was no bag there."

"What became of it, then?"

Question and glare were general. No one was imprudent enough to venture a reply.

"How about you, Harkway? Did you see a bag when you stopped the car? I mean in the rumble seat."

"Gosh, I can't remember."

"Something happened to that second bag! It didn't fly off over the meadows."

The police chief's anger exploded into action. Seizing a paper knife he attacked the bag on the chair. One catch broke. The knife slid into the crack beneath the lid, bent in a dangerous arc, and the other catch broke; the lid of the bag snapped back and the knife flew across the room to fall unnoticed.

We crowded about Standish, all of us silent, too amazed for speech. The pigskin bag was heaped with currency. Hundred-dollar bills, ten-and twenty-dollar bills. Stack after stack, fitted shoulder to shoulder, still wearing the paper halters provided by banking houses.

"There's a million dollars there," said Harkway in an awed whisper.

He was wrong. There wasn't a million. After a double count, some twenty minutes later, John Standish announced in weary baffled tones that the bag contained exactly $108,000.

CHAPTER FIVE

The Open Door

It was long past midnight when Standish glanced at the wall clock, sighed and said he guessed we could call it a day. Needless to say Jack had not explained the $108,000. Neither of us could imagine why Elmer Lewis had carried a small fortune in an ordinary pigskin bag. Obviously the money had a connection with the dead man's mysterious business in Crockford, but the wildest speculation carried us no further.

Fingers cramped with weariness, Minnie Gray took down Standish's rapid questions on the point, and Jack's flagging answers. Her record is before me now. It is both diffuse and repetitious and I am consulting it only as an aid to memory.

"You say Lewis himself put the bag in the front seat of your car?"

"Yes, sir."

"You had no idea of its contents?"

"Certainly not!"

"A hundred and eight thousand dollars is a lot of money, Mr. Storm. Did you get any hint from Lewis how he meant to use so large a sum?"

"I've just said I didn't know he had the money."

"Did you receive any impression from his manner that the bag was valuable?"

"None whatever."

"I believe you said Lewis watched his property from the rumble seat. By rising, from time to time, and looking through the window at you."

"That's correct."

"Still you didn't suspect he was anxious about his bag?"

"We've covered that. I thought the man was crazy. Not a raving lunatic, but certainly a little touched. We were annoyed by his peeping till Lola drew the curtain."

"You weren't frightened?"

"I wasn't; he made my wife jittery."

"How about the missing bag? Can you describe it? Was it similar to this one?"

"I really didn't notice. My impression is it was somewhat smaller."

"Did it feel heavy?"

"I didn't handle either bag; so I can't compare them. I wasn't interested in Lewis's luggage."

Standish stared at the open bag with its cargo of heaped-up bills. No one in the room had ever seen an equal amount of money. We all were fascinated, and I confess my eyes kept straying there. Beautifully engraved, green and orange and brown, those bits of paper spoke of ease and luxury, of furs and jewels, of security in a world grown insecure. They spoke no further.

The police chief's gaze moved again to Jack. "Possibly Mrs. Coatesnash may be able to explain the purpose of the money. I hope so."

"You sound doubtful. Surely it is to be expected she will be better able to explain than I am. She knew Elmer Lewis—I didn't. She wrote to him—not to me. He came up from New York on her business—not on mine."

"Mrs. Coatesnash will do all she can. I'll vouch for her willingness. My only regret is she's so far away."

The interrogation continued. Hours later Jack rebelled. He flipped, a final cigarette to the pile beside him. "You have pumped me dry. I'm signing off. I have one more thing to say. I object to your methods. Strenuously. There are other lines of investigation in this case. Why don't you follow them up, and give me and my wife a rest?"

"Interested parties, Mr. Storm, seldom approve of police methods in a criminal investigation. Speaking candidly, I'm far from satisfied with the story you've told tonight. Far from satisfied."

On that note, abruptly, Standish decided to call it a day.

Allowing for possible delays, an answer to his cable could not be expected before noon on Saturday. He warned us to anticipate further questioning, stretched and rose.

"We seem to be at a temporary stalemate. A great deal depends on the cable I receive tomorrow. Mrs. Coatesnash may be able to throw some light on the situation."

At his apparent lack of conviction my heart sank. Jack got stiffly to his feet. The small room which I had virtually memorized during the hours we sat and talked in circles was rank with the odor of dead smoke. The fire flickered low, expired. Minnie Gray yawned, gathered her notebooks, dropped into a handbag those neat, accurate, damning reports, and slipped away. Outside a wagon clattered across the cobblestones. Milk bottles clinked and a sleepy driver shouted at his horse.

I reached for my coat. Standish intervened. "You must put up with us a little longer, Mrs. Storm."

I paused, confused. Jack laid down his hat, turned slowly. "Then we aren't going home? Is that what you mean? Are we under arrest?"

The police chief was falsely jovial. "We have to make sure you two will stick around. So far you are the backbone of our case!"

He made a phone call. In silent sympathy Dr. Rand offered Jack his whisky flask and took a drink himself. The three policemen declined, though I thought Harkway looked rather wistful. As the wait lengthened, he stepped out to the hotdog wagon and brought back greasy paper bags. A constrained group, we were drinking coffee and eating sandwiches when old Judge Calkins waddled in. He was a portly gentleman with a prejudice against Italians, Middle Europeans, and New Yorkers. He had been summoned from bed and was eager to return to it. He decided at once that Jack and I should be held as material witnesses, and promptly set a prohibitive bond to guarantee that we would remain in Crockford. We couldn't have raised a quarter of the sum, and I was wondering where I was to lay my head that night when Dr. Rand unexpectedly came to our aid.

"That figure is ridiculous," he informed the judge, "but I think these kids are unlucky and honest. I'll go bail for them."

"With what?"

"With my expensive, well-appointed and completely modern house. I exclude my library, of course."

The judge and the doctor were friends. They argued amiably over the value of the house, which the judge insisted was papered with mortgages, and the upshot of this bickering was that Jack and I went free. I guessed that Standish wasn't pleased by the physician's kindly interference; the pompous little Blair plainly was not; and even Harkway seemed doubtful.

Frowning then, Standish added a few last instructions. We were to go straight to the cottage; we were to remain there, awaiting a call from headquarters; we were not to discuss the case with outsiders. The policemen went into a huddle, and Jack and I departed. Dr. Rand, who accompanied us to the street, wouldn't listen to our fervent thanks.

"I was glad to help out. If your conscience is clear—and I think it is—you have nothing to worry about."

"Then we won't worry."

"That house," said the physician meditatively, "is all I own in the world. I've lived there a long time and it suits me perfectly."

He was gone. Jack and I looked at each other. The village was dead as Pompeii, the stores closed and barred, the echoing sidewalks empty. The street lights, all six of them, had glimmered out at midnight. I felt light-headed from strain and exhaustion. Jack took my arm.

"Standish didn't believe a single word I said."

"Anyhow we're not in jail. I wonder if both of us could have wedged into it. I could have kissed the doctor."

"It's preposterous," said Jack bitterly, "we should need bail. Standish knows damn well we won't light out. Where have we got to go?"

"New York."

"New York, hell! We would be arrested at the first station. That's exactly the sort of break they're waiting for. That bag of money looked bad. Very bad. It provided a motive."

"A motive for whom?" My voice shrilled. "For you? It's nonsense to suppose you would murder a man you didn't know for money you didn't know he had!"

"Where's proof I didn't know him? Where's proof I didn't know he had the money?"

Our car detained by the police, was to be examined for fingerprints and searched for further evidence. We walked to Crockford garage to hire a taxi. The news of the murder had preceded us. Two sleepy-eyed drivers drifted out of the office to stare. Al Loomis, owner of the three taxis that served the village, personally drove us to the cottage.

It was after two o'clock when we reached home. The rain was long since over. A thin, clear breeze stirred the tree tops, and the rank meadow grass bent sibilantly before it. A high moon shone whitely upon the open field beyond the cottage, over a stone fence to the left, and etched in sharp relief the black woods that separated us from the next house on the road. Throughout the dreadful evening my mind had been pulling toward this spot. As I alighted to experience the impact of deep, country silence I regretted that we had not stayed in town. Dark and quiet, forlorn and lonely, our home had never seemed so alien, or less a place of comfort and of rest. Until the taxi disappeared, Jack and I stood in the driveway, watching. Then, "Let's not talk tonight," said he. "I'm dead."

I shivered, loath to proceed. "I wish we had left the lights burning."

Jack was tired and querulous. "We're home, Lola. You've been a good girl. Try not to go to pieces now."

He guided me across the muddy drive, past the well to the kitchen door. Like most country people, except on rare occasions, we used the back entrance. Jack produced his key, preceded me into the house. I stepped reluctantly into the inky blackness, paused and waited for him to find the light. Suddenly from the darkness came the sound of a collision followed by a cry of rage and pain.

"What was it, Jack?"

"That damned cellar door just knocked me cuckoo." Immediately he switched on the light, glared at the door which led to the cellar, transferred the glare to me.

"You should know better than to leave it open."

"I didn't leave it open, Jack."

Our nerves were on the ragged edge. In the yard I had wanted sympathy and had received none. Now I myself declined to offer solace. Promptly we found ourselves engaged in a pointless, bitter, matrimonial wrangle.

"You left the door open, Lola, as you habitually do. There's no sense denying it. You went down to bank the furnace."

"I closed the door when I came up. I remember closing it. You must have gone down later on."

"I haven't been in the cellar since morning."

"You must have been."

"I say I wasn't!"

Kicking shut the disputed door, Jack stamped off, nursing his head and muttering darkly. When I entered the bedroom, he was already half undressed. Without speaking further, he climbed into bed. A few minutes later I joined him, put a timid hand on his averted shoulder.

"Jack, I'm positive I closed the door."

"You win, dear. You closed it, and the little people opened it."

"I'm serious, Jack. Really serious. Are you certain you didn't go to the cellar after I did?"

"Is this another cross-examination? I've said repeatedly I was certain."

"Then how did the door get open?"

"For God's sake, Lola, let me get some sleep."

Almost at once I heard his heavy breathing. Moonlight poured into the bedroom; the night was quiet. I desperately wanted to sleep, but I was in that condition of exhaustion when sleep becomes impossible. I turned and turned again, unable even to close my eyes. My nerves were taut, my senses preternaturally acute. I felt a thin chill breeze although the window curtain stood motionless; I smelled the salt of the Sound and the damp, earthy odor of the fields; I heard the subdued rustle of mice in the attic.

I couldn't rid my mind of that door. Again and again I went over my trip to the cellar. Again and again I saw myself shutting the door. My certainty became an obsession. I longed to compel Jack to admit he had been mistaken.

"Jack," I whispered. "Jack."

His heavy breathing continued unabated. I assumed another position, tossed and rolled. My eyes wandered, and in wakeful desperation I studied the bedroom doors. Three doors, one to the bathroom, one to the living room, one to a shallow clothes closet. I examined the closet door. Jack's necktie hung around the knob, and the shadow of knob and necktie were weirdly printed upon the floor. Gradually my fixed gaze grew hypnotic. My lids were drooping shut when suddenly I felt a wave of cold surprise. The shadow on the floor was moving. I stared. Slowly but definitely the shadow advanced across the floor and toward the bed.

For a moment I lay rigid. My heart hammered, perspiration chilled my forehead and I seemed frozen to the bed. I looked again at the shadow, then raised my eyes to the closet door. Very quietly the door was opening out into the bedroom.

I shrieked.

The door flew open. A man with a blurred, black face rushed from the closet, across the bedroom into the living room. Jack flung back the covers, sat up.

"What was it?"

"Someone in the closet—a Negro."

The kitchen door banged. Instantly Jack was out of bed and out of the bedroom. A second time the door banged. Clad only in a thin nightgown, I, too somehow got outside and into the yard.

Two figures were running through the moonlight. The man who had hidden in the closet was far in advance, half way across the stubble field beyond the fence. He ran like an animal, crouched low, arms swinging. Hampered by a late start and bare feet. Jack was steadily losing ground. As I gained the fence, the black-faced man plunged into the woods at the edge of the field, disappeared. Jack put on a fresh burst of speed.

"Come back," I screamed.

Jack didn't turn or hesitate, but darted on and out of sight. This bit of foolhardiness, typical of him, can make me angry now. As I saw him vanish across that empty moonlit field I felt a terror such as I had never known before. I clambered over the fence, reversed myself, and shot back into the cottage, thus, as Jack admitted later, exhibiting a higher degree of intelligence than he had shown. I reached the telephone. I retained sufficient wit to realize that Standish was six miles away, and when a sleepy operator finally answered, I put in a call for Silas. He answered at the second ring, but he sounded sleepy and his questions were intolerably slow and stupid. Frantic, I demanded that he come at once.

"Directly I get some clothes on, Mrs. Storm."

The Lodge was more than half a mile distant. Reminded of my own apparel, I snatched up a bathrobe and slippers, hesitated long enough to try the police station—I got no response there or at Standish's home—then ran outside into the stubble field, loudly calling Jack and watching for Silas. I had hoped he would take the short cut through the pasture. His bobbing lantern a few minutes later approached by the road.

Hatless, coatless, muttering to himself, he *was* hurrying. As he scrambled through the barbed-wire fence, and as I dragged him toward the woods, I poured forth a confused, incoherent story.

"Who was in the closet?"

"I don't know. It was a Negro."

"There aren't many Negroes around Crockford."

"I don't care who was in the closet," I cried, maddened by his stupidity. "I don't care how many Negroes are in Crockford. I want to find Jack. You've got to help, me."

At this point it developed that Silas was unwilling to enter the woods. He proposed returning to the Lodge to get his dog. I plunged in alone, and I suppose his conscience pricked him, for he followed, though he stuck close beside me. Together we started beating the bush, calling, calling. I had a flashlight. Silas, who had prudently armed himself with a stout stick, swung his lantern to and fro. Giant circles danced eerily through the tangled underbrush. Twigs crackled, the wind sighed overhead, a rabbit fled past like a shadow. Silas and I grabbed each other's hands in mutual terror.

Five minutes later the hired man stumbled across a pair of outthrust feet. Bleeding and senseless, Jack had been roughly shoved into a clump of briars. We drew him into the open.

I pushed Silas aside—he was near collapse—and knelt upon the ground. Blood smeared Jack's cheek and forehead; he lay deathly white and still. He didn't hear me when I called his name.

CHAPTER SIX

The Hell Hole

Between us, Silas and I carried Jack into the cottage and laid him upon the bed. Although he had not stirred during the journey, his pallor was less intense. As I wrapped a comforter about his feet and adjusted a pillow beneath his head, he moved a little and groaned deeply, wearily. I sent Silas to heat a kettle of water. When he brought in the steaming kettle I began to bathe Jack's forehead.

"Well," said Silas almost cheerfully, "we got him back all right."

"So *we* did," I said.

He was impervious to irony. He shambled to the closet, peered curiously inside and muttered that our intruder had chosen a strange hiding place—a fact which had earlier occurred to me. Just then, however, I could not appreciate the hired man's speculations. My tone was short.

"Go and phone for Dr. Rand."

I continued my ministrations. The savage head wound, clotted with blood, matted with blond hair, abruptly thrust from my mind a certain tentative theory. Until then I had thought that, running as he was, headlong, into the dense blackness of the woods, Jack might have crashed into a tree and knocked himself unconscious. This wound was the result not of accident, but of a singularly brutal attack.

Silas returned to report that Dr. Rand would come at once. We were to put ice on Jack's head and a hot-water bottle at his feet. We were to do nothing else until the physician reached the cottage.

"He said quiet was the best medicine."

Shortly afterward Jack opened his eyes. Too sick and nauseated to discuss what had happened in the woods, he was sufficiently himself to protest against a doctor.

"I'll be o.k. in the morning."

Following his prediction, he was again violently nauseated. Silas promptly suggested that the patient rise from bed to walk backward across the room. This remedy was culled from Mrs. Coatesnash's store, and according to Silas, had been effective in the case of a young relative who had tumbled from a haymow.

"You can lean on me, Mr. Storm, if you feel sickish. I promise it's a sure cure. With my own eyes I saw it work with little Willie. Mrs. Coatesnash swears it saved his life."

Jack decided to remain where he was.

Dr. Rand had assimilated his quota of excitement for one evening. He arrived at the cottage, disposed to make light of Jack's injuries. Silas's telephone report had been garbled and uninformative; furthermore, Jack was shakily sitting up.

The physician jovially approached the bed. "What's this I hear about your chasing bandits in the woods? Don't you know enough to carry a flashlight?"

Immediately he commenced the examination his face sobered. He asked Jack many questions. He had him shake his head. "Do you feel any pain?"

"Lord, yes."

"Is it concussion?" I asked quietly.

"I think not." Dr. Rand looked at Jack. "You're a lucky young man. That's a nasty wound. You missed a bad injury by a very narrow margin."

"I think myself I missed death by a narrow margin."

The statement went uncontradicted. Dr. Rand turned, gave me a few instructions and ordered Jack to report the next day for an X-ray. Just to be sure. Then snapping shut his bag, he paused hesitantly.

"Exactly what did happen? I'm curious."

"I was running in the woods, running hard. I stopped to listen. Someone hit me."

"From behind?"

"Yes."

"You didn't see what it was?"

"No."

Silas put in his two cent's worth. "Mrs. Storm said it was a Negro. That don't seem likely to me. Only three Negroes live in Crockford and they're respectable folks."

Dr. Rand turned sharply to Jack. "I thought you didn't see who it was."

"Lola thinks," Jack replied, "it was a Negro."

The remark was oddly framed; Jack's glance was odd. I knew him better than the others; I realized he was holding something back. The physician addressed me.

"You saw the man?"

"When he came out of the closet. I glimpsed his black face as he rushed through the bedroom."

Silence fell. Clear in the minds of three of us rose a scene on the streets of Crockford; a noisy, babbling crowd, a parked automobile, a rigid, upright body sitting in the rumble seat. We had, that night, played a part in one murder. Within nine hours of the murder this attack had occurred. Dr. Rand's eyes traveled again to Jack's wound.

"It runs through my mind that I did you a poor favor tonight. Apparently you'd have been better of if you had stayed—downtown." He paused. "Of course, it's possible there is no connection."

Silas was baffled by the trend of the conversation. He interposed a quick, inquisitive question. "Connection, doctor? What are you talking about?"

"Please don't interrupt, Silas." To the physician Jack said, "How could there be a connection? No one wants to kill me."

"Make no mistake! Someone tried to kill you."

When I accompanied Dr. Rand to the door I asked him how he could be so positive. "After all, Jack has no enemies."

"He has one deadly enemy. Whatever you may imagine, your husband was not the victim of an unpremeditated attack. His assailant didn't strike with a stone or a branch torn from one of the near-by trees, as you may suppose. He struck with a heavy, blunt, metal weapon."

"How can you know that?"

"I found bits of rust in the wound."

Having alarmed me thoroughly, he advised me to go to bed and get some rest. His car roared in the yard outside and I returned to the bedroom. Propped high with pillows and still extremely white, Jack was energetically directing Silas in a search of the closet. The hired man crouched on hands and knees, staring owlishly and fruitlessly at the closet floor. Except that several garments had fallen from hangers and lay about in untidy heaps, there was no evidence that a black-faced man had hidden there within three feet of our bed. I put a stop to the search.

Bought by the promise of an extra fifty cents, Silas agreed to spend the remainder of the night on the living-room sofa. Pie seemed decidedly uneasy, and I thought it fortunate that he knew nothing about the murder. An uncourageous man, he was sharp enough to sense that certain facts concerning the evening had been withheld. This further impaired his morale.

"Can I keep the lights burning?"

"Certainly."

"The light in the kitchen, too?"

"As many as you like."

I closed the door on him. Jack retained sufficient spirit to flash a grin. "Silas isn't much of a port for the Storms."

Then, as he spread his open palms upon the coverlet, his grin faded. "Look at my hands, Lola."

"They're filthy!"

"That isn't dirt. That's soot."

Uncomprehendingly, I stared. The palms of both hands were black; a smear of dense black discolored the back of the left hand.

"But Jack, how can that be? There isn't any soot in the woods. Where did you get it?"

"From the man who knocked me out. I think I must instinctively have caught at him in an effort to fight back. In fact, I'm sure I did."

"But, Jack…"

"Look at the knob on the closet door. The inside knob."

I went to the door. The white china knob was a grimy black. I extended an experimental finger; particles of soot came away.

"You didn't see a Negro," said Jack from his pillows. "You saw a man who had covered his face and hands with soot or burnt cork. You saw a man who had disguised himself."

I spent a restless night. At dawn, leaving Jack asleep, I rose and tiptoed through the living room. The sofa was empty. I heard Silas moving in the cellar. I established his identity by taking what would have been a silly and unthinkable precaution—twenty-four hours earlier. I shouted down.

"Is that you, Silas?"

"Yes, ma'am."

"What are you doing?"

"Looking for dues."

"I don't suppose you've found any."

Silas's voice, satisfied, and, now that day had dawned, chipper enough, floated upward.

"I found out how that fellow got in."

Immediately I descended the unstable wooden stairs. Dusty, musty, damp, smelling of faint, strange odors, the cellar of the cottage was an untidy catch-all which we referred to privately as the Hell Hole. For generations the Coatesnash family had accumulated possessions and for generations had stubbornly-clung to them. In every available corner Mrs. Coatesnash had stored superannuated articles she considered far too good to throw away. The assemblage included a decrepit phonograph with a painted horn, three bottomless reed chairs, ancient electric fixtures, a horrible, marble-topped dresser, a camp cot, an old mattress, a three-legged table poised drunkenly against a whatnot whose seams were bursting with dampness. It included bits of broken never-to-be-mended china and bric-a-brac gleaming on shelves along with empty ginger-ale bottles and preserve jars. It included a long, unpleasant roll of carpet which had not seen the light in forty years.

In the midst of this ruin of the past glowed a modern furnace pink with heat. Near by stood Silas, squinting at a pile of coal which mounted to a small window above. At once and certainly I knew where our intruder had got his disguise. Coal dust. In three rapid minutes, with coal dust, a white man could make himself a black man. It had been coal dust on Jack's hands and on the doorknob. Coal dust from our own cellar!

As I left the stairs, I had the queer feeling that Silas also, independently, had arrived at and would suggest the possibility that the intruder had smeared himself with coal dust. We had planned to impart only to the police our information regarding the disguise. For an instant I wondered if

Silas were as stupid as we had thought him, or if we had considered him stupid merely because he was unlike ourselves. Had he glimpsed Jack's hands? Had he seen the grimy door knob and drawn his own conclusions?

"Right here, Mrs. Storm," began the hired man in his flat, shrill tones, "is where the fellow got in. He busted that window-pane, unlocked the window and slid down the coal."

I picked my way to the spot. Silas pointed out the broken window-pane, the bits of shattered glass sparkling on the browned grass outside. I said nothing. Standing beside the hired man, in daylight, in the cellar of my own home, I was swept by an appalling sensation of fright and insecurity. The pane could be mended. Bars could be wedged across the window. Still I knew that never again would I feel safe in the pretty little country cottage. At length I spoke calmly, steadily.

"You must show this to the police, Silas."

With which I went back upstairs. Awake now and livelier than he had any right to be, Jack was clamoring for coffee. We were breakfasting from a card table pulled up beside the bed when Silas entered with a final, disquieting piece of news. Our poker had disappeared.

"You're sure you saw it yesterday?"

"I used it yesterday."

"Maybe you mislaid it."

"I don't mislay things, Mrs. Storm. I keep that poker beside the furnace. It was there yesterday. It's gone now."

After breakfast, despite Jack's protests, Silas and I went out to search the woods. We didn't locate the poker. As I remember, I didn't say in words to Silas that we were hunting for the poker. He knew. He was as certain as was I that our own poker was the blunt, heavy, metal weapon which had struck Jack unconscious to the ground.

With the sun glinting down, at eight in the morning, last night's woods were anything but sinister or mysterious. The trees, mostly elms and oaks, grew in a sparse narrow band between two wide fields, our own, and the field which belonged to the Olmstead place. I had not previously felt the lack of neighbors. Now the brown farmhouse, shuttered, unoccupied, depressed me by its very emptiness. As we patiently wound in and out the winter trees, examining the soggy ground, I said to Silas:

"When are the Olmsteads opening their place?"

"Some time in May. Mrs. Olmstead asked me to start her gardens in April. She's a nice lady, talks too much, but you will like her."

Empty-handed at the end of an hour's search we plodded back toward the cottage. A car shot past on the road and pulled into our drive.

John Standish was alighting when we arrived in the yard. He had not heard the news of the attack, and was wholly absorbed with the murder. He greeted me with tempered cordiality.

"Good morning, Mrs. Storm. Is your husband up? I'd like to ask him some additional questions."

"You've had an answer to your cable?"

"Not yet."

"Then why are you here?"

"The second bag turned up this morning. A farmer driving along the road outside Durham found a packed bag tossed behind a signboard. We believe it to be the missing bag."

I looked at him blankly. "Durham! But that's miles beyond New Haven. We weren't there."

"That is what I want to establish—if I can."

Standish waited for my reply. I realize now that he was deliberately watching my reactions, seeking, in my first instant of surprise, to trap me into some admission that the detailed story we had told him was untrue.

I disappointed him. "We were nowhere near Durham. Not within miles of it. If you have found the bag on a road outside Durham, someone put it there—not Jack, not I. Someone else."

"I hope that's true."

"What was in the bag?"

"A man's pajamas, bathrobe and slippers, toilet articles, a magazine and a couple of fresh shirts."

"No letters? Nothing to identify Lewis?"

Standish shook his head. "I'm afraid the identification is going to be tough. Lewis himself made it tough. A funny thing. The man's own extraordinary behavior is hampering the investigation of his murder."

I had forgotten Silas. A choking sound recalled him to my attention. He was gazing pop-eyed at Standish and me, as though simultaneously we had taken leave of our senses.

"What are you talking about? What murder? No one told me anything about a murder."

I said shortly, "Last night a man was murdered in the rumble scat of our car. Shot through the heart. I can't tell you any more."

Silas sank to the running board of Standish's machine. He turned a mottled gray. His first thoughts, his first words dwelt upon himself. "If I'd known about it I never in the world would have spent a night on your sofa."

"Then it's as well you didn't know!"

While he sat huddled on the running board, I gave Standish an account of the man who had hidden in the clothes closet. The police chief listened intently, stepped over the fence and examined blurred, valueless footprints, and decided, before speaking to Jack, to go to the cellar. Silas obstinately refused to accompany him. The news of the murder had destroyed his interest in clues.

"Let the chief look for himself. I got my work to do. I ain't going to mix myself in murder."

He rose, ambled across the yard and started up the hill toward the

Coatesnash mansion. In a way, I suppose Jack and I had served him a mean trick; it was natural he should resent it. Nevertheless, I was exasperated by the solid self-interest of the type he represented. Country people, suspicious of the law fearful of newcomers, anxious above all else to keep their own skirts clear of trouble—how I hated them! Jack and I had been good to Silas, yet he could see us hang without too great perturbation.

Standish and I went to the cellar. After glancing around its gloomy confines, speculating upon the whereabouts of the missing poker and studying the broken window, the police chief suddenly climbed the steps that led to the lawn. I followed him around the house. He stared at the broken glass scattered outside the cellar window. He looked inside at the coal. Then, grunting, he stooped, picked up a fragment of glass, and dropped it in his pocket. I was curious.

"What's that for?"

"One never knows," was the evasive reply, "what might be useful."

How a bit of rain-washed glass could be useful was beyond my ability to conjecture. Puzzled, I escorted him into the house. He nodded to Jack, expressed jocular sympathy, crossed the bedroom and peered at the closet door knob. His face assumed a peculiar expression.

"No fingerprints. This evidently is to be a case without them. There was none on the car, except yours and your wife's." Returning to the bed, he glanced at Jack's bandaged head. "Have you had a doctor?"

"We called Dr. Rand last night."

"You did!" Standish at once stepped out to telephone the physician.

I strongly suspected that he had doubted the attack, despite the circumstantial evidence provided by Jack's bandages, the coal dust on the knob, the broken cellar window. A few minutes later my suspicion was verified. Having spoken to the physician, Standish was now entirely convinced and—I thought—obscurely relieved. He was also friendlier.

"The doctor is willing to swear you were murderously attacked. No question of accident. Now-it's up to us to decide why."

Jack gingerly fingered his bandages. "That sounds like a large order."

"On the contrary, it seems to me the simplest point in the whole business. A man with a soot-blackened face hides in your closet, runs outside, with you hot on his heels. You rush into the woods; you stop to listen; perhaps you make a move as if to turn. Immediately he smacks you from behind. Why? Because he is afraid to have you turn."

"You mean," said Jack slowly, "he was afraid I might recognize him?"

"Exactly. Even with his soot-blackened face, he was afraid. Mr. Storm, you know the man who struck you down last night."

The solution seemed infinitely horrible to me. "If that is so, why did he run across the open field? I saw him clearly in the moonlight. So did Jack. Why didn't he run to the road? It's much darker there."

Standish frowned. "He was in a hurry to escape."

"The distance to the road is the same. It's easier to run on a road than on a stubble field."

"Perhaps he didn't think."

Jack sided with me. "It's a queer thing to say, but I believe he did think. That man ran like a person with an objective—straight ahead. He led, you understand. I followed."

"He may live in one of the houses farther down the line. Who owns the next house? The Olmsteads? They winter in New Haven, don't they?" Standish spent an interval in reflection. "Just on chance I'll have a look at that place this afternoon." Jack stirred restively. "The whole affair seems senseless. Meaningless. Why should anyone break into our cottage and hide in the closet?"

"You say you have no enemies?"

Jack smiled. "Not that sort of enemies."

"Then," said Standish "we can eliminate a design upon your personal safety as the motive."

Jack nodded in agreement.

The other continued. "Next we will eliminate robbery. You drove up in a taxi. As you entered the back door it would have been easy for a thief to leave by the front door. The black-faced gentleman didn't do that. Instead he did what no run-of-the-mine burglar ever does. He hid himself."

I shivered. "He was waiting for us."

"No, Mrs. Storm. I believe he was waiting for someone else."

"For Elmer Lewis!" exclaimed Jack.

Bewildered, I interrupted. "But Lewis was dead when we drove up. Dead in Crockford, murdered."

"Your intruder may not have known that. You have said Lewis wanted to come to the cottage, insisted upon coming. Isn't it possible he expected to meet someone here?"

"Do you mean to say he expected to meet a man hidden in the closet with a poker in his hand? Am I to believe that?" Standish smiled vaguely. "Strange things happen, Mrs. Storm. After all, Lewis had one enemy. Why not two?"

"It seems a trifle thick," Jack said doubtfully. "Two separate plots on the same man's life in a single evening! Lewis was an odd duck, but he wasn't simple. He went to considerable pains before he set out on his trip— cut the labels from his clothes, shaved his mustache, wore those glasses. One would think he might have taken a few elementary precautions to protect himself."

"He did," said Standish grimly. "I didn't tell you two last night, but Lewis was armed. There was a gun in his overcoat pocket. And his right hand—you will remember—was jammed in the pocket."

"Under the circumstances," said Jack, "it might have been wiser if he had carried a gun on his lap."

"Lewis anticipated trouble," said Standish, "but my hunch is he didn't anticipate what happened. He had provided for contingencies which—" the policemen looked around the bedroom "—which might occur in this cottage."

An automobile—our own car, by the way—chugged into the drive, came to a noisy halt. Blair popped out of it and strode purposefully across the yard. A moment later the little deputy swept into the bedroom, clothed in the authority of the law and the neatest uniform that Crockford has ever seen.

"Well?" said Standish.

Blair whipped out two white envelopes, and handed them to his superior. They were the cablegrams, long awaited, one signed by Luella Coatesnash, the other by the head of the Paris *Sûreté*. Standish opened the envelopes, rapidly perused their contents. Jack couldn't conceal his eagerness. He stretched out his hand.

In silence Standish surrendered the printed sheet. I read over Jack's shoulder. The message was short. It follows:

"ELMER LEWIS HANDLED NO BUSINESS FOR ME HAVE NEVER HEARD THE NAME. PLEASE CABLE EXPLANATIONS.
LUELLA COATESNASH."

CHAPTER SEVEN

The Voice on the Telephone

For a long interval no one in the bedroom moved or spoke. Together Jack and I stared at the printed words which had deepened materially the embarrassment and danger of our situation. I was not precisely surprised, but I was angry and discouraged. A few minutes earlier Standish had been discussing the case in quite a friendly fashion, and now it seemed to me the atmosphere had subtly altered. Jack refolded the white paper, returned it to the police chief.

"And the other cablegram?"

"The other is a confidential report from the French police and merely verifies what you read. Mrs. Coatesnash was interviewed at her hotel this morning, expressed her willingness to be of assistance, but was helpless. Evidently she is bewildered at being drawn into the matter, and can neither explain who Elmer Lewis is or how he happened to use her name."

"That," said Jack, "is impossible for me to credit."

Few outsiders had the temerity or the bad taste to criticize a Coatesnash on her own home grounds. The pompous little deputy, whom Luella had never so much as spoken to, bristled like a wet cat. Standish looked cold and alienated. This was a situation we were to face throughout the coming days; whenever our interests conflicted with those of Mrs. Coatesnash, inevitably we lost.

Said Standish, "I've known Luella Coatesnash since I was a boy in knickerbockers. In some ways she may be peculiar, but she is a fine old lady. I have the utmost confidence in her integrity." Jack half rose in bed. "Isn't it important that Lewis lured us to New Haven by using her name? Isn't it strange? How is it to be explained?"

Blair displayed his claws. "There's only your word for that tale, Mr. Storm. Your word alone!"

"There's my wife's word! If you were sufficiently enterprising you might discover the telephone operator who put through the call. Those girls listen in on everything. Have you done anything about tracing the call?"

"You bet we have! The local exchange has no record of a long-distance call made here yesterday afternoon. They don't keep records of local calls, but neither of the girls remembers ringing this number at all. They're both smart girls."

Standish glanced at his assistant in brusque reproof. "For the present we will accept that the telephone call was made, exactly as it's been described. We will accept that Elmer Lewis announced his intention of coming to Crockford on business for Mrs. Coatesnash. We will accept that Lewis, for a reason of his own, lied. Now where does that get us?"

I said, "It gets us back to the spot where we left off last night."

"Not quite," said Jack with a suspicious mildness. "Today we have cleared Mrs. Coatesnash. We've done it on the strength of a single unsupported statement. Which is no mean feat!" Standish said patiently, "How could Mrs. Coatesnash be expected to recognize the name Elmer Lewis if the man were using an alias? She might be acquainted with him under his right name. On the other hand, she might never have heard of him.

"The Coatesnash family is one of the most prominent in Connecticut. It would be very easy for a stranger to pick up the name, to learn certain things about Mrs. Coatesnash, to discover she was abroad and to take advantage of the fact."

I chimed in, "It wouldn't be easy for a stranger to know we are tenants of hers. Elmer Lewis knew it. He knew about the cottage. He knew the make and model of our car."

Standish swung around to face me. "It's easier than you imagine for unscrupulous persons to gather information about you, information you can't dream they possess. Particularly when a large city is concerned. Let me show you. You've lived in Crockford since January—three months—and during that period you have returned to New York several times. How many times?"

"Five or six."

"On those occasions you saw friends, visited restaurants, theaters, attended parties. You talked. What did you talk about? Let me guess. You talked about your life in the country; you mentioned your landlady. No doubt you described her, spoke of her eccentricities, the small differences of opinion between you. By and large, many people heard you were living in this cottage, just as many people saw you driving about in the gray roadster."

I became alarmed. "Our friends have nothing to do with this. It is entirely out of the question."

"I haven't finished yet. These friends, also, talked. Don't you see that idle gossip, started by yourself, may have traveled far and fast as gossip does, may have reached the ears of people who are not your friends and whom we cannot locate, until, at last, perhaps, it came to the notice of someone who had a use for it? Aren't you willing to admit that Elmer Lewis, a stranger, might still have known a great deal about you and Mrs. Coatesnash? Enough to make, or delegate someone to make, the phone call?"

Fascinated, as I always am, by logic that is quick, flashing and—fallible, I nodded. Jack said sourly:

"That sounds well, but it misses on a pretty important point. Until last night our residence, our car, our landlady weren't of interest to anyone except us. Our friends talk enough, but they have livelier material for conversation."

Standish was, for the moment, checked. A small-town man at heart, he liked to picture New York as a metropolis of plots and counterplots, a vast mysterious center of conspiracy and crime. Jack seized his brief advantage.

"A while back we were going over possible reasons for Elmer Lewis's behavior, and I suggest we continue. We decided he was scared, so his gun, his alias, his feeble disguise fit in. But the rest of it doesn't fit in. Why didn't he take a cab from the station? What purpose did he hope to serve by tricking us into driving him over from New Haven? What was in his mind? It's a cinch he didn't climb into our rumble seat to make it simple for his murderer."

Standish reluctantly abandoned his darkling vision of New York. Jack's questions made him restless. "Certainly it's extraordinary we don't know more about Lewis by this time. We can assume he was wealthy, an important figure in his own world. Why don't his friends and relatives appear? Even in New York, few men transporting a hundred thousand dollars in currency can drop out of sight."

"Have you established he was a New Yorker?"

"He came to New Haven from New York. The conductor remembers him. The porter remembers him, clearly. Lewis allowed the darkie to carry one bag, and insisted upon handling the other himself. Apparently that was the bag containing the money."

Standish then enumerated various steps taken in the investigation. The press had been given free rein in the hope of obtaining additional information, and Boston, New York and Philadelphia newspapermen were already flocking to the village in droves. Metropolitan police, without result, had checked over the several "Elmer Lewises" listed in the city directory. Also without result, they had got in touch with the large New York banks. No one of these banks could report the recent withdrawal of $108,000. In Crockford prominent business men—including the baker, the plumber, the coal merchant, practically everyone except the unpopular Greek fruit dealer—had been requested to view the body which lay in the local undertaking parlors.

Elmer Lewis remained unidentified.

"I still believe," said Jack, "Lewis is known in Crockford. What's more, I think Mrs. Coatesnash knows him. If not as Elmer Lewis, then under some other name. Have you ordered her friends to visit the undertaking parlor?"

"Certainly not!" said Standish. "In the first place, I haven't the authority; in the second place, I don't consider it necessary. I did communicate with Darnley and Elliott, the New York lawyers in charge of her affairs. Mr. Darnley was out of town; Mr. Elliott kindly offered to appear for Mrs. Coatesnash any time I call on him."

"No one can say," remarked Blair, "that Mrs. Coatesnash isn't cooperating."

Jack suppressed his exasperation. "Very well, we'll drop the lady. But if Lewis wasn't acquainted in Crockford why did he come here? Are you proposing he was shot down by someone who had never seen him before?"

Standish studied the pattern in the carpet. "There's always the chance of a homicidal maniac."

"It's an astute maniac who picks a man carrying a hundred and eight thousand dollars. The notion of a maniac is patently absurd," snapped Jack. "The only positive factor in the whole mess would seem to be the motive for Lewis's murder. The motive was money. Lewis was killed by someone who knew he had a hundred and eight thousand dollars and who wanted it. As it turned out he didn't get it. But he tried. The bag that disappeared last night and reappeared this morning was seized in mistake for the bag up front with Lola and me. Isn't that your idea?"

Standish had to smile. "You have a logical mind, young man." Jack's summation had appealed to him, and I saw it reflected, at least in part, his own reasoning. I felt a lightening of spirit. The police chief hesitated. "In a way, the second traveling bag hasn't been a bad break for you, Storm. For the life of me I can't see how you could have planted it in Durham—unless you had accomplices."

Jack said dryly, "I don't wonder you're puzzled. We met Lewis at five o'clock, arrived in Crockford at a little past six. From six-thirty until two we were steadily in your company. We left our car downtown, took a taxi home. Meantime, of course, we might have cached the missing bag somewhere. But Durham is a good fifty miles away. No doubt you asked our taxi driver if he took us to Durham, stopping en route so we could recover the bag."

The sarcasm proved a boomerang. "That's just what I did. It helped me decide you hadn't gone to Durham."

That was sensible enough but disconcerting. Although the second bag had developed a point in our favor, my spirits sagged. Henceforth I realized that an official microscope would be directed upon all our acts, and I didn't like it.

Standish now demanded a list of the New York friends with whom we stayed while visiting in the city—in case they might have a line on Lewis. Jack's frayed good nature gained additional tatters. The desired list obtained, his brisk-stepping deputy at his side, Standish departed. In a husbandly fashion Jack immediately passed his irritation on to me.

"A bird brain—though I doubt Blair could compete with a really sagacious bird—could comprehend that Luella's friends should be investigated, not ours. She may be the great white cow of Crockford, but she's greedy, grasping, filthy rich. She's financially able to engage in shady transactions involving a hundred thousand dollars: we aren't. And as for our unfortunate friends—put them all together and they aren't worth a hundred thousand cents."

Outraged, indignant, Jack attempted to settle down but couldn't rest or sleep. I brought his pad and pencils to the bed posed patiently for a sketch which he hoped to sell to a humorous magazine. He wasn't feeling humorous. Toward the middle of the afternoon he tore up his sheets of drawing paper and announced an idea. He wanted to cable Laura Twining. "What for? She'd only show the cable to Mrs. Coatesnash." Jack threw the fragments of his sketch into a wastebasket. "She might not. Laura's something of a dunce, and I admit she always played the devoted slave, but I've a sneaking notion she harbored an occasional rebellious thought. We don't know what she's thinking now. If she has any suspicions in this case I'd like to share them."

"A cable costs a lot."

"It might be worth a lot."

"Besides we'd have to go to town. You should stay in bed."

"Something tells me" said Jack, "that the less I stay in bed while the investigation proceeds without me, the better. I've never craved a good close look at an electric chair."

"Don't they hang in this state?"

"Neither do I fancy rope."

We were joking, but we were scared. Blair, who had arrived in our little car, had left it parked in the garage. While this was not exactly an official procedure, it was typical of Crockford and of Standish in his more pleasant guise.

I hadn't wanted to go to the village, and after reaching there I discovered how right my instinct was. I suppose normal curiosity was to be expected, but what Jack and I were subjected to went beyond any decent limits. Our appearance in the small gray roadster created a sensation. Doors flew open, windows flew up, shopkeepers darted from stores, people stopped dead on the sidewalks, necks craned from passing cars. The town was crowded with Saturday shoppers, and if anyone missed seeing us, it wasn't for lack of trying. Main Street was one long stare—a cold, unfriendly, measuring stare.

"I feel like Gary Cooper," said Jack.

He sounded chipper, but he didn't look it. Only a moment later at the telegraph office, we discovered that our errand was useless. The doors were closed and locked; we had both forgotten that in Crockford telegraph service ceases on Saturdays at noon.

"We can cable Monday," Jack said.

I said, "We should have stayed at home."

"Nonsense. This costs us nothing. Let the public have its fun."

And then we saw a friendly face. Dr. Rand, whose office overlooked the square, spied us through his windows, hurried forth to scold Jack for getting out of bed, and finally dragged him off for an X-ray. "It only takes a minute, and you can't grow another head." Jack returned in a more cheerful frame of mind.

Unfortunately, as was again impressed on us, Dr. Rand was not the whole of Crockford. An incident in the grocery store was more typical of village sentiment. Elsie Crampton—who represented the woman's club opinion and didn't care who knew it—was at the vegetable counter when we went in. She saw us, started, and then instantly swept out the door, leaving three pounds of cabbage swinging on the scale. Hahneman's, it was plain, could not contain the three of us.

A few minutes later there was a traffic jam at the post office. Half of Crockford found it needed stamps at the moment we stopped for mail. Jack pushed through the crowd, unlocked our box. The postmistress—as the village had it, a widow woman—leaned from her window to wag a humorous finger.

"You've got one letter, Mr. Storm, that I been wishing was written on a postcard."

Along with a dozen of the interested, I glimpsed a thin French envelope, a foreign stamp, Luella Coatesnash's cramped, old-fashioned script. I felt an edged surprise. Luella had never written to us before. Why now? The widow woman chuckled at her ancient joke; the crowd gawped. Jack stalked outside.

Safe in the car, we read Luella Coatesnash's note. Mailed ten days before, chatty, diffuse, dwelling on the beauties of Paris, it told us none of the things we desperately needed to know. That was a friendly letter. Nothing else.

"It's too damned friendly." Jack's eyes narrowed. "Why should Luella take it in her head to write us?"

I, too, was puzzled. Our relations with our landlady, as I have said, had not been social. For the two months we lived within a stone's throw of her home she had not troubled to call. Yet now we were blushlessly addressed as "Dear young friends." Neither Jack nor I could fathom the apparent change in attitude.

We put away the letter and forgot it.

That was a mistake. I believe now if we had considered the small mystery more important, if we had speculated more earnestly upon the motives which might have caused Luella Coatesnash to write the letter, if we had recalled her character with more exactness, we might have saved ourselves and others from grief, worry and disaster.

The road home went past Brownlee's undertaking parlors, a dusty establishment bedecked with leather furniture and extravagant Boston ferns. The night before, Alfred Brownlee, the sad-eyed proprietor, had taken mournful charge of the mortal remains of Elmer Lewis. Today the body lay on display in a rear room on the chance that identification might be had. A knot of people was collected on the sidewalk, peering through the glass windows.

"There's Harkway," Jack said, suddenly.

Just then quitting the undertaking parlors, the traffic cop hailed us. Jack stopped the car.

"Any news?"

"None yet." After glancing around, Harkway added in a low voice, "Unless you call it news that I've been put on the case." Although he offered the expected congratulations, Jack looked perturbed. "You're to represent the State?"

Harkway nodded. "I was detached from traffic duty today Standish and I are going to work it out together."

He spoke cheerfully, and seemed much set-up over the promotion. Good news for him, it sounded like bad news to me. In Connecticut before State police enter a homicide case, the local police must either request their aid or show themselves helpless and in the dark. I felt sure Standish had not requested aid. Harkway's promotion then meant two things. It meant that twenty-tour hours after the event the local investigation had got nowhere. It meant also, despite Harkway's lip service to cooperation, that Jack and I would be under the observation of two rival police organizations.

Flushed slightly with new authority, Harkway asked a few brisk questions about the attack upon Jack. He had received a report from Standish, but wanted to view for himself the closet, the broken window, the footprints in the field. When he proposed to accompany us to the cottage, we could not, of course, refuse.

As the policeman climbed into the car, a woman emerged from Brownlee's, came swiftly down the steps. The Harris Tweed suit, the modish hat seemed familiar. The woman passed the car closely, cast one look at us, passed on. The Storms had received the cut direct. The woman was Annabelle Bayne.

"It's a well-known fact," Jack said cheerfully, "that those big, brown eyes are often myopic. Strange, too. I wouldn't have dreamed that Annabelle Bayne was quite as near-sighted as she seems to be."

I smiled, but I was shaken. So shaken that it didn't occur to me to wonder what Annabelle Bayne had been doing at the Brownlee funeral parlors. Or why she had gone there.

Twilight was gray in the west when we started down the bumpy back road which wound to the cottage. At the Olmstead farmhouse, shuttered and melancholy, bearing the depressing aspect of a summer place in early spring, we saw John Standish poking about the yard. He came over to the car to speak. The meeting between him and Harkway confirmed me in my belief that he had not welcomed outside assistance. Their greetings were polite, but not effusive.

Harkway spoke a shade too jovially. "Found anything here, Chief?"

"Nothing." Standish peered gloomily at the porch of the cottage, ankle deep in dead brown leaves. "I thought maybe the house had been entered last night. Apparently not. I've gone over the doors and windows."

"Then you've come to a dead end?"

"Looks that way." The failure to discover evidence of an unlawful entry into the farmhouse discouraged Standish. For the time being he discarded an idea he had entertained, quite without realizing that he had brushed upon a part of the truth. The man who had hidden in our closet had been running toward the Olmsteads'. Also he had run in that direction with a purpose.

Harkway, Jack and I drove on. Daylight was fading rapidly. The two men would have gone at once into the field, but first I insisted upon a thorough tour of the house. With some little show of male superiority, they looked under beds and examined the closets until I was satisfied. Then they went outside.

The house seemed very quiet. I began to pare potatoes for an early supper. Following the footprints, Jack and Harkway moved slowly toward the woods. Pan on my lap, I watched at the kitchen window. When they had progressed some yards the telephone rang. Four shrill rings, twice repeated.

I ran to answer. In response to my voice came another voice, dreadfully familiar. The voice of the afternoon before! For an instant I was stunned, too appalled literally to speak or move. Then I stammered: "Wait a minute. I can't hear you."

The telephone was located near a window overlooking the field. Covering the mouthpiece I pounded the glass until Jack turned, saw me understood. He started running toward the cottage, Harkway close behind.

The voice said, "You can hear this. I have other business for you and your husband, and I don't want the law messing in it. Keep your mouths shut, both of you. That goes for the cop you brought out from Crockford this afternoon."

Jack and Harkway burst into the cottage. I beckoned them toward me. As I handed the receiver to Harkway, I said into the mouthpiece, "What other business? I don't understand."

My ruse failed. Very stealthily, as the exchange took place the caller hung up. Harkway heard nothing, and the line was dead.

CHAPTER EIGHT

Identity of a Corpse

For some thirty seconds, in an attitude of tense suspense, Harkway, Jack and I clustered around the telephone. Then Harkway said, "There's no one on the line, Mrs. Storm. Who was calling? What's the shooting for?"

"It was the same voice that phoned yesterday!"

At once the policeman attempted to reach the operator, but country telephone service is never good and several precious minutes elapsed before he obtained any answer. It was then too late to establish the source of the call.

The girl at the Crockford exchange was vague and uninformative. "I'm sorry. I've been awfully busy. We're always rushed at supper time."

"This is vitally important."

"I can't help it. I may have handled the call, but I don't remember it. Let me ask Edna."

The second operator was similarly unproductive. Warning both girls to pay special attention to our number and to listen in on any future conversations that seemed suspicious, Harkway replaced the instrument and, looking very disappointed, turned to me.

"Now tell me what your caller said. In detail."

"There isn't much. The voice simply said that Jack and I were to be prepared for further orders."

"What orders?"

"I didn't hear. The connection was broken then."

Harkway made a nettled gesture. "No use crying over spilled milk, I suppose, but it does seem too bad we flubbed the business." His dark face brightened. "Anyhow, we've got another chance. Those girls will watch this line like hawk?. When the third call comes we'll nail your caller."

I personally considered the man behind the mysterious "voice" too clever to be caught in such a simple trap. He would, I felt, anticipate our move and provide against it. Harkway commenced a worried pacing of the floor.

"How about the voice, Mrs. Storm? Could you identify it this time? Did it seem more familiar?"

I shook my head reluctantly. I was confirmed in my previous conviction that the voice had been deliberately and skillfully disguised, that I had heard it elsewhere in a different connection, but further my mind refused to go. However, as I concentrated upon the conversation I recalled something that did seem of real importance. I turned in some excitement.

"There's one curious thing I haven't mentioned. Evidently the caller knew you were here with us. At any rate he spoke of the policeman at the cottage."

"What's that!"

"He warned me not to tell the policeman at the cottage about the call. Now how could he have known you were here?"

Jack's eye kindled. "He must have seen the three of us together as we left the village. Or when we met on Main Street. Or as we drove here in the car."

Swiftly we attempted to tabulate the persons we had seen that afternoon, but as we did so the realization came upon all of us that the task was hopeless. Harkway spoke firsts "It could be almost anyone in town."

"But," said Jack, *"in town.* I knew all along local people were concerned. That call was made by a local man."

Harkway glanced thoughtfully at his neat blue serge. "Also it was made by someone who knows me as a policeman when I'm not in uniform!"

With that and after requesting us to communicate with him or Standish in the event of another call, he returned to the village.

Jack and I sat down to a dismal supper. Jack was suffering from an over-active day, his head was aching and he scarcely touched his food. I also ate little. The second phone call following so swiftly on the first, the insolent boldness of the caller and his knowledge of our movements, had shaken me more than I was willing to admit. I cleared away the supper things. I curled up on the couch.

"Being rung up by a murderer," I said presently, "isn't my idea of the peaceful, country life."

"If it's any consolation," said Jack with a thin smile, "it couldn't have been the actual murderer who rang us up. It was our old pal—the black-faced man in the closet."

"How can you know that?"

"Figure it out yourself, Lola. It's really quite simple."

After a puzzled moment I saw why Jack was right. Both phone calls had been made by the same voice. Lewis himself had been aware of the first call, had met us in accordance with the telephoned directions, and, except that his violent death intervened, eventually would have wound up at the cottage. Obviously then both phone calls had been made by the mysterious individual who awaited Lewis, crouched among the frocks and coats in my clothes closet.

"Even so," said Jack, "the closet man remains a riddle. Either he was astoundingly persuasive, or else he had some strong hold on Lewis. I favor the strong hold myself. It's quite a trick to persuade someone to fill a bag with money, ride twenty-five miles with two people he's never seen before, and be prepared to walk into a house where you're nicely set to ambush him."

"You think the closet man meant to rob Lewis?"

"Rob and—murder him."

Jack's tone, the look in his eyes, made me shiver. He said, "It isn't pleasant to think about, darling, and I hate to sound hard-boiled but I hardly believe Elmer Lewis—as a human being—was worth what you're feeling now. He was a bad egg, Lola. If anything's certain, that is."

I said weakly, "We saw him only once."

"Once was plenty. Elmer Lewis had an evil face—and you needn't say that's just my artist's eye. No honest man needs travel disguised, under an alias, as Lewis did. We can be sure that when Elmer Lewis climbed into our car he was bound on some illegal mission." Jack went on soberly, "It looks as though the gentleman met with the double-cross, but my guess is that circumstances had been reversed Elmer Lewis would not have hesitated to plant the knife in someone's back. Be realistic, Lola. Isn't that how he struck you?"

I had to nod. I remembered my own distrust of Elmer Lewis, the antagonism and aversion which had flared when first I saw him walking along the sidewalk through the crowd. It seemed quite logical that such a man should have earned himself two mortal enemies. One enemy who had killed him, and another who had been set to kill. But there my reasoning faltered. I could see no way in which we could connect those shadowy figures, a way in which we could identify them. And I retained the uneasy feeling that the repercussions of Elmer Lewis's murder which had affected Jack and me would continue to affect us until the mystery was fully solved.

By bedtime I was so apprehensive that. Jack proposed we ask Silas to stay in the house again. The pasture path which climbed in an almost vertical line from the cottage to the Lodge was shorter, but it was also very steep and I preferred the road. Jack who carried a flash, preceded me. I remember the smell of the spring night as I followed. I remember hearing the rattle of tiny sliding stones, and seeing the stark outlines of the box and elm trees on the Coatesnash lawns as we rounded the hill. Monstrous shadows enveloped the mansion; it looked bleak, forbidding formidable.

Iron gates barred the driveway which gave on the road, but they were purely ornamental, since a line of leafless bushes grew on either side of the stone supports. Jack held back a bush, and somewhat nervously I crept through the hole. We were trespassing, and I couldn't forget how much Mrs. Coatesnash would dislike it if she knew. I think Jack felt the same. We hurriedly mounted the bone-white drive—it glittered in the moonlight—and, our steps instinctively hastening, passed Hilltop House and descended to the Lodge in the rear.

Silas had retired. Spirited pounding finally roused him. He refused to spend another night on the sofa—flatly and without equivocation.

"No, siree, Mr. Storm. I'm staying here."

"Maybe you'll let us take Reuben."

The hired man glanced doubtfully at the small sand-colored dog which yapped at us from the doorway. Jack produced dollar bill, and cupidity won. We got the dog.

"The better man of the two at that," said Jack, as with one accord we turned down the short cut home. A brisk ten minutes' walk carried us there.

Reuben wasn't exactly a comfort. The small dog had an insane aversion to mice—guests common to country cottages—and throughout the night he barked frantically. I was too tired to care. I slept fitfully, but slept.

The next day—Sunday—I observe is listed in my rather sketchy notes under the heading: "Plague of the Reporters." It occurs to me that I have not dwelt sufficiently upon the fervid and hysterical attention which metropolitan newspapers were taking in what they termed the "Rumble Seat Murder." Columns were printed, editorials lamented the mystery of the $108,000 corpse, front-page space was filled with maps of Crockford, dotted diagrams of Main Street, and the like. Special writers descended like locusts on the village, set themselves up at the principal hotel, burned holes in the blankets, ran up enormous telephone tolls, and, I believe, gave Mr. Bemis, the town's despairing liquor dealer, a new lease on life. Amateur detectives every one, and an undoubted nuisance—Harkway always insisted that he trapped a reporter under his bed—they trotted in and out of the Undertaking parlors, camped on the police station steps, and demanded interviews from everyone who had the remotest connection with the case.

Sunday was a dead day in the investigation. Standish and Harkway fled from the station and locked themselves in a room at the Tally-ho Inn. Dr. Rand, described in the public prints as "an elderly, short-tempered eccentric," barricaded himself in his home, detached his doorbell, pulled down his shades and was at peace.

Jack and I bore the brunt of a mass attack. Since we declined to talk, the reporters—there must have been a score of them—genially set out to wear us down. Our telephone rang until I removed it from the hook, our doorbell rang steadily from ten o'clock until noon—at which point Jack discovered some ingenious soul had wedged it with a match. We had locked the doors but wheedling voices called through keyholes that we were missing visits from old school friends. Sob sisters smoked on the steps and tossed butts and matches to the lawn. A card game was staged in the garage, and I hate to think about the number of empty bottles we found discarded there.

At four o'clock, uninterviewed but photographed—and the photograph of me adjusting my stocking remains a sore spot to is day—we escaped by the back door to exercise Reuben. Until darkness we stayed away. Returning, we were cheered to discover that hunger had vanquished the press.

At eight o'clock on Monday morning an especially enterprising New

York newspaper telephoned the cottage. The *Globe* had learned that Jack was an artist; the *Globe* would like signed sketches of the various personalities who figured in the case—the two investigators, the coroner, ourselves, and, if possible, a drawing from memory of the victim. Sleepy and annoyed. Jack was on the point of curt refusal, when I intervened.

"Ask them what they'll pay."

Negotiations were resumed. It was suggested quite sensible that the sketch of Elmer Lewis might result in an identification. The possibility appealed to Jack, and I must confess the surprising sum of money offered appealed to me. But when the *Globe* further stipulated that Jack must deliver the sketches in person both of us were dismayed. It seemed unlikely that we could obtain permission to leave the township.

Eventually, however, we drove to town to broach the proposition. First we called upon our bondsman. Dr. Rand admitted us cautiously, and only after peeping through the curtains to *see* who was ringing his bell. He was agreeable and even enthusiastic about the venture. "It will do you a world of good getting to the city, give you a sense of perspective. After yesterday I could use a sense of perspective myself! A murder's a bad thing, but I'm not sure newspaper men aren't worse." The final decision he then said must be left to Standish, and with Standish we anticipated difficulties. To my surprise the police chief readily granted Jack permission to make the trip. "Sure, run along to the city. Take your wife if you like—probably do her good. All I ask is that you be back by noon tomorrow."

I was too naive to dream of looking a gift horse in the mouth or to speculate at any ulterior reason for the police chief's amazing affability. Jack did his sketches, I approved them, and that very day we started gaily, lightly, off to town.

It was mid-afternoon when we alighted at the Grand Central Station. Until I set foot on Forty-Second Street, breathed in the smoky, familiar air, I hadn't realized how much I missed New York. The day was gray. Leaden, low-hanging skies could not diminish the splendor and the wonder of my favorite city. Granite towers soared toward the heavens in the same remembered way. The same lovely furred women strolled into hotels to keep appointments. The same well-dressed, ill-shaped business men rushed past. The same newsboys cried their wares. We were home again, lost in the anonymity of preoccupied crowds, rubbing shoulder to shoulder with the most tolerant people one can ever hope to meet. People who didn't care who we were, or what we had done or were about to do. Jack looked at me.

"Swell," he said "swell."

He snared a taxi and departed toward the offices of the *Globe*. I went to get a decent shampoo and manicure. Afterward we met in an uptown hotel for tea. Jack was stimulated by the enthusiastic reception of his sketches, and by the tonic of the city.

"I," he said, "feel great. You look great. Cute haircut you've got there—

I like it. Now that's set—how would you like to take an independent step in solving the mystery of Elmer Lewis?"

"What step?" I asked cheerfully.

"Do you remember that firm of lawyers Standish mentioned the other day, those lawyers who handle Mrs. Coatesnash's affairs? Hiram Darnley and Franklyn Elliott? Well, they've got a suite of offices downtown—and T thought we might go there and have a talk with them."

"A talk about what?"

"About Elmer Lewis, stupid." Suddenly Jack was quite serious. "Mrs. Coatesnash is the great white cow of Crockford, but in New York, thank God, she's only a person like us. Darnley and Elliott is a reputable firm—I asked at the *Globe*—and I don't believe they'd shield a client they thought involved in a serious crime. Anyhow it won't hurt to go and see."

"Certainly not," I said.

It was all as casual as that.

Darnley and Elliott occupied a twenty-story office building's topmost suite, an entire floor. It was a most luxurious place. The etchings on the walls, the thick soft carpets, the expensive sunshine on the floor, the unusual quiet, testified to taste and money.

In the outer reception rooms a very pretty secretary tapped at a noiseless typewriter. Jack paused before her. He asked for Hiram Darnley.

"Mr. Darnley is out of town."

"Then may I see Mr. Elliott?"

The stenographer smiled. "Mr. Elliott is also out of town. He is due here at four o'clock."

I was already doubtful of our mission, but Jack pulled out a chair for me and calmly settled near the door to wait.

At four promptly the door opened. A short, stout man, astonishingly light on his feet, came quickly in. The secretary rose at once.

"Good afternoon, Mr. Elliott. These people have been waiting…"

"I can't be bothered now. I'm busy. I'll be busy the rest of the afternoon. Get rid of them."

Franklyn Elliott vanished. The girl looked apologetically at us. Jack, who hadn't moved since the lawyer's entrance, addressed me in a low, excited voice:

"Did you recognize Elliott? He was in the New Haven station this morning. I saw him boarding the Crockford bus."

A buzzer sounded on the secretary's desk. She lifted a telephone, spoke, turned and said to Jack:

"What is your name, please? What business have you with Mr. Elliott?"

"My name is Jack Storm—my business is personal."

The girl relayed the information. She hung up the telephone. She looked surprised.

"Mr. Elliott can give you fifteen minutes, if you don't mind waiting a few minutes more."

We waited.

I experienced a certain qualmish feeling as we entered the private office. New York's expensive sunshine barred a thick rust-colored carpet. I had a hazy impression of Durer etchings and cheerful draperies. Behind a lovely rosewood desk, either a museum piece or a skillfully faked antique, legs crossed, sat Franklyn Elliott.

He wasn't alone. A middle-aged woman—obviously an employee—was seated in a chair beside the desk. She was crying. She balled her handkerchief, got up and stumbled from the room. Elliott didn't say anything about her.

He turned to us and I studied his round, rather pleasant face. His head was a trifle large for his short body, was bald and he carried it well. He looked like a man who might collect Napoleonana, and, glancing at his desk, I wasn't surprised to see a small bronze of the Emperor. Elliott caught my eye and smiled.

"A great general—Napoleon, and one of my admirations. Now won't you sit down and tell me what I can do for you?" We sat down. Jack hesitated. Politely interested, the lawyer leaned forward. The silence lengthened. Elliott glanced inquiringly at Jack, then at his watch. Jack flushed but still said nothing. At that moment, as he admitted later, he was strongly tempted to leave the office without a single word. I would have followed gladly. I realized belatedly how absurd was our idea of presenting our suspicions of Luella Coatesnash to this man. If Elliott knew anything to his client's disadvantage, anything which might assist our case, certainly he was capable of keeping such information to himself. From my first glimpse of him I firmly believed that he would do so.

"Well. Mr. Storm?"

Jack at last got under way. "I suppose you've seen newspaper stories. A man who introduced himself as Elmer Lewis was murdered in my car; he was carrying a great deal of money. So far—chiefly because I had the opportunity—I seem to be the favored suspect. Indeed the only suspect. In the two days since the murder the police have accomplished nothing. They haven't even managed to identify the victim."

"You're mistaken there, Mr. Storm."

"I don't understand."

"Elmer Lewis has been identified."

"When? By whom? How do you know?"

The fat man fixed unblinking eyes upon us. "I have just returned from Crockford. I identified the body this afternoon." Elliott paused. "Elmer Lewis was Hiram Darnley, my legal partner."

CHAPTER NINE

The Woman at the Keyhole

Not until we were aboard the New Haven train and bound for home did Jack and I appreciate Franklyn Elliott's talents as an inquisitor. From us he had learned all we knew. From him we had learned nothing. Why Hiram Darnley had chosen to masquerade as Elmer Lewis, why he had carried $108,000 in currency, why he had announced himself as engaged in a business transaction for Luella Coatesnash—to these questions Franklyn Elliott merely replied that he did not know. He was tactful, courteous, adamant. In vain Jack sought to draw him out. "Weren't you in your partner's confidence?"

"To an extent, yes. In this particular instance, no. Unfortunately, I was away on a hunting trip when Hiram left the office Friday."

"Then you don't know why he came to Crockford?"

"I haven't the remotest notion. Naturally I've been curious. So curious that I took the trouble to question Hiram's secretary. You saw Miss Willetts. She was badly hit by the news. She was closer to him than anyone else, and she says he received no communication from Mrs. Coatesnash at this office."

"How about his home?"

"He lived at the Chatham Club. I imagine the police will check there." The stout man smiled faintly. "My own sleuthing instincts didn't carry me quite that far. In any event, it's difficult for me to believe that Hiram heard from Mrs. Coatesnash after she left New York. We both saw her on the day she sailed—in fact, I saw her off—and at that time her affairs were in perfect order. The estate is handled by the firm—it seems incredible that Mrs. Coatesnash could have engaged in any private transaction with my partner. On the other hand, I can't conceive why he should tell you so. The whole affair sounds fantastic—completely unlike Hiram Darnley."

"There's the money itself," said Jack, slowly. "Surely it can be traced now. Where did the money come from?"

"I presume it came from my partner's bank account."

Jack hesitated. "This is extremely important to me, Mr. Elliott. Is it possible the money belonged to Mrs. Coatesnash?"

Elliott's urbanity lessened. "Certainly not! Your suggestion is incredible! In the first place, we hold no power of attorney from Mrs. Coatesnash, so Hiram could not have drawn on her account. In the second place, he had an ample fortune of his own."

Abruptly Elliott wearied of our questions. He rose to signify that his good nature and the interview were at an end. He escorted us to the door.

"My best advice to you, Mr. Storm, is to leave the conduct of the investigation where it belongs—in the hands of the authorities. Amateurs only succeed in annoying people who haven't the time or patience to be annoyed."

Dispirited, Jack and I turned for information to the evening papers. Although headlines cried the fact of the identification, the stories which dealt with the career of the murdered lawyer offered nothing helpful. Hiram Darnley, survived by an invalid wife, a patient in an up-state sanitarium, apparently had lived a blameless and a public life. He was fifty-one, New York born and bred. In 1908 he had finished at Harvard Law School and gone immediately into private practice. During the war period he had covered himself with distinction in Belgian relief work and later served this Government as a dollar-a-year man. On the strength of his wartime reputation he had twice run unsuccessfully for Congress. Thereafter he had resigned political ambitions to bury himself in the law; with Franklyn Elliott he had represented several of Manhattan's best-known corporations. The list of his clubs was impeccable. The resume of his activities, both legal and political, contained no hint of scandal—no suggestion of moral turpitude.

"The man," declared Jack, disgusted, "was a whited sepulcher, and far too good for a wicked world."

We left the newspapers on the train. Both of us knew that the real story of Hiram Darnley had not been printed. We reached the cottage very late, and were surprised to find John Standish and Harkway awaiting us. Jack was glad to see them, but I think I noticed even at the time how quietly the two men received his comments on the identification of Elmer Lewis, and how silently they rose from the front steps and followed us into the house.

I was exhausted and excused myself immediately and started to retire. "A moment, please," said Standish. "I want to talk to you."

I paused, startled by his tone. His morning affability had inexplicably vanished; his face was stern and cold. I looked toward Lester Harkway, but the younger officer managed to avoid my eye. Very much disturbed, I sat down, Standish turned to Jack.

"I understood you were going to New York to sell some drawings. Isn't that what you told me?"

"Yes, of course," said Jack.

"Then why did you call on Franklyn Elliott this afternoon?"

Jack stared. "How did you know that?"

"You don't deny seeing Elliott?"

"I saw him, yes. But I wonder how you knew. Did you have us followed?"

There was no reply. Standish leaned forward in his chair and what he said next was, to say the least, incomprehensible. "I've tried to treat you fairly, Mr. Storm. But you're very much mistaken if you believe you can keep from me facts which I'm entitled to know. I don't care what your motive is! If you've been intimidated, if you feel you need protection, I'm prepared to give it."

Jack was too staggered to interrupt. Standish rose from his chair—and with his next words suddenly all was clear. "You received a second telephone call at this cottage on Saturday. Your wife told Lester Harkway here that the message had been interrupted." He looked at me with those cold, hard, alienated eyes. "You lied, Mrs. Storm. Why did you lie? Why did you say that message was interrupted? You know as well as I do that you were told—or ordered—to go to town for an interview with Franklyn Elliott. I insist you tell me the purpose of that secret meeting! I demand to know what occurred this afternoon in Franklyn Elliott's office!"

I was stunned. The reasoning, mistaken as it was, had a certain-frightening plausibility. The mysterious telephone call, our sudden request to go to the city, our failure to mention Franklyn Elliott because we hadn't dreamed of seeing him. There were other things, however, which I didn't understand. Did the police suspect the lawyer of having a hand in his partner's murder? Why else would Standish attempt to establish a link between the three of us? Why else would he charge conspiracy and silence on our part?

Jack repeated precisely the words of our talk with Franklyn Elliott and explained as best he could the impulse which had conveyed us to the lawyer's office. He explained to a man who listened, but who plainly didn't believe a word he said. Standish's attitude became apparent when he departed, for Lester Harkway stayed. There was no explanation; the young policeman simply stayed.

The inquest was to be held on Thursday, and our understanding was that we were to be kept in "protective custody" at least until the verdict had been handed down. It was an awkward situation and one which I resented. No one likes being under guard, and I like it less than most, although I must confess that Harkway did his best to be unobtrusive. He even tried to be of service around the house. In the morning he neatly made his bed and offered to help me with the dishes. He spent considerable time at the telephone. He always closed the door, but I gathered that the investigation was in full cry and that Standish was out of town. It was plain enough that Harkway didn't wish to discuss the case, but at Wednesday lunch I brought it up.

"Why do you suspect Franklyn Elliott? And what do you suspect him of?"

"I wouldn't exactly say I did suspect him," said Harkway cautiously. "But what we're up against in Hiram Darnley's death is beginning to look like a conspiracy—and, in a conspiracy, plenty of people *could* be involved." His meditative glance reminded Jack and me that we could be involved.

Jack hardly ignored the glance. "A conspiracy! Are you seriously suggesting that the murderer had an accomplice? What's your evidence for making things so complicated? We've got two plots on Darnley's life already, two people to account for and now you propose a third!"

"Not necessarily." Again Harkway hesitated. "Standish has suggested, and it doesn't seem unlikely, that the man who hid in your closet and the actual murderer might originally have been confederates in the same plot."

Jack stared at him. "I don't follow you. Darnley was murdered long before we reached the cottage, and the black-faced man certainly didn't know it, else he would not have waited here. That…doesn't look like team work."

"Suppose," said Harkway slowly, "the plot didn't operate on schedule. Suppose it went off the rails. Doesn't that make the situation less confusing?" He added thoughtfully, "You've heard of the double-cross. Well, a hundred and eight thousand dollars is a lot of money. A cold-blooded murderer who saw a chance to grab a fortune might not pause to consider a confederate. He might be willing to forget previous—arrangements."

It was a logical theory. I could see that Jack was much impressed. But my own special leaning is usually toward facts. I said, "Is there any way of fitting Franklyn Elliott into such a picture? I'm sure that Standish doesn't trust him."

"I shouldn't sit here talking." Harkway said candidly, "but there's no harm in saying this. We haven't a scrap of real evidence to tie up Elliott with Darnley's death. You need evidence to take before a court. A hunch won't go far there."

"But your hunch must be based on *something!*'

"It's based on nothing more than Franklyn Elliott's attitude," said Harkway slowly. "Personally, I'm inclined to think any suspicion of Elliott is moonshine. But this is true. He spent four hours in the station Monday, and when he got through talking he hadn't said a thing. Not one damn thing about a man who'd been his partner seven years. Also he seemed a little over-anxious we should write off the murder as an unsolved mystery."

I was disappointed. "Had he a motive for wishing Darnley dead?"

"None at all," Harkway said at once. "Or none that we can find. Standish was in the New York office yesterday, talking to the help. It appears that Darnley's death will actually cost Elliott money. Darnley was the senior partner; he ran with the society crowd and drummed up the business. Offhand, you'd say Elliott had every reason for wanting Hiram Darnley alive—every reason for wanting us to catch the killer. That's just it; he evidently doesn't care to have us crack the case, or at least he doesn't choose, to help."

I asked if Elliott had an alibi for the night of the murder, and Harkway laughed. "You don't ask a big-time lawyer if he has an alibi. As a matter of fact, Elliott told us voluntarily that he'd been on a hunting trip. He has a place in the Catskills."

"Was he there alone?"

"He said he went out with a guide days. The guide went home nights. Standish looked up that place on the map after Elliott left," ended Harkway, "and it's two hundred and ninety miles from here. That, Mrs. Storm, is one hell of a distance!" Thursday came at last, a bright clear day, a day of blue skies and-white drifting clouds. In Connecticut an inquest is always held in private—decently, behind closed doors. Jack, I knew, would be the leading witness, and I was very grateful that the ordeal would take place in private. What I didn't take into my calculations was human nature, and I wasn't prepared for those crowds who poured into Crockford merely on the chance of glimpsing the actors in a tragedy.

Harkway, Jack and I drove downtown together. Long before we reached Town Hall, we had to abandon the car and walk. Sidewalks and streets alike were jammed with sensation seekers. Jack and I were identified at once, and Harkway had all that he could do to force us through. I thought for a time I wouldn't escape with the clothes on my back, and I still remember that determined young woman who wanted to seize my scarf for a souvenir. And what she said. She said indignantly. "You won't need a scarf in the death house."

As I sit here now it seems incredible those words were ever spoken. But on that bright blue day of the inquest, that angry, defrauded young woman—I saw her long afterward behind a counter in the Crockford bakery—represented the majority opinion, the ingrown, prejudiced opinion of a small New England village. The opinion, in short, of most of Crockford.

It was ten past two when we battled our way into Town Hall. The hearing was to be held in the court room upstairs, and the jury, chosen that morning, was already closeted there with Dr. Rand, who, as coroner, was presiding. After the uproar outside, the lower floor seemed queerly quiet and empty. The room where the witnesses were to wait their turns to testify seemed also very quiet, although two people were sitting there. Dennis Cark, the grocery boy, was seated near the door. He wore a brand-new suit, and he looked small, subdued and nervous. Beyond him, in a far corner of the room, sat a wan, colorless woman whom I did not immediately identify. Her head was bent and she was weeping silently into a crumpled handkerchief.

"Darnley's secretary," whispered Harkway. "Name's Anita Willetts. She's come to confirm the identification."

I remembered then the stricken woman I had seen in Franklyn Elliott's office. I said, "Where's Elliott?"

"He sent word this morning he was ill. Miss Willetts came instead."

"I thought Elliott *had* to come."

"No," Harkway said slowly, "No. At this stage he has a legal right to refuse to leave the State of New York. A coroner's inquest is not a trial."

Trial or not, Jack and I were there and I bitterly resented Franklyn Elliott's absence. I fancied Harkway also resented it, though discretion kept him quiet. Jack and I sat down and Harkway tiptoed off upstairs.

"I'll get a line," he said, "on what's going on."

I knew precisely what was going on. John Standish, I had been informed, would make an opening speech, and, from that locked and curtained room three flights above, I almost fancied I could hear the rumbling accents of his voice, explaining to the members of a local jury at what date and hour, under what circumstances, and exactly how he had found a dead man in our car. A dead man and a bag which contained over a hundred-thousand dollars. I was convinced he would not mention Franklyn Elliott.

"You," said Jack suddenly to me, "are the greenest-looking woman I ever saw. Go over and get yourself a drink of water. And say to yourself as you go, 'the Storms may be down, but damned if they'll ever admit it.'"

I went past Dennis Clark to the water cooler. Anita Willetts didn't look up from her chair, but wept steadily on. I saw her fumble for another handkerchief, and I put mine in her hand. She looked up then from reddened, swollen eyes, hesitated and finally took the handkerchief.

I drew a glass of water and drank it slowly. "You're Lola Storm, aren't you?" said Anita Willetts, presently. A certain awkwardness in her tone made me nod and turn at once to leave. She did something which surprised me. She leaned out, and patted my hand. "Sit down, my dear. You needn't leave. I feel quite sure you and your husband didn't murder Mr. Darnley."

She had obviously adored the dead man, and I was deeply touched. I was disconcerted when she added shrewdly, "If you'd wanted to kill him, you had only to drive him on to your cottage. Or so it seems to me." She must have seen me flush, for she added, "I don't mean to be offensive, but it was odd, your picking him up. But then—" and again her eyes overflowed "—Mr. Darnley had been acting so oddly I can't help believing your story is true. In a way I feel responsible for the dreadful thing that happened to him."

"You feel responsible!"

"Because of that money he carried in his bag," said Miss Willetts, evidently grateful for a chance to unburden her mind. "I got that money for him, Mrs. Storm. Every noon hour for two weeks I cashed checks for him at his various banks. I used to feel extremely nervous coming back to the office with several thousand dollars in my purse, and Mr. Darnley made me nervous by his attitude. He warned me to tell no one about the money, particularly I wasn't to let anything slip to Mr. Elliott. I thought it was all wrong then, and that last day when he told me he was making a trip, and started off to the train with those two bags, well, I think I knew he would never come back."

"You saw him start to the train," I said excitedly. "You knew he was coming to Crockford!"

"No, Mrs. Storm. He told me he was going to Chicago."

She had little more to add. She had been shocked, perplexed and bewildered by the whole affair. When she had last seen Hiram Darnley in the office at one o'clock on that Friday afternoon, when he had picked up those traveling bags, he had worn a mustache, he had been dressed in quiet, impeccable taste. "He was," said Miss Willetts sadly, "a most fastidious dresser. I've seen the clothes he wore up here, and I can't conceive how he could bring himself to put them on."

Presently she was called upstairs to testify. Dennis Cark followed her. It was four o'clock when Lester Harkway appeared at the door and said, "Well, Mr. Storm, it's your turn next."

Jack took a long breath and rose. I rose, too. I knew it wasn't exactly legal, my going to the court room while Jack testified, but I didn't expect to yield the point without a battle. None was necessary. Harkway conveniently looked away when we reached the proper door, and I slipped in. The policeman even found an inconspicuous chair for me, and though Dr. Rand, who was presiding from a raised bench which overlooked the room, certainly saw me, he gravely pretended not to.

I stared hard at the members of the jury! I was prejudiced perhaps, but I didn't like their looks. Jack was sworn immediately. It was explained to him that the hearing was informal, and it was not explained that the informal hearing might well pave the way to a charge of murder. That was understood.

The room was very small and, since the windows had been curtained, dark. A single naked electric bulb burned overhead. The furniture was the poorest grade of pine; faded, worn linoleum was spread upon the floor. But the machinery of justice—even in a cheap and illy furnished court room—has a certain frightening, impressive quality. As I remember it, I felt I needed air.

When Jack began to speak I relaxed. He talked to Dr. Rand as simply and naturally as though the two of them had been alone, and I know his manner had its effect upon the jury. I watched them.

"He's going over great," Harkway whispered.

His tone seemed abstracted, and I noticed that his eyes were fixed upon a door set in the wall near the jury box. "What's that?" I whispered.

"The jury room. I've closed that door twice already. It keeps coming open."

He rose, tiptoed past the jury, closed the door again and leaned there against the wall. From the witness chair Jack said, "My only connection with Hiram Darnley came through Luella Coatesnash. I believed at the time I met him and I believe now that she sent him to me."

"Wait a minute before going on," said Dr. Rand. "I want to put this cablegram in evidence." Whereupon he read out the following message, received the day before from Paris: "I did not request Hiram Darnley to telephone the Storms or to go to Crockford. I cannot understand his actions or his use of the name Elmer Lewis. I have not communicated with Darnley since leaving America. Luella Coatesnash."

Jack turned white. "That cablegram," he said, "is a lie. A palpable, unmitigated lie! I have some rights here, and I insist..."

"Control yourself," began Dr. Rand. "You're out of order, you must..."

He, too, broke off. The members of the jury were surging to their feet. There was a violent commotion near the box, and at first I couldn't see what was happening. Then I saw. The door to the room beyond was open, and Harkway had seized and was struggling with someone who had been crouched at the keyhole, listening there. It was a woman. One arm shielded her face from view, and then she dropped her arm, ceased struggling and I saw her clearly.

It was Annabelle Bayne.

There was a stunned silence. Then, in cold fury, Dr. Rand rose from the bench. "What were you doing in the jury room?" Annabelle Bayne pushed back the hair from her face. "Eavesdropping," she said clearly, "what do you suppose?" Before, in his outraged astonishment, he could speak she whirled on Jack. "You! Listen, you! I wanted to see how far you'd go in blackening the character of a very old woman who isn't present to defend herself. That, my fine lad, is a pretty low way to defend yourself from a charge of murder."

If I ever saw outright hatred in a human being's eyes, I saw it in the eyes of Annabelle Bayne as she looked at Jack.

CHAPTER TEN

The Man with a Bag

Annabelle Bayne turned on her heel and started to walk quickly from the court room. I've never seen an angrier man than Dr. Rand. "Come back here!" he shouted from the bench. "You're by no means finished with this court."

For a moment I think she meant to defy the order, but I suppose his tone alarmed her, for she turned around, came back and quietly sat down. She seemed perfectly self-possessed, and as Jack resumed his testimony she even smiled to herself. An odd, contained and scornful little smile it was.

A moment later Jack stepped down. He had finished his story in an aura of anti-climax. The jury was inattentive and uninterested. Jack's future and mine were at stake, but the jurymen were watching Annabelle Bayne.

"Now, Miss Bayne," said Dr. Rand, "you will kindly take the stand."

The coffee-colored hat went up, the strange eyes flashed, and for a second time I fancy she considered open defiance. She thought better of it, rose and sauntered slowly forward.

"This is quite beyond me," she said, as she languidly took the oath. "I know nothing about this case."

"You know why you hid in the jury room. That's a serious offense. Explain it!"

"I've told you what I was doing there," she said sullenly. "Luella Coatesnash is a friend 6f mine, an old, very dear friend, and I was determined to hear what was being said behind her back. What that man—" she looked hard at Jack "—was saying. I've heard of the rumors and lies he's been spreading. And I've resented them. Luella Coatesnash scarcely knew Hiram Darnley. He might have been her lawyer, but she hardly ever saw him, and she had no conception of his character."

The jury overlooked the significance of her statement. Aggravated by her manner, Dr. Rand did not. His voice gained a quick, new interest.

"Will you please explain that?"

I thought the witness looked frightened. "Explain what? What is there to explain?"

"Were you acquainted with Darnley? Did you know him well?"

"I did not!"

"You have inferred you were more familiar with his character than

Mrs. Coatesnash was. How does that happen?"

"Oh, I see." She touched the handkerchief to her lips, glanced up brightly. "I see what you mean. Darnley visited Mrs. Coatesnash here in Crockford many years ago. I met him in a casual way, and took a strong dislike to him. Although Mrs. Coatesnash trusted him implicitly, I considered him stupid, for all his reputation as a brilliant lawyer."

"Then you did know him!"

"If you choose to call it that. I saw him only twice."

"When was this?"

Annabelle Bayne said slowly, "Many years ago. In June of nineteen-twenty. Jane Coatesnash was buried that month, you may remember. Mr. Darnley came to Crockford for the funeral."

Suddenly Harkway, who was listening closely, walked to the coroner's bench, leaned over and whispered something to Dr. Rand. The coroner started. He turned to Annabelle Bayne and said sharply, "Did you see Hiram Darnley's body while it lay in the undertaking parlors here?"

She began a glib denial. Her clear brown eyes met my eyes—and then, I suppose, she remembered. She was, for a moment, shaken, definitely alarmed. Her voice faltered, recovered.

"Yes, I did see the body. It bad almost slipped my mind. I dropped into Brownlee's Saturday afternoon on my way home from town."

A dead silence fell. She appeared not to notice. Her restless hands lay still; her chin rose at its proud, usual tilt. The coroner spoke gravely.

"Hiram Darnley was not identified until Monday morning. Why didn't you go to the police and identify him on Saturday?"

"I couldn't identify him."

"You couldn't!"

"I didn't recognize him," she said rapidly. "I hadn't seen the man in fifteen years. His appearance was not memorable or striking. I wouldn't have known him from Adam if I had met him walking down the street."

I knew she lied. Evidently Dr. Rand shared my opinion. He tried hard—quite without result—to shake the witness. Annabelle Bayne stuck stubbornly to her denials, until finally she left the stand and departed from the court room. With her went the material of drama.

The inquest developed nothing further. At five o'clock the members of the jury retired. Their deliberations were mercifully short. At twenty minutes past the hour Jack and I heard the only verdict which the evidence would allow. Hiram Darnley had met his death at the hands of a person or persons unknown.

What that stolid country jury really believed I cannot say. Probably most of the jurymen believed that Jack and I had murdered Hiram Darnley or knew who had. But there must have been a minority who like myself, thought Annabelle Bayne could tell more than she had told. For like all juries, the members of that secret panel talked, and it seemed to me that after the coroner's inquest Jack's and my position in the village became somewhat easier.

We met John Standish in the lower hall. He congratulated us bleakly on the verdict, and indicated that the "protective custody" was to be lifted, and that Harkway was to report in the morning at the station. The investigation evidently was to be tirelessly pursued, but where it was going and in what direction Standish didn't say.

Harkway accompanied Jack and me to supper at the Tally-ho Inn, a guest this time and not a guard. We talked about the inquest. We talked about Annabelle Bayne.

"Why," said Jack, "has she such a vigorous dislike of me, and why is she shouting so loudly in defense of Mrs. Coatesnash? Why, for that matter, should the two be friends? Offhand, I'd say they were poles apart."

The policeman gave us a curious glance. "Haven't you heard about Jane Coatesnash? Annabelle Bayne was her chum. After the girl's death, she and the mother became very close. In a way, it's an odd relationship."

I thought personally that fifteen years would put a pretty severe strain on a sentimental loyalty. I said so. Harkway buttered a piece of bread.

"Then you don't know about the girl?"

"Only that she's dead. Why? Is there more?"

"I'm not a very good source." The policeman reached absently for the coffee pot as I was about to pour, encountered my hand, flushed, permitted me to fill his cup. "Thank you, Mrs. Storm.

To get back to Jane Coatesnash—if you want the straight facts, it might be better to go to the newspaper files."

"The newspapers!" I felt a prickling at the roots of my hair. "What do you mean? What happened to the girl?"

"Jane Coatesnash was drowned," said Harkway.

I must have looked disappointed. At any rate, he smiled, then proceeded to tell us all he knew of the tragedy which had blasted Mrs. Coatesnash's life. The story, still whispered about the village, was singular, to say the least.

Fifteen years before, Jane Coatesnash, then a student at Mather College for Women (located high in the Berkshires), had left the campus on a shopping trip. It was her nineteenth birthday. Wearing an expensive fur coat, a gift from her mother, she had started to town to buy a matching hat and gloves. Thereafter she had been seen no more.

"The girl vanished," said Harkway. "She vanished like a puff of smoke."

A cool salt breeze drifted into the dining room, stirred the cheerful draperies, blew lightly across the table. Jack's eyes and mine met. Between sips of coffee Harkway continued the narration. After twenty-four hours of what he termed criminal delay, the college authorities telephoned Mrs. Coatesnash. She went immediately to Mather, accompanied by Annabelle Bayne. A frenzied private investigation followed; detectives buzzed up and down the streets of the sleepy little town; thousands of dollars poured into the search. Three days later the story of the missing heiress appeared in every newspaper in the United States. Police of 48 States were on the lookout for a brown-eyed girl in sables. Scores of amateur sleuths participated in the public hullabaloo, lured on by the hope of a $25,000 reward.

Harkway drained the dregs of his coffee. "No one ever collected the dough. It was posted for months."

"You said the girl was drowned."

"She was drowned. Jane Coatesnash disappeared in February. Five months later, in June, a couple of fishermen picked up her body in the Connecticut River."

Jack said, "Murder? Suicide? Accident?"

Harkway spread his hands. "The body had been weeks in the water. You couldn't tell what had happened. The police followed the usual routine, and wrote it off as accidental death."

"In that case how could they be sure of the identification?"

"The local dentist identified the body from work he had done on the teeth. There was a bracelet too, as I recall it, a bracelet that had belonged to the Coatesnash girl. She was drowned, all right. Everyone was satisfied on that count—everyone except the mother."

Jack looked a quick question.

"Hope dies hard," said the policeman. "People are likely to believe what they want to believe. Also there was one queer angle. The fur coat wasn't found. Mrs. Coatesnash did everything to trace the coat; you can find advertisements requesting information in newspapers a few years back. Nothing ever came of them; nothing could. But I hear Mrs. Coatesnash, as she got older, went a little potty on the subject. Local people will tell you that she expects to see her daughter coming around any corner, looking just as she looked fifteen years ago." Hark way folded his napkin. "I'm not acquainted with the old dame myself, but that sounds exaggerated to me."

The sad little story had reached its sad conclusion. Hark-way had no other information, and presently he left us. Jack and I lingered in the dining room, talking, speculating, trying to fit together the murder of Hiram Darnley and the fifteen-year-old tragedy. Why we should have believed there was a connection, I do not know. But we did believe it and our instinct was correct, although the link eluded us for days.

Many times Jack and I have driven past the village burial ground, a calm and lovely place on a wooded hill. We had often planned to examine the quaint old-fashioned stones; that night, for the first time, we walked through the scrolled iron gates. A white moon shone upon the city of the dead, and silvered brief graven paragraphs which perpetuated the memory of forgotten lives. We discovered the plot we sought, paused before a mausoleum of gray granite that bore the Coatesnash name. Luella's husband lay inside. Beside the mausoleum, a slender marble shaft pointed like a finger toward the sky. There was no name on the shaft, simply the engraved inscription: *"Sacred to the Memory of My Only Child"*

Silently we returned to the car.

Jack proposed the beach road home. It was longer, but on a moonlit night enchanting. The opening of the Crockford summer season was still weeks away, and the neighborhood which would ring with music and with laughter was dark and silent, touched with beauty and a kind of piercing melancholy. The only lights for blocks twinkled from the windows of an old stone house, obviously built years before the plague of country clubs and summer cottages transformed the shores of Long Island Sound. Set upon a natural rise, surrounded by extensive grounds, it commanded the deserted landscape.

Jack was driving casually and he barely missed a small car without a tail-light, parked beside the road. He cursed, jammed on his brakes. I grabbed his arm.

"Who's that?"

"Don't do that, Lola!"

"Look, Jack, look."

Jack looked. A short stout man, burdened by a bag, was walking ahead of us along the beach. It was impossible to recognize him from the distance, but he seemed familiar. Jack got out of the car. I got out.

The man ahead turned into the grounds of the stone house. We crept closer, watched him stroll up a wooden sidewalk, mount steps, knock. Annabelle Bayne opened the door. We saw her clearly as light gushed forth from inside. We identified her guest.

It was Franklyn Elliott.

CHAPTER ELEVEN

A Light in a Window

Hand in hand, with instinctive caution, Jack and I moved away from the lighted dwelling. Sand whispered sibilantly beneath our feet; the waves of Long Island Sound sighed against the beach; overhead the white moon spent itself in prodigal glory. We were too bewildered, both of us, for speech.

After pleading illness as an excuse to avoid the coroner's inquest, Franklyn Elliott had come openly to Crockford. But had he come openly? I tried to recall the strolling figure. It seemed to me there had been a furtiveness in the lawyer's attitude, a surreptitiousness in the very way he walked. And certainly Annabelle Bayne had admitted him with suspicious speed.

We approached our car. Jack paused beside the other car—a yellow roadster—looked into the empty seat, lighted a match, stooped to examine the license plates.

"New York plates, Lola. This must be Elliott's car. He probably drove up from town this afternoon. Sure, it's his car. His initials are on the door."

By this time I had my fill of sleuthing. Frankly, I didn't wish to encounter Franklyn Elliott, particularly in this vicinity. When Jack proposed that we drive on a distance, stop and watch for him, I declined at once, but eventually Jack wore me down.

A sheltered spot a little off the road and well known to Crockford swains lay near by. The night was clear but cold; we had the place to ourselves. Jack switched off the lights, and silently we settled down to wait. Perhaps half an hour later the yellow roadster shot past toward the village.

We started in pursuit. There was little traffic; we easily kept the car in sight. Elliott drove at high speed; Jack kept fairly close behind. Soon we found ourselves in the center of the drowsing village.

The advance car pulled abruptly to the curb, directly in front of the Tally-ho Inn. We parked across the street. It was past eleven. The restaurant was long closed. The adjoining lobby, revealed by plate-glass windows, was empty except for the yawning clerk.

Franklyn Elliott alighted from his car, removed two bags and walked boldly into the hotel. He crossed the wide, old-fashioned lobby, approached the desk. The clerk roused. The clerk was Bill Tevis, a perennial college boy, who attended school one semester and worked at the Tally-ho Inn the next. He and Elliott held a short conversation. Both men stepped into the clerk's office. Presently Elliott emerged, started up a broad stairway leading to the rooms, climbed out of sight.

Bill Tevis came outside and got into the yellow roadster. Jack crossed the street.

"Hi, Bill! Where you going?"

A little surprised, Bill answered readily, "To the Inn garage. I'm putting up the car for a guest."

"Look here, old man. Do you know who your guest is?"

"Sure," said Bill. "What's it to you?"

Jack hesitated. "I've been parked across the street looking in. I noticed something peculiar. That man didn't register."

Bill would have driven off at once, but Jack said quickly, "You weren't born yesterday. It's against the law to assign people rooms unless they register, and you know it is. You can't convince me Franklyn Elliott registered. I was watching."

The college-boy clerk became defiant. "He took my room. So he's my personal guest, not a hotel guest. What's against the law about that?"

Jack shrugged. "Standish might not be keen about the arrangement if he learned about it."

Bill turned sulky. "Go ahead and be a heel. Run to the cops if you want to."

"I don't want to," Jack said slowly, "and I won't. I'd hate to get you into trouble. But why did you agree to such a queer arrangement?"

Bill snapped on the ignition. "I like my job, that's why. Mrs. Coatesnash owns the Tally-ho Inn, in case you're interested. And Elliott's her lawyer."

Jack was baffled. "Didn't Elliott explain?"

"He said he didn't want police to find out he was here until tomorrow. Else they might think it funny he didn't show up for the inquest. He said he was here on private business."

Which was all we could gather from Bill Tevis.

More mystified than ever at the end of the crowded day, we went home and to bed. The morning papers—we recklessly bought Boston, New York and New Haven editions—devoted columns to the inquest, and it was surprising the amount the newspaper men had found out about a supposedly secret hearing. Even the incident of Annabelle Bayne was printed. I was about to toss the papers aside, when Jack whistled and handed me a copy of the New York *Globe*.

The *Globe,* pursuing devious methods of its own, had scored a journalistic beat. An enterprising girl reporter had tracked down the shop where Darnley's clothing had been purchased, a small second-hand store in the upper regions of the Bronx. The proprietor, an alarmed little Jew, clearly remembered the well-dressed gentleman who had appeared on March 20th to trade his own expensive apparel for "the shoddiest stuff you've got in the place." As indisputable proof, he produced—and the *Globe* photo-graphed—the garments Hiram Darnley had worn when he left his office.

It was information of a sort, but again it led to no conclusion, except the inescapable conclusion that Darnley had been bound on some illegal mis-sion. But what was the mission? We did not know. What was the purpose of the money? We did not know. We had many questions, and not a single answer. We didn't know why Darnley had climbed into the rumble seat of our automobile, why he had treated us with such marked incivility, who had telephoned or why. Reconstructing the crime or piecing together any background which might explain it was out of the question.

It was seven days after the murder, and we were completely up in the air. Our theories were non-existent. Our brains were addled. We turned to tangibilities. Two people provoked our attention. They were Annabelle Bayne and Franklyn Elliott. We suspected both the lawyer and the lady of possessing knowledge which might aid us materially in a better under-standing of the case. We attempted to concoct a sensible method of tapping these twin sources. A method eluded us. We had called upon Elliott in New York and had been fobbed off with polite evasions. To seek an interview with Annabelle Bayne, I suggested, would be like seeking an interview with an Arkansas bobcat, and Jack laughed and agreed.

I collected the scattered newspapers and carried them to the kitchen kindling box. Unannounced, Silas shambled up from the cellar. As usual, his errand was financial. For the sake of my peace of mind, we were keep-ing Reuben at the cottage. The stipend to Silas was twenty-five cents per day; he now thought fifty more equitable.

"You agreed to twenty-five."

"I can't help it, Mrs. Storm. I'd really like the dog myself.

It's lonesome at the Lodge. Specially nights."

The murder had affected him to a surprising degree, and his cowardice infuriated me. He jumped at shadows and refused to enter the cellar until, to the ruin of electric bills, we left burning there a permanent light.

Jack said he probably didn't enjoy the company of a pair of putative murderers, and I know I was increasingly exasperated by his habit of slip-ping noiselessly into the kitchen and not speaking until I discovered him. I had an uneasy feeling that he might be peering at me from around any corner—peering and wondering.

We haggled over Reuben's price, settled finally at thirty-five cents a day, with the privilege to Silas of breaking the bargain whenever he chose. He went off, doubtful and dissatisfied.

I washed the dishes, tidied the house and took the expensive Reuben for a walk. At four o'clock the dog and I were engaged in a game of ball when a smart car rolled suavely into our driveway. I turned around to look at it. Annabelle Bayne alighted and walked slowly across the lawn. I dropped the ball, stood, stared. She reached my side, laughed a little nervously, but was otherwise composed.

"Please let me say my piece before you order me off the place. I've come to say I'm sorry for what happened yesterday. I—well—let's say I was mistaken. Will you forgive me?"

I simply couldn't find my voice, Jack emerged from the cottage, stared as I had stared, and then she was upon him repeating the same astonishing apologies. She had hated him yesterday, but today it seemed she wanted to be his friend. Jack recovered himself sufficiently to remember what I had forgotten—that we desired a talk with Annabelle Bayne. He invited her into the house. She went eagerly.

"Such a darling place," she murmured. "Mrs. Storm, you have perfect taste."

"Mrs. Coatesnash," I said shortly, "is responsible for the taste. We rent the cottage furnished."

"Now you're being modest. You've moved the couch and changed those chairs." Her bright eyes darted to the walls. "And you've taken down the dreadful portraits. Uncle Will and Aunt Maria and Cousin God-Knows-Who. I wonder what became of them."

"I think they're in the attic," said T. "Have you been here before?"

"Often. As a child I almost lived here, played here every day. Jane Coatesnash and T used to come to see Jane's aunt, who had the cottage then. There were trunks in the attic full of ridiculous clothes, and we'd drag them out and put them on—you know how children are." She assumed an air of sweet appeal. "Would you mind too much if I went through the house?"

Taking permission for granted, she linked an arm through mine and we began the tour. Her eyes flashed everywhere. She saw the attic; she found the battered trunks; she saw the cellar and pointed out the broken tea pot which she and the long-dead Jane had used for tea.

She sighed. "What fun we had! Those days were the happiest of my life."

Last we went into the bedroom. Annabelle had no associations here; at any rate, she mentioned none. Still she seemed loath to leave. She spoke of the curtains, the rugs, the furnishings. She covertly examined the doors. She approached the closet.

"Is this where your burglar hid?"

"Who told you there had been a burglar?"

She smiled amusedly. "You haven't lived in a small town long. Do you think you can keep anything a secret in a town the size of Crockford? You'll learn, Mrs. Storm you'll learn."

"Then you've heard all about it?"

"From a dozen different people."

Reentering the living room, she settled gracefully in an easy chair. Jack and I exchanged a glance of deep perplexity. Annabelle was clever, but so were we. If she had hoped to convince us that her call was merely friendly, she had failed. What did she want of Jack and Lola Storm?

She finally told us. "You're in a jam. I am, too. Since—" she smiled faintly "—since that foolish exhibition yesterday, I've had plenty of policemen in my hair. I'm a selfish beast, and my own troubles probably made me think of yours." She laughed.

"Made me realize that since I was innocent, so could you be. There's human nature for you! Anyhow, I thought this. Standish is nothing but a stupid, routine village cop. Harkway is very little better. Between them they'll never solve the case. But the three of us—if we pooled our resources—might solve it."

The words were smoothly spoken, and entirely unconvincing. Jack said dryly, "Where do you propose we begin?"

She had her idea ready. "First, you must dismiss Luella Coatesnash from your mind. Whatever you were told by telephone, it's absurd to imagine she had anything to do with Darnley's coming here. I know. Although Mrs. Coatesnash was fond of Hiram Darnley, she was on purely formal terms with him, had been for many years. I doubt she's talked to him a full ten minutes since those days at Mather."

"Mather? Was Hiram Darnley present during the search for Mrs. Coatesnash's daughter?"

"Indeed, yes. He spent days there, hardly ate or slept, did all that was possible, and more too. I say it, who disliked him. Afterward Mrs. Coatesnash felt eternally grateful."

"Weren't you," Jack said carefully, "in Mather at that time?"

"Yes, of course. I stayed until we gave up hope."

"Then how does it happen you told Dr. Rand you had seen Darnley only here in Crockford?"

"I lied," said Annabelle Bayne, without an instant's hesitation. "I should warn you that I'll always lie to save myself a little trouble. Of course, I recognized the body, but I owed Hiram Darnley nothing, didn't even like him. My name is poison in the village anyhow, and it seemed best to just keep quiet." I decided then that Annabelle was perhaps more clever than her audience. Seemingly she had shown all her cards; in reality she had told us only what we already knew. She had chosen the time and place; No one heard the damaging admission except myself and Jack.

"Suppose," said Jack, and gave her a level look, "we do drop Mrs. Coatesnash from our present calculations. Must we also drop Franklyn Elliott?"

"Elliott? Oh, you mean Darnley's partner." The straight brows drew together. "I hadn't thought of him at all. Surely you don't suspect"…"

"What," said Jack, "is he doing here in Crockford?"

"Here in Crockford!" The brows went up, the full mouth framed an astonished circle. "Is he in Crockford? I understood he was too ill to leave

New York."

Apparently Annabelle Bayne had decided the time had come once more to lie and save herself a little trouble.

Shortly afterward, innocent that we had trapped her in deception, still chattering volubly, she left. We followed her outside. Silas crossed the yard, bound on his evening trip to the furnace. She stopped him to request that he appear at Bayne Place to clip her privet hedges. Beside her smart, low-slung car the four of us stood together in the thickening dusk.

Darkness was falling almost visibly, blotting out the fields and trees. I happened to glance up the hill toward the Coatesnash mansion. I squinted. It seemed to me I had seen light flicker behind one of the upper-story windows. "Silas," I said, "did Mrs. Coatesnash leave you keys to the big house?"

He started. "No, ma'am. She said she didn't want me poking in her things. The house is locked up like a drum."

"Then," I said "someone has broken in. I just saw a light on the third floor."

The darkness blurred Annabelle Bayne's expression. Her voice was cool and unexcited. "You probably saw a reflection from headlights passing on the hill road."

All four of us stared toward the vague bulk of the great white house. The chimney shaft rose stark and clear, the cupola had lost its gingerbread in shadows. A second time light arced across an upper-story window. Silas and Annabelle Bayne exchanged a look, a complicated look, a look I couldn't comprehend, a look which inferred the dimmest sort of understanding. And yet strangely I sensed an antagonism between the two. So they might have looked at each other if one of them guessed something of the other and dared not speak it out.

"It's only a reflection," said the woman indifferently, and the hired man bobbed his head in vigorous agreement.

"No one could get into the house, Mrs. Storm."

"Why should anyone want to?" queried Annabelle.

Whereupon she stepped into her car and drove off toward Crockford. Silas, too, shambled away. Jack and I lingered in the yard. The light did not reappear.

The ringing telephone summoned us inside. Dennis Cark was on the wire. The grocery boy had telephoned reluctantly and admitted it. On the way to the cottage, Annabelle Bayne, he said, had stopped in the grocery store. At first, she made an attempt to conceal her mission, eventually revealed it.

"She tried to find out," said Dennis Carle's thin, troubled voice, "how much you owed the store. We wouldn't say, but she went on to the drug store and asked there too. Don't tell my boss I told you. I promised not to, but I thought you had a right to know."

Jack and I regarded each other in mingled wonder and aggravation. Annabelle Bayne's curiosity had mounted to amazing heights. Evidently she was anxious to learn just how great was our need of money.

I said to Jack, "Perhaps she wanted to know if we could use a certain sum of money—say a hundred and eight thousand dollars."

CHAPTER TWELVE

Two New Suitcases

No better method of heightening curiosity has ever been devised than the unsuccessful effort to turn curiosity aside. By denying the existence of the light. Annabelle Bayne and Silas focused our minds upon it. Because of their behavior, the light gained an importance. Why had they lied? The answer seemed obvious. For an unknown reason they wished to prevent an investigation of the Coatesnash house.

The scene on the lawn had another specific effect. From the moment he sturdily forswore the evidence of his own eyes, we suspected Silas. We added him to a list which had consisted only of Annabelle Bayne and Franklyn Elliott. "People Who Need Explaining," we dubbed them. A strange dissimilar trio—the lawyer, the sharp, clever writer, the jack of menial trades.

As in the case of the others, our suspicions of Silas were irritatingly indefinite. He acted oddly, but from motives we could not penetrate. With quickened interest we considered his change of manner since the murder, his growing nervousness, his extreme unease. Previously we had put down his condition to an ignorant fear of the law. Now it seemed that Silas might fear something more sinister and more explicit.

"But what?" Jack sat for a speculative interval. "Look. Lola. This sounds fantastic, but think a minute. Why wasn't Silas the man who hid in the closet?"

"Silas wouldn't need to break into the cottage. He has keys."

"But...".."

I shook my head. "It won't do, Jack. You have forgotten I dashed inside and phoned Silas. The Lodge is fifteen minutes hard running from the woods. Silas could not have run from there and reached his telephone by the time I rang him up."

"Then he answered right away?"

"Immediately. It was barely five minutes after you and the black-faced man disappeared.

"Immediately?" Jack frowned. "You phoned late at night, yet Silas always goes to bed with the chickens. And sleeps like a rock."

"What are you getting at?"

"Did he answer *too* quickly? He knows we would call on him in case of trouble. How did he sound? Is it possible he was waiting beside the phone

Friday night expecting trouble here?"

"He sounded sleepy."

"That doesn't signify. How fast did he get down here from the Lodge?"

"Not fast at all. He came the long way round. I remember because I watched the pasture path. I was annoyed when I saw him coming by the road. If Silas expected trouble, he thought of his own skin first. He wouldn't set foot in the woods till I went in."

I felt we were unduly complicating the already complicated situation. The picture of Silas seated at his telephone filled with a inexplicable anxiety did not appeal, to me. It argued a craft which I could not concede him.

Late in the evening Jack and I decided to trespass upon our landlady's grounds. It was an imprudent decision, but we had arrived at a state where action seemed essential. The light which had shone briefly and mysteriously in the deserted dwelling was a powerful lure. As Jack said, sometimes a great deal depends upon trifles. Also, as he didn't say, sometimes it is well for the innocent to avoid even the appearance of evil.

We planned carefully, deliberately delaying a start until eleven o'clock. Once Silas was safely asleep, the danger of discovery would be slight; if caught we were prepared to say we had strayed thoughtlessly from the road. Jack armed himself with a good, stout monkey wrench—he didn't own a gun—and, accompanied by Reuben, we set forth on our illegal jaunt. The yellow dog hung at my heels; he disliked the darkness and the sounds of a country night.

Silently we mounted Strawberry Hill, taking the short cut through the rocky pasture. Jack used a flashlight sparingly. The path familiar in the daytime presented unexpected ruts and turnings and long vistas of inky blackness that were, I must admit, dampening. We almost ran into the Lodge. Reuben emitted a yip of pleasure, which I stifled instantly. We waited. Silas slept on, undisturbed.

Softly calling the dog to follow, we crept ahead, past the vegetable gardens, past the grape arbor to the rear of the mansion. At the irregular patch of dead lawn, where on sunny days Mrs. Coatesnash had walked with Ivan, we brought up sharply. One by one Jack illuminated the third-story windows of the big white house. A close inspection disclosed one unshuttered window at the extreme left. Narrow and uncurtained. Jack spoke in a whisper.

"Is that where you saw the light? Could you place it?"

"I think that's right."

"Wait here."

He tiptoed to the rear doors—there were three—separately examined each. He rattled the knobs, causing my heart to beat uncomfortably. He returned to report rear doors and windows locked and apparently impregnable.

"Two of the doors wouldn't budge a fraction of an inch. I believe they're barred from the inside. The basement door isn't barred, but it's sure as hell locked."

"You made a lot of noise," I said nervously. "Someone might be inside and have a perfect right there. We don't know Mrs. Coatesnash didn't lend her keys."

"Silas would have known about it if she had. I wish I had a ladder. I would like a closer look at the upper windows."

Fortunately—or so I felt—our equipment did not include a ladder. Unsatisfied, Jack inched along the lawn searching vainly for possible marks of a ladder used by someone else. Then, when I was reaching a pitch of nerves and impatience, he proposed to give the front grounds and entrances a similar examination.

By this time the whole expedition had begun to seem both impertinent and pointless. I protested. I wanted to go home. I said so. We went around to the front of the house. Thick boards covered the two front doors; shutters cloaked the first floor windows. Nothing suggested illegal tampering. Leaves choked the walks and porches, maple seed wings littered the steps. Relieved by non-success, I concluded that the mysterious light had a natural, innocent—if elusive—answer.

Past an elaborate rock garden an untidy graveled path twisted to the main road which bent around the hill to join our own road. In our vocabulary this route was termed "the long way home." I started toward the gates. Disappointed, Jack turned to follow. His flashlight made a great arc as it traversed the steep slope of the garden.

I gasped and stopped on the path. Beside me Jack stood rigid. In the daytime we would have missed what we now saw clearly—an oblong patch of earth in the garden, black and freshly dug. A patch vivid in the flashlight's glare, standing forth from the intense surrounding darkness, a patch of queer shape and size—about four feet in width and six feet in length. Although the earth had been skillfully roughened, it resembled unmistakably a level grave.

An owl shrieked near by. Reuben bristled and I felt my hair rise on end. Jack dropped his flashlight. He sheepishly picked it up, scrambled over the rocks, knelt and thrust out his hand. His whisper was piercing.

"The ground is soft. Something is buried here." He swiftly returned to me. "You stay here with Reuben. I'll need a spade."

I clutched at him hysterically. "What are you going to do?"

"I mean to find out what's buried there."

An argument ensued, incoherent, bitter, touched with the horror of the place and situation. Convinced that the light, the cunningly hidden grave, the Coatesnash house impinged upon the murder of Hiram Darnley, Jack was fanatically determined to complete his evening's work. He should, of course, have delegated further investigation to the police; he flatly declined. He believed they would disregard any evidence which tended to incriminate Mrs. Coatesnash, unless the evidence were final and conclusive. In the end, his vehemence conquered me—though there was one thing I refused to do. I would not remain alone in the rock garden.

For a curious reason, Reuben stayed. As we turned to go, his head went up, he sniffed the air, barked and bolted into the leafless laurel bushes. I felt a thrill of icy fear.

"What's there?"

Jack was impatient. "A woodchuck probably. Come on."

"Reuben," I called. "Reuben."

"Let him catch his woodchuck. Come, Lola, let's get this done."

With an odd reluctance, which I laid to the happenings of the evening, I obeyed.

I do not like to think about the return trip to the cottage—the stumbling along the road, the protracted hunt for a spade after our arrival, the darkness and the quiet. Once or twice I fancied I heard the distant barking of a dog. Five minutes later when we hurriedly retraced our steps through the pasture, I was sure of it.

"It's Reuben, Jack."

"He's got the woodchuck."

"It doesn't sound like that."

As I spoke the barking rose to frenzy, became a yelp of anguish, subsided to a moan—to nothingness. Jack broke into a run. Half a minute carried him past the Lodge. He shot through the grape arbor, circled Hilltop House to the right, disappeared.

Reuben lay in the rock garden. Kicked into unconsciousness, bloody and pathetic, the dog sprawled beside a wide, shallow, gaping hole. The excavation revealed every sign of haste. Clods and mounds of dirt were scattered in four directions; swift, deep shovel bites were visible. Also visible were smeared footprints.

Kneeling beside the dog, Jack looked up dully. "Rotten luck beat us, Lola. I ran around the house the wrong way."

In explanation he turned his flashlight upon the gaping hole in the garden. From the excavation, leading across the grass, blurred marks showed where something long and heavy had been dragged away. These marks led directly to the left and toward the house, vanishing in the gloom of the trees. If, when Jack dashed around the house, he had happened to run to the left, he would have solved our mystery then and there. But he made the wrong choice. He ran to the right, and thus missed a dark figure scurrying along the opposite side of the mansion, hauling a heavy burden.

With Reuben wrapped in my coat, we started again for home. The marks on the brittle grass stopped abruptly at the cellar door. The door was closed. Jack tried the knob. His fingers touched a key in the lock.

Immediately, unhesitatingly he turned the key and entered the cellar of the Coatesnash house. He collided with an ashcan, pushed past, strode to the furnace, pried it open, peered inside. A film of ancient ashes rose chokingly. His instant hunch had failed. There was nothing there.

Leaving the injured dog near the door, I joined him. He put his mouth to my ear.

"Let's go upstairs."

A desperate situation requires desperate remedies, and the situation, I felt, was desperate. It appeared certain that whatever had been buried in the garden was hidden within the house, if we were to search, it must be tonight. Tomorrow would be too late.

Such logic sustained me very little as we began our surreptitious tour. My tongue clove to the roof of my mouth, and if ever a person felt criminal, I did. We gained the first floor, paused at the entrance of the cavernous drawing-room, where long ago we had sat at tea. Luella Coatesnash's personality lingered like a vapor there. I seemed to hear the tapping of her cane, to smell again her cloying lavender scent, to see the diamonds on her hands and the splitting taffeta of her gown.

A drapery rustled; something pattered across the floor. A mouse or a rat probably, but I gasped and grabbed at Jack. The darkness filled itself with shapes and forms. Behind every shrouded piece of furniture, beyond every unseen corner, lurked a crouching, waiting figure. I felt certain we were not alone in the house. The key in the basement lock—might it have been left to lure us in? Had we walked into a trap?

Jack pulled me on. He paused at the flight of stairs which climbed to the upper floors. His quick, excited breath stirred my hair.

"We may find what we're hunting in the third-floor room."

Setting my teeth, I started up the stairs. The journey was less difficult than I anticipated. The curving banister was reassuringly solid, the carpets were thick. In absolute silence we moved upward. We easily located the room with the unshuttered window. At the corridor end, a door stood ajar.

We crossed the threshold. Jack snapped on his flash and I looked around a cheerless storeroom. Dusty trunks, bags, boxes, broken furniture jammed the place. Blinking, I surveyed the decidedly unmysterious surroundings and turned to speak. With a report that resounded throughout the house, the door behind banged shut and something bounced on the floor. Severely shocked, I didn't realize what had happened.

"Lola!"

"It's all right. I bumped the door."

"The knob's come off."

"It's here on the floor."

I picked up the china knob and handed it to Jack. He stepped to the door. A moment passed. I said nervously, "Well, why don't you put it back?"

"I'm afraid I can't." Jack's voice was queer. "The outside knob and the shank fell through on the other side. You've locked us in.

Under other circumstances the immediate shift in attitudes might have had a humorous side. Thoroughly alarmed by the mishap, Jack lost his burning interest in the Coatesnash house and wanted only to get us out of it. As for me—temporarily, anyhow—I was too apologetic to be frightened.

Jack hammered at the door. It was two inches thick and fabricated of solid oak. It didn't budge beneath his stoutest efforts. Nothing he tried would serve in place of the missing knob and shank. He tried to fit into the hole in the door his finger, his fountain pen, his palette knife. The door remained firmly closed. The single window offered the only other egress from the room. After minutes of frantic, futile labor, Jack pushed up the window and poked his head into the raw spring night. He doubtfully examined the overhanging gutter.

"Do you think you can make it to the roof, Lola?"

I looked out and up, and firmly declined to try.

"If I went first and pulled you up…"

"I prefer staying here."

Jack then proposed that he ascend to the roof, climb down by the grape arbor in the rear and return through the house for me. Once he got hold of the shank and knob which maddeningly lay in the hall he could easily open the door for me. It was a solution I didn't like, but I hardly dared object.

With a sinking heart I saw Jack go out the window. Half standing, half sitting, he attempted to draw himself to the roof. He is a strong and acrobatic man, but the gutter was old and rusty. A piece tore away, ne grasped air, and for one dreadful moment I thought he would plunge to the ground below. I insisted that he abandon the effort. He refused. He tried again with me clinging desperately to his knees, wondering how long I could support his weight if he should slip. This time the gutter held, and in some miraculous fashion he got to the roof. Leaning over the edge, he whispered a few final encouraging words and vanished.

For a while I remained beside the window, too terrified to move. Jack had left me the flashlight and the wrench. A monkey wrench is a singularly inadequate weapon. I laid it down. Minutes slowly passed, and gradually I felt a little better. If anyone were in the house, surely the loud report of the door would have brought that person to the scene. No one came.

I changed my cramped position, began to study the confusion of objects in the storeroom, shifting the flash from a box piled high with shoes to a box filled with hardware—old electric fixtures, locks, bits of plumbing, and the like—from a battered wardrobe trunk to a sagging, springless couch.

The room was bitterly cold. I tiptoed to the couch, pulled its faded coverlet across my knees. Fumbling in my coat I pulled out a squashed pack and lighted a cigarette. I flipped the match to the floor. As I bent to extinguish it, my hand touched leather. Tucked underneath the couch were two traveling bags, brand new and thick with dust. Both were initialed L.T.

How long I sat staring at the bags I cannot say. L.T must stand for Laura Twining. But what were her bags doing here? Why hadn't she taken them to Europe? The very questions were disquieting.

I pulled out the bags, snapped the locks. My perplexity and uneasiness intensified. Both bags were packed, just as Laura Twining would have packed them. Stout shoes wrapped in tissue paper, cotton stockings wound in careful balls, a crepe kimono folded across a hanger. The bags contained every garment I had seen the spinster wear; the bottle-green foulard so peculiarly unbecoming, the black poplin used for every day, the darned housedresses, the shapeless raccoon coat, the purple velvet hat. Laura Twining had planned to take the bags. A waterproof toilet case provided with fresh toothpaste, a tin of talcum, a bar of jacketed soap, insisted that she had. Why not, then? I recalled the orderly workings of her mind. That she could have forgotten her luggage seemed beyond belief.

Why should the bags be in the storeroom here hidden beneath a couch? I continued the exploration, caught my breath. In the second bag I came upon three things. I found the dress Laura had intended to travel in—the gray poplin trimmed in lace, pressed and ready to wear, and yet not worn. In the pocket I found a letter of credit, pathetically small, and an unused passport. Laura's passport. The photograph smiled timidly, apologetically as Laura herself had smiled when she asked me if I thought the poplin dress was suitable for shipboard.

I felt a sickening dismay. A conviction long avoided rushed inescapably upon me. Laura Twining had never sailed to France. If not to France, where had she gone? In awful fascination my mind returned to the rock garden and to the excavation there. Sitting in the storeroom, her pitiful possessions spread before me, I felt quite certain that never again would Jack and I be annoyed by friendly little calls from Luella Coatesnash's dull companion.

I began automatically to repack the bags. I stopped suddenly. Someone was moving in the hall outside. I tried to pull myself together. It must be Jack, come back into the house for me. But I hadn't thought he would be so soon. I went to the door.

"Jack," I whispered. "Jack."

There was no answer. The footsteps ceased, and all was quiet. Someone lurked beyond the door, motionless, listening, waiting for me further to betray myself.

I crouched against the panel. I heard from the other side the flare of a match, a rattle along the floor, and then, most terrible of all, I heard the sound of the steel shank as it was forced through the hole in the door. Slowly the door began to open. I resisted frantically. Inch by inch the steady, insistent pressure forced me back. The noiseless, terrible contest continued. My strength and will gave way. The door opened wide. I was trapped in the corner, pressed against the wall.

Footsteps, regular, unhurried, came into the storeroom, crossed to the couch. The thick darkness kept its secret well. I could see nothing. The couch coverlet rustled; leather scraped on wood. A pause, long and ominous. Then the unhurried footsteps returned to the door, again paused. I prepared for the end. Whoever had entered the room knew that I, or that some person, was also there. I opened my mouth to scream, made no sound.

The door began to close, slowly and deliberately as it had opened. Fantastically, in the darkness, I heard a low soft chuckle. The door shut smartly; the shank was swiftly withdrawn, and was dropped to the floor on the other side. I heard it fall.

Three minutes that were like hours dragged by. Certain my visitor would not return, I tottered to the couch, found the flashlight. Laura Twining's bags were gone. I was alone and imprisoned once more.

CHAPTER THIRTEEN

A Splinter of Bone

Gravel pattered at the window-pane behind me. A sharp, small noise like the rattle of broken beads. I tottered to the window. Jack stood on the ground below. His coat was torn, his cheek was bleeding, but to me he looked very nearly perfect. Then to my consternation he called in loud and cheerful tones:

"I'm alive and whole. I had a devil of a time getting down that arbor, and…"

I leaned out into the night. "For heaven's sake be quiet. Something dreadful's happened."

I heard him gasp, but he asked no questions. "I'll be there in a minute."

A little later his footfall sounded in the corridor beyond the storeroom. Once more the steel shank slipped through the door, once more the knob was turned, and the door was opened. This time, though, I felt the blessed clasp of Jack's arms, the warmth of his kiss on my lips. I tried incoherently to talk and I know that I wept from sheer relief. Clinging together, we started through the pitch-black silent house toward the lower floor. I recall little of that swift and noiseless journey, but as we started down the cellar stairs I did become vaguely aware of the change in temperature. The previous bitter chill had vanished; the basement dampness stirred with a feeble, humid warmth. A strange odor assailed the nostrils, an odor misty and unsubstantial, yet faintly acrid, like rubber drying in the sun. Then, suddenly, from the darkness came a whimpering moan.

"What was that?"

Jack's arm tightened at my waist. "It must be Reuben. Poor little devil, I'd forgotten we left him here. Come, Lola."

I sensed the strain and urgency in his voice, the speed with which he hurried me outside. But I was glad enough to go. Jack returned for Reuben, and shortly afterward was at my side.

We ran most of the way to the cottage, stumbling along in the dark, Jack with Reuben nestled under his coat. Under the cheerful light of the living-room lamps it became evident that Reuben was less seriously injured than we had thought. But the little dog was bruised and bloody, and my rage at his condition was a tonic to my nerves. While Jack busied himself with iodine and bandages, and I grew angrier every minute and less afraid,

I got my story fully told.

I can remember now Jack's whitening face, the look in his eyes, how he rested his cheek against mine, how he said: "Maybe you're a bum house-keeper, love of my life, maybe you don't sew the buttons on my shirts, but you do have your points. Go on, weep on my shoulder. Collapse! You're entitled, to a week of prostration. You've earned it."

That made me laugh. But Jack's kiss wasn't a joke. We had a moment of our own, before I said honestly, "The truth is, I was scared stiff. So scared that I haven't the remotest notion who the man in the storeroom was, what he looked like or anything else."

"I think," said Jack, "I know what he looks like. And both of us know why he ran such a desperate risk to get those bags." Jack was silent for a long time. "You must have noticed how warm it was on our second trip through the cellar. And that curious odor. While we were trapped in the storeroom, Lola, something was being burned downstairs. Burned in a hot quick fire. I examined the furnace when I went back for Reuben. It was still warm. I found this in the ashes."

From his pocket Jack removed a tiny, charred object. It was a splinter of bone, very narrow, about three inches long—a fragment broken from a larger section. We stared at each other. Our eyes asked questions with implications almost too terrible to put into words.

Jack said, "You're certain you saw Laura's passport?"

"Positive." Suddenly I found myself near tears.

Jack took my hand, and held it hard. "It's a ghastly thing to think about, but there it is. Laura Twining has been murdered, Lola, her body burned. Ghastlier still. I'm convinced I know who's back of it."

I only looked at him.

"In all her many talks with the French police," Jack said carefully, "Mrs. Coatesnash has consistently omitted one important fact—the fact that the woman who started to Europe with her never arrived there. That's significant, isn't it?"

"But how…"

"Do you recall," Jack asked, "the day the *Burgoyne* sailed? Do you remember the Coatesnash car passing us on the road? Who was in the car besides Laura?"

Before me rose the unforgotten scene. It was a sunny February afternoon. I saw an ancient limousine rush past us and away toward New York. I saw baggage heaped in the car, saw Mrs. Coatesnash's cold still nod, saw an English mastiff crouched on the floor, saw Laura Twining's averted profile. At the wheel, facing his task with obstinacy and ignorant conceit. I saw a third familiar figure.

I said, "Silas was driving."

"Well?"

A series of possibilities paraded through my mind. Like scenes from a motion picture, rapid and chronological: A decrepit limousine halted on a deserted backwoods road; a terrible struggle occurred in the car with a strong and sullen man in the leading role; a body was carried back to a big white house and hastily buried; a proud old woman pursued a predetermined plan, traveled on to New York, and sailed alone.

The events which might have occupied that sunlit afternoon seemed clear enough, but I hit upon no motives. What motive had Mrs. Coatesnash for the murder of her companion? What motive had Silas?

I considered the relationship between Silas Elkins and Luella Coatesnash—the hired man's serf-like demeanor toward the lady, her bland acceptance of it. Assuming that Mrs. Coatesnash desired to hurry Laura Twining from the world, I was almost ready to assume that Silas could be bullied, persuaded or ordered into assisting the bloody purpose. Almost— not quite.

Logic faltered when I weighed his character and particularly his cowardice. Silas had the physical stamina, the strength for murder. Had he the courage, the cool and steady nerves, the will? The unknown whom I had encountered in the storeroom must surely be the murderer. That person had possessed to an extraordinary degree cunning, determination and intrepidity. Silas hardly possessed such attributes. Or did he? Could I have struggled with Silas and failed to recognize him?

Chin sunk in his palms, forehead knotted, Jack also pondered the string of evil possibilities. On the chair Reuben stirred and moaned. Jack stroked the dog's head. Slowly his expression changed.

"We've been overlooking something damned important. Reuben."

"Reuben?"

"I thought it was Silas who was at the big house tonight, scaring you to death, vanishing with the bags. Well, it wasn't. This fellow here lets him out," Jack said ruefully. "Reuben wouldn't have barked at Silas, in the first place—under any circumstances. And in the second place, Silas wouldn't have needed to maltreat his own dog so he could escape from us into the house."

That logic was unanswerable. Reuben hated strangers, but was always friendly to those he knew. But if it had not been Silas in the big house—and eventually we decided it had not been—it was still possible that he suspected someone else was there and for Mrs. Coatesnash's sake meant to shield that person from our curiosity. Did Annabelle Bayne also suspect? Who was the mysterious third person?

Abruptly Jack turned and faced me. "What do you think of Franklyn Elliott as a candidate? Maybe he was on the hill tonight. He has courage, imagination, subtlety, all the talents of the top-flight criminal."

I said dryly, "A pretty conclusive definition of a man you've seen exactly twice."

"Twice was plenty. Elliott knows more than he's told, a good deal more. Here's something else. His profession is against him. He is a law-yer"—here Jack developed a favorite theory of his own—"and successful lawyers are notoriously the most lawless class on earth. They're trained to consider evidence in a special light, as something to use, or something to hide and destroy. They make fortunes in contriving evasions of justice. Elliott would probably stop at nothing to assist a rich client. And the Lord knows that Mrs. Coatesnash is rich."

I thought Franklyn Elliott would stop at digging up and burning the body of a murdered woman—to oblige Mrs. Coatesnash or any other client I said so.

"It's nonsense, Jack. I don't trust Elliott, but we've no real proof he isn't a reputable lawyer. Nothing beyond a lot of vague suspicions."

"He ducked the inquest and made that secret call on Annabelle Bayne."

"That's true enough, but..."

"This isn't vague!" Jack rose suddenly from his chair. "Do you remem-ber Elliott's telling us that he went down and saw Mrs. Coatesnash off to Europe? Laura wasn't aboard the *Burgoyne;* she couldn't have been. Has Franklyn Elliott said one word about her absence? You bet he hasn't. He's let us all believe that Laura was safe in Paris."

It was long past three o'clock. A distant rooster crowed shrilly. I wasn't sleepy. I was confused, dissatisfied, bewildered.

What we had learned at Hilltop House, what we had inferred, appeared to lead not toward, but away from, the original mystery. How could the events which had taken place that night be connected with the murder of Hiram Darnley? Superficially the grim-faced wealthy lawyer (our first vic-tim) and the penniless spinster who had drunk our tea seemed worlds apart. I accepted that Darnley had been slain for money. Laura had no money. She was dull, colorless, unprovocative. So far as I could see there was nothing about her to invite murder.

Luella Coatesnash was the single link between the dual mysteries. Hilltop House belonged to her; Darnley had been her legal representative; Laura had been her companion, her closest confidante.

Presently Jack roused from his own thoughts. "I've been busy trying to tie up Darnley and Laura. Maybe I've got somewhere. I don't know. I've been wondering if there might not have been a motive for Darnley's murder other than that money." He gave a short laugh. "I'll admit that Mrs. Coatesnash would hardly conspire to kill a man for money. The money which Darnley carried must fit in of course, but if Mrs. Coatesnash had him murdered it must have been for another reason. I've thought of one good sound reason, and only one, why she might have wanted Hiram Darnley and Laura Twining out of the way."

"What is it?"

"Think it out yourself, Lola. Concentrate on Mrs. Coatesnash, on the kind of woman she is. How could you hit at her? How could you bring her to the point of murder?"

"You'll have to spell it out for me," I said slowly. "Unless—" I hesitated "—unless you're thinking about her grand old family name."

Jack smiled his satisfaction. "That's it precisely. As I see it, you could hit at Luella only through her family, her infernal pride of race. Now let's go on from there. Suppose Laura Twining and Hiram Darnley shared a piece of information, a secret, a shameful secret that concerned the Coatesnash family. The honor of the family sounds unmodern, old-fashioned, but Luella doesn't live in a modern world. She belongs to the generation which cheerfully faced death before disgrace."

"Still…"

Jack waved aside the interruption. "Wait a minute. Luella learns those two know the secret. Maybe Laura and Darnley threaten her with it. She sees disgrace, a grand old family toppling in the mud; she can't bear the village knowing, snickering, whispering behind her hack. She…" Suddenly Jack's eyes blazed. "The daughter, Lola! Jane—remember Jane? Remember the curious drowning? Darnley headed the search. Could he have learned something then, something about the girl, something kept quiet for years, but something hot enough to be news today in Crockford?"

"But where and how and when did Laura and Darnley meet? We have no knowledge they ever did. Laura came to Mrs. Coatesnash after Jane's death. Darnley hadn't been in Crockford since then until the other night. Or we don't know he had."

"Laura has been in New York."

"Darnley was a hard-headed business man. If he actually had a secret, why would he choose a chatterbox like Laura to confide in?"

"They may have discovered it simultaneously. The thing for us to do is to establish a friendship if we can. Find out how well they knew each other. Find out everything about them both."

Shortly afterward Jack belatedly telephoned to the police. He disliked the task of outlining our evening's questionable activities, but I for one was happy to delegate my own share in any further speculation. I was intolerably weary. Also I have a pragmatic mind, and though Jack's theory was ingenious, I wanted some solid, substantial evidence to support it.

Standish could not be raised by repeated ringing, but eventually Jack roused Lester Harkway. The young policeman asked excited questions, and promised to leap into clothes and come out at once. As Jack replaced the telephone, the clock on the mantel struck four. Four long silvery notes. Someone began to pound at the cottage door.

I looked at the clock. I looked at Jack. He went quickly to the door, called out, "Who's there?" A moment later he returned with Dr. Rand. The physician was haggard and worn; his coat was a mass of wrinkles; his shoes were caked and muddy. He walked wearily, gratefully to the fire.

"It's a lucky thing for me you artists and writers never go to bed. I saw your lights from the road and chanced your being up. Do I smell coffee?"

"Will you have some?"

"Will I! Two cups, if it's handy, no sugar, but I favor lots of cream. Also I'd like to borrow a gallon of gas. My car ran out down the road a piece. Second time I've been caught in twenty years. Not bad, considering…but maybe after all we should have stuck to the horse."

He took a chair near the fire and yawned prodigiously.

"Babies have a talent for selecting inconvenient hours to make a start in life. It's a wonder their mothers put up with it. I wonder I do myself." He rubbed his fingers through his skull-white hair. "I had a nasty shock tonight. It comes to me I'm getting old, damned old—senile, practically. An hour ago I brought Alice Shipman's baby into the world; eighteen years ago I brought Alice into the world. That's bad enough, but it's not the worst of it. The first baby I delivered in Crockford was Alice Shipman's mother. Thirty-eight years ago almost to the day—thirty-eight years! Does that qualify me for the firing squad, or doesn't it? No man should be permitted to outlive his arteries." He yawned again. "There's no money in babies; there never was. People have them, doctors deliver them, and no one seems to make a penny out of it. Did you ever read Swift's *Modest Proposal?* Swift suggested that Irish infants be substituted for pork in the retail markets. I've often thought his notion should be applied in Crockford. God, I'm tired. Will you tell me why any sane man takes up a country practice?"

We couldn't tell him. I brought the coffee. He drank three cups, instead of the threatened two. His shoes were muddy. He borrowed a tea towel and polished them. He fell to discussing the inquest. He said heatedly that Annabelle Bayne should be ducked as a public nuisance. He regretted the passing of old New England customs which had possessed a certain social value.

The clock struck the half hour. The physician glanced at it. "Good Lord, is it that late? What *were* you kids doing up? Don't you ever go to bed?" He eyed Jack disapprovingly. "You were knocked unconscious less than a week ago. You should take care of yourself. You're looking pale around the gills." The sharp gaze was transferred to me. "You look a little peaked, too." He peered into my face, felt my wrist, wagged his head. "Saffron eyes at twenty. A jumpy pulse. Wretched color. If you youngsters don't start sleeping occasionally, when you get my age you'll have no nerves worth mentioning."

"It's fortunate we didn't turn in tonight," Jack said at once. "We've covered a lot of valuable ground. Most of the credit is due to Lola, but between us we've practically worked out a theory for Hiram Darnley's murder."

Immediately the physician lost interest. "After drinking your coffee and toasting my feet at your fire, I probably shouldn't criticize. However, one of the advantages of age, one of the few, is offering unsolicited advice. Polite young people feel obliged to listen. If I were you, young man, I'd pick something better to occupy my time." He sniffed. "The village is overrun with amateur detectives, poking and prying and chattering among themselves. Ghouls, the lot of 'em! Why class yourself and your wife with a collection of morbid louts? You look normal. So does she." Jack grinned. "Sure I'm normal. So normal that I actively resent the possibility of being arrested for a murder I didn't commit."

"Bosh! If Standish had planned to arrest you, you'd be behind bars now. So long as you behave yourself, you're safe. Safer than you'll be if you begin sticking your fingers in a policeman's pie. When they want your help, you can be sure they'll ask for it."

I poured oil on the troubled waters. "You don't get the point, Dr. Rand. Jack and I are outsiders, and we've been made to feel it. We've been questioned and harassed and spied on and the rest of it, and Mrs. Coatesnash has gone scot-free. Anywhere else—in New York, say—she'd have been forced to come back from Paris."

"In a measure I agree. If I had charge of the investigation, Mrs. Coatesnash would have been ordered home. She ought to be here. There's no question of it. However, I gravely doubt that murders are solved by youngsters who sit up till five in the morning celebrating. They're solved by evidence and by policemen who go out and dig it up."

The physician's thorny mood did not invite an account of our evening. I changed my tactics. I called on guile. "Anyone has a right to be interested where his own safety or convenience is at stake. As ours is. And the case has been badly handled. This evening, for instance, Jack and I have been discussing a person never mentioned in connection with it. Laura Twining. We think that Laura should have been interviewed by the French police."

Dr. Rand chuckled. "The French are a smart race. The *chef de Sûreté*— or whatever you call him—probably took a good look at Laura and decided to save his eardrums."

"She *was* a great talker. She used to come here afternoons and wear us out." I added innocently, "Have you known her long?"

The physician studied me severely. "What are you up to, young woman? I suspect I'm being pumped. Of course, I've known Laura Twining long. Met her ten years ago when she started working for the old lady. She—Laura, I mean—has the worst sinuses and frontals I've ever seen. I've treated her for years. Would you like a report on the hay fever attack Laura had in nineteen-twenty-seven?"

"Skip it, please."

Dr. Rand was again thoroughly aroused. "Curiosity is a curse; even legitimate curiosity is. It has broken more hearts and opened more graves and caused more trouble, I do believe, than all other human emotions combined. What tree are you barking up now? Why these questions about Laura Twining? Are you supposing that anemic, dried-up old maid could tell you anything about Darnley's death?"

"Lola," said Jack, endeavoring to interpret my remarks, a habit of his which I detest, "was merely using Laura as an example of the mismanagement in this case. If Laura had ever met Hiram Darnley, and she probably had, the French police should have questioned her."

"Why, in the name of heaven? The police can't question everyone who had a nodding acquaintance with Hiram Darnley."

"Then she did know him!"

"Trapped, by God!" Dr. Rand made a sound, half exasperated, half amused. "Certainly Laura knew Darnley. Quite well. He got her the job with Mrs. Coatesnash, recommended her from New York. Anyone in the village could tell you as much." He rose from his chair. "I see I must flee for my life. You will be demanding professional confidences next. The fact that Laura and Darnley were acquainted adds up to nothing. Sensibly, it doesn't." He looked from Jack to me. "But then you don't appear to be in a sensible mood. Either of you!"

Irritated as he was, Dr. Rand remembered his need of gas. While Jack was siphoning a gallon from our car, Lester Harkway rode up to the cottage and joined the two men in the garage. Preferring to hear our story without an auditor, he restrained his questions.

"Good morning, doc. You're out early."

The physician chilled at the "doc."

"The Storms have been good enough to entertain me a while. They're bright young people. Somewhat nosy, but then detective work takes nosiness. I should warn you they've gone in for sleuthing. If you don't solve your murder soon, they may beat you out of the glory."

Harkway smiled a shade smugly. "Anyone who cracks the case will earn my gratitude."

"How's Standish? Where's he? Usually you two are thick as thieves— never see the one without the other."

"John's out of town. He went yesterday to Osage, New York, to interview Darnley's wife. That's why I'm here."

"Oh! So you were expected."

Dr. Rand gave Jack a straight look. He refused a lift to his car. "I like the exercise." He picked up the gasoline and plodded toward the road. Jack and Harkway watched him vanish in the distance, the tin bucket bobbing at his side.

CHAPTER FOURTEEN

The Missing Annual

Over coffee Harkway heard the story of our evening. Directly afterward we started for the Coatesnash house. It was six o'clock.

Dawn was rising in the east, like the spreading of a slow stain. A bleak, colorless dawn. We climbed the pasture path. The rocks and trees and turnings that by night had been so fearsome were now merely gray and dull and ugly. Clothed in naked trees rose Hilltop House, cupolaed and hideous. The Lodge squatted in close attendance like a meek and anxious servitor. Unchallenged, we wound past the smaller building and on to the grape arbors.

Harkway had pocketed the key to the cellar door. We went there first. Quite undramatically the policeman thrust the key into the lock, twisted it. The lock grated, but did not budge. Again the lock grated. Harkway frowned.

"Sure this is the right key?"

"Certain. Here let me try it." Jack's knuckles whitened as he vainly exercised his force upon the key. His face looked queer. "It seems to stick."

"It doesn't," amended Harkway doubtfully, "appear to fit." Jack was nervous and annoyed.

"The key did fit last night. Let me try again."

"I don't think it's necessary." Harkway dropped to one knee and, taking out a pocket magnifying glass, scrutinized the lock. A small brass circle, slightly rusted. He handed Jack the glass. "Was this particular lock on the door last night?"

"I didn't notice the lock; I simply turned the key."

Harkway said slowly, "I believe the lock has been changed since you were here. Done pretty carefully, but if you look closely, you will see certain traces of the job." He moved his finger around the rusted circle. "Do you see the particles of raw wood? And over here—the fresh scratch?"

Jack stood up. "I see, yes. But where did the second lock come from? Crockford isn't New York. Where could a second lock be got in the middle of the night? They don't grow on bushes." Harkway hesitated, and I perceived his bewildered groping. He scratched his jaw. "The lock isn't new."

Suddenly and definitely I hit upon the origin of the second lock. A recollection of the cluttered storeroom flashed into my mind. I recalled the cardboard carton filled with odds and ends of hardware—bits of plumbing, window fastenings, a graceful wrought-iron hinge, a bunch (of string-tied keys and old discarded locks. Jack turned to me.

"Did you say something, Lola?"

"There were locks in the storeroom; I think this may be one of them."

"In the storeroom!"

"Old locks—junk. The place was jammed with trash."

Jack gnawed his lip and I understood, if Harkway did not, the workings of his thought. He was remembering our case against Franklyn Elliott. Small as it was, this bit of evidence weighed in the lawyer's favor. A straw to indicate his innocence. Even if Elliott had the manual skill to change a lock—which seemed unlikely—he hardly could have obtained the second lock. Such a presumption required far too intimate a knowledge of the house. The person who had gone to the storeroom and found a lock there must have known precisely where to look for what he wanted.

These speculations slid rapidly through my brain. Abandoning our efforts with the cellar door, we circled around the house. We had been prepared for surprise, and consequently were not surprised by what we saw. There was no hole in the rock garden. There were no swift blurred footprints. The marks on the grass remained, but in a form changed and characterless. They had been trampled over; other marks had been superimposed; it was now impossible to trace the course which had led from the garden to the cellar door a few hours earlier.

Jack blinked. "A thorough clean-up."

"Very thorough. Queer thing—the deliberation of it all. The business must have taken plenty of time and calculation—changing the lock, filling in the hole, spoiling the marks. A cool customer, the chap last night." Harkway spoke absently. His eyes rested upon the rock garden, narrowed. "Can you show me the spot where you saw the hole?"

Surmounting the rocks, Jack halted at a patch of loose black earth, which in the dull dawn light resembled not a level grave, but a recently prepared, quite unsinister flower bed. "Here's the place."

Harkway joined him. They both got down on hands and knees and crawled about, searching for something which might have been overlooked. Nothing had been.

A line of leafless snowball bushes marched somberly along the road at the foot of the garden. I guessed rather than saw a stir of movement there. I squinted. The movement became perceptible. Both men were occupied, and as I opened my lips to summon them, the bushes parted. Silas Elkins stepped forth and hastened up the slope toward the searchers. He looked angry and aggressive.

"What do you think you're doing?"

Harkway stood, brushed his trousers free of gravel. I had never thought of him precisely as an agent of the law. I did now and evidently so did Silas, for at once he lost his defiant swagger and moderated his tone.

"You got no right here. Mrs. Coatesnash left me in charge. I was to keep trespassers off."

"We will pass the matter of our rights." Harkway indicated the plot of earth in the garden. "What do you know about this?"

"What is there to know about it?"

"I'm questioning you. Please remember it! Have you been digging in the garden recently?"

"I dug the crocus bed, if that's what you're driving at. Mrs. Coatesnash told me to. Prepare the crocus bed, she said, the last week in March."

"When did you prepare it?"

"The last week in March."

"Exactly when?"

"A couple days ago, Wednesday, I guess." Silas glared at the policeman. "You got no right to ask me questions. I don't need to answer."

"You'll answer or I'll take you down to jail. Are you saying you haven't worked in the rock garden since Wednesday?" The threat of jail had again deflated Silas. "I got finished Wednesday morning. I put in fertilizer and was waiting for it to work. I figured on setting out the bulbs today."

Silas was a farmer. He had sharp eyes and the perspicacity of country people. If he had prepared the crocus bed on Wednesday, he certainly would have observed signs of previous digging and quite probably would have encountered something buried in the softened ground. He denied noticing anything unusual. The second alternative was equally black. If Silas had not prepared the crocus bed, then he was lying, cither to protect himself or someone else. The destruction of the evidence needed to verify our story—the filled-in hole, the smeared marks, the changed locks—had required time, energy and particular knowledge. Silas had these things.

I studied his face, mute, stubborn and unreadable. Again I attempted to place him as the marauder of the night before; except for the detail of Reuben, he slipped perfectly into the part. My thinking traversed a worn, monotonous trail. Reuben would not have barked at his master; Silas would not have kicked into insensibility his own dog. Yet he must be involved. In what way? Flow?

In my effort to implicate Silas I viewed the affair from a different angle. I had assumed that the person who had dug the hole also filled it in. It occurred to me that there might be two separate individuals—one person who had prowled the night-black grounds, and a second person who had later concealed all traces of the first. Silas could be the second person. I believed he was.

Harkway had heard about the dog. At this point I am positive his thinking was similar to mine. He looked thoughtfully down the garden slope.

"Why were you hiding in the snowball bushes?"

"I wasn't hiding. I was working—pruning the bushes."

"You were spying on us!"

"I say I was pruning them bushes."

Harkway moved deliberately down the rocky slope. Silas gave a short alarmed cry and followed. There were no pruning shears in the place where he had crouched. There was, however, a spade. It had a bright red handle. Mrs. Coatesnash marked her tools to discourage borrowing. Harkway kicked at the spade. "Do you use this for pruning?"

Silas was a little white. "I hadn't got rightly started. I was going back to the. Lodge for my shears."

"What were you doing with the spade?"

"Loosening the dirt a little."

"Where? Show me."

The earth surrounding the snowball bushes was hard and unbroken. Silas again contradicted himself. He had only begun the spading, he said, when he noticed us. He was confused and frightened. Harkway peered at the spade. Bits of loam adhered to it.

"Where did you use this spade?"

Silas said nothing. Harkway turned and stared significantly at the garden above. "I'll tell you where. I'll do more. I'll tell you exactly how you've occupied your time this morning."

"I just got up."

"You've been up for hours," snapped the policeman, "and busy every minute. Suppose I list your various activities. It may refresh your mind. You changed a lock on the cellar door; you trampled over certain marks on the lawn; you filled in a hole that was in the crocus bed last night. You were polishing off your work at the crocus bed when you heard us coming around the house. You ran down here, concealed yourself, watched a while, and then conveniently discovered us."

Silas wet his lips. "You're crazy. I don't know what you're talking about."

He entrenched himself in obstinate denial. The strength of the stupid supported him; his own denials seemed to convince him he was the injured party. He resented our presence; he bitterly resented Harkway's manner. His alarm lessened and his indignation grew. Shown the lock on the cellar door and the key that did not fit, he glanced suspiciously at Jack and said:

"Mrs. Coatesnash didn't leave you keys. I ain't surprised your key won't work."

"It worked last night."

"Nobody gave you permission to be on the grounds last night. If I'd a heard you, you'd have got a load of buckshot for your trouble. Keep off these grounds. I mean it, you better keep off these grounds."

Harkway interrupted the tirade. "Bring me the key to the door."

"I got no key."

"Stand back then. I'm going to break it down."

Silas unloosed violent objections. "You got to have a court order. Let me read your order."

"I'll get the order later."

At once the policeman launched himself upon the door. The wood groaned beneath the onslaught; for all his slenderness Harkway was a powerful man. Silas darted forward. Jack grabbed and held him. A second time Harkway plunged against the panels. The hinges squeaked agonizingly, the lock broke, the door gave and Harkway stumbled inside.

Silas, Jack and I entered in a noisy, argumentative body. The hired man continued to threaten and object. We might as well have listened to him, and Harkway could have spared himself his high-handed and illegal effort. The cellar had undergone the same careful transformation that had occurred outside. The furnace was stone-cold and empty: there were no ashes, no clinkers, no traces of a hot quick fire. The third floor told a similar tale. The storeroom door stood invitingly open but the floor was freshly swept—innocent of footprints—and the window was closed and shuttered. The broken door knob had been repaired.

"Where's the box you saw, Lola? The box with the locks?"

"Here it is."

"Any locks there?"

"None now."

Silas shot the three of us a look of baleful triumph. "What did you find? Nothing is what you found. The bunch of you," he ended violently, "are no better than common burglars. I'm going to report that busted door. Don't think I'm not!"

If this were acting, it was most effective. A later scene, puzzling and bewildering, played in an identical key, took place at the cottage. Outraged and indignant, Silas stalked ahead of us to regain his injured dog. His wrath rekindled when he examined Reuben; he quit his job on the spot and demanded his pay in full.

"I'm through with folks like you! Folks that would mistreat a helpless little animal. You've half killed him."

"Reuben was hurt last night—kicked by someone on the Coatesnash grounds. We had nothing to do with it."

"I want my money."

Jack wrote the check. Silas pocketed it and picked up the dog. Reuben weakly licked his hand. Silas looked down. His lips twitched, and I realized that even the dour, unpleasant Scotchman could be tender.

It was too much for me. Silas loved Reuben as he loved no other living being. Why, then, should he shield the person responsible for the dog's condition? Harkway and Jack admitted an equal perplexity. The results of our night's adventure boiled down and diminished. To show for hours of hazard and grave danger we had one tiny object—a splinter of charred bone.

The men decided that the bone should be delivered to Dr. Rand for analysis, and that he should hear a full account of our evening. Typically enough, so Harkway told us, the physician's laboratory was modern and well equipped and he could provide us with as complete and accurate a report on the piece of bone as any osteologist in New Haven. I had no desire, however, to be a member of the party. I should have gone to bed. Instead, when Jack and Harkway went to Dr. Rand's offices, I requested that they drop me at the village library.

I had a plan of sorts. As I have said, Laura Twining was an omnivorous reader and I had often heard her mention the "lovely qualities" of the town librarian. She and "dear sweet" Anna McCall were friends, if you stretched the term. I had guessed in advance the pallidness of the relationship; by reason of visits to city tea rooms I had identified it. A camaraderie built on air, the sort that exists between women unattached and insecure. Bloodless, feeding itself on little gossips, trips to the movies, a rare, shared dinner. Laura Twining had lived a life so solitary that I knew no better place to go for information.

Anna McCall had the pale, bespectacled look common to librarians. Neat head bent, she was addressing notices when I stepped inside. She saw me. Her facial muscles stiffened. I walked firmly to the desk. Anna McCall informed me promptly that I hadn't lived in Crockford a sufficient time to be eligible for a card. Her tone dismissed me. She addressed another envelope.

I mapped out a quick campaign. "I don't want a card. I have a message for you."

She laid down her pen and frowned. "For me?"

"I had a letter from Laura Twining this morning and she asked me to give you her regards."

"So she wrote to you!"

The implication was unmistakable. I read both jealousy and irritation. I followed up. "Hasn't she written you?"

"Not a line." Indicating a lack of interest, the librarian poured the notices into a basket and started to carry them away.

I hurriedly intervened. "Just a minute, Miss McCall. You're a friend of Laura's, and I would like to talk to you. The letter bothered me—it sounded strange, unhappy—as though Laura were afraid of something, or terribly worried. I thought she seemed changed in February, before she started on her trip. What did you think?"

Like many lonely people, Anna prided herself upon imagined talents in reading human character. Torn two ways, she hesitated long enough to say, "Laura isn't exactly a happy person. But then, who is? I must say I've never known her to be afraid of anything, except being old and dependent. Maybe you got the wrong idea. Things look different written."

"Then she didn't seem strange to you—when she called to say good-bye?"

The other woman stiffened. "As it happens, she didn't say good-bye to me. Too busy, I suppose." Miss McCall sniffed. "If Laura needs help she knows where to write. Furthermore, she *should* write."

Rising with the notice-basket, she marched to the letter box. I pursued her. "Please, Miss McCall, this is more important than you realize. Important to Laura and to others, too. What did you mean—she *should* write? Is there a reason she should write you? A special reason?"

Anna McCall displayed a flash of involuntary aggravation. "She always wrote before. It's inconsiderate of her not to now. She walked off with a library book that's weeks overdue. I've sent her several notices. Not a word in reply."

Slight material for the imagination, this minute variation from the ordered pattern that had used to govern Laura Twining's life. Still—odd. Laura had been fussy in social duties, punctilious, yet she had neglected to bid a friend good-bye and had failed to return a borrowed book.

I said politely, "I hope it hasn't caused you trouble."

As if regretting the momentary confidence, Anna McCall withdrew into her shell. "We've had no calls for it, but any missing volume breaks up our files, and Laura knows it does."

I felt an idle curiosity. "What was the book?"

"One of the Crockford high-school annuals."

"A high-school annual!"

"Curious, isn't it?" My surprise apparently echoed a similar surprise in the other's mind. "What Laura wanted with a nine-teen-twenty high-school annual I can't imagine, but she should certainly see to getting it back."

Since I believed that never again would Laura Twining stroll through a sunny day, stop for a sundae, pause later at the library to exchange a book, I made no reply. Anna McCall studied me closely. "You said this was important, Mrs. Storm. In what way? How? Is Laura sick? Is she in serious trouble? Is that why I haven't heard?"

My fancy was running thin. "It's nothing definite. It may be just a case of writer's imagination. I thought—I think she is unhappy, disturbed. More than ordinarily."

"You aren't," Anna McCall said suddenly, and definite hostility crept into her voice, "thinking Laura is concerned with your own difficulties?"

"No, indeed!"

My haste failed to carry conviction. "May I see your letter. Mrs. Storm?"

"I didn't bring it down."

The librarian said almost angrily, "I'm sorry I ever spoke about the book. It simply slipped Laura's mind, but in a town the size of Crockford people will talk about and twist anything."

"I won't mention it."

A nod, not quite relieved, and Anna McCall was gone. Far too restless to turn the pages of a magazine, I occupied myself with the provoking problem of the missing book. A seed catalogue would have been a less unusual choice of reading matter. Except to members of a graduating class or to their families, a high-school annual is the dullest form of literature. I recalled the volume I had edited in student days. A medley of silly personal jokes and youthful prophecies, a lengthy, detailed account of dinners, picnics, dances, pages of photographs. Why had Laura Twining concerned herself with the absurd activities of the Crockford high school class of 1920?

Absently I traced the figures—1920. Women wore long tight skirts in 1920 and began to bob their hair; men predicted widespread use of the radio and tinkered with crystal sets; an Ohio Senator ran for President. 1920—sixteen crowded years ago. Suddenly like a bell, the year rang in my mind, became particular, distinct from 1919, distinct from 1921. In June of 1920, Jane Coatesnash had been graduated from the local high school. In September of 1920, she had gone off to college and to death.

CHAPTER FIFTEEN

A Lady of Mystery

The missing high-school annual revived my thirst for information. I wanted to learn more about Jane Coatesnash, a good deal more. Beyond vague gossip I had little positive knowledge of the girl, her death and disappearance. I determined to adopt Harkway's suggestion and to consult the newspaper files.

The Crockford public library was not citified enough to boast a periodical room. Outdated publications were stored in the attic. I climbed a flight of stairs to a musty, dusty space lost beneath a maze of overhanging eaves. Stack after stack of yellowing newspapers climbed to the sloping room. They gave forth an odor of dry rot and decay. A heap of magazines, fallen, spread like a pack of cards, strengthened the illusion of neglect and disuse.

In the wan illumination I saw two things. The dust on the floor was marked by footprints where someone had walked; a round smudge before one of the newspaper stacks indicated that someone had sat or knelt there a short time previously. I approached the newspapers. I simultaneously discovered that each stack contained issues of the Crockford *Blade* for a particular year, and that directly before the 1920 stack was the smudge on the floor. Wondering who else had possessed an interest strangely like my own, I briefly studied the smudge, then spread a handkerchief, dropped to my knees and pulled out a bundle of papers.

Except as to year, the issues of the Crockford *Blade* were not chronologically arranged. I desired reports for two months only. February 1920, June 1920. These eight weeks covered the disappearance and search, the sad conclusion of the mystery.

The task I set myself was dull and tedious. Beside me mounted a discard pile. I paused once to read the society notes of January 2, 1920. On January 2, fifteen years before, Jane Coatesnash had entertained at luncheon. She received her "many friends in the lovely Coatesnash drawing-room"; she presided at a table "bedecked in larkspur and delphinium"; she wore a "Paris frock, taffeta in the new apple green." With my knowledge of her death falling like a shadow across the printed page, Jane Coatesnash clothed herself in vividness and life. I saw her in the apple green; I saw the Coatesnash drawing-room in a different light; I grasped at and dimly understood an old woman's overwhelming, uncomprehending grief.

I resumed my labors. Perhaps fifteen minutes later I paused, listened. Someone had come into the attic. I was quite sure of it. Someone had quietly climbed the stairs and stood now, watching me. I turned.

Annabelle Bayne and I stared at each other from opposite corners of the dusky room. A smile curved her lips. I spoke first.

"Good heavens! How you startled me. Why didn't you speak?"

Her hand sketched an airy gesture. "I hated to interrupt. You were so intensely occupied." Her bright, quick glance included me, the papers on my lap, the papers on the floor. "What on earth are you doing?"

I didn't propose to say. Her smile deepened, and she passed the silence negligently. "Never mind, Mrs. Storm. I can guess what you're hunting and you're simply wasting time. Those months are gone."

"What months?"

"February and June of 1920. The months that carried Jane's story. They've disappeared. I know. I looked this morning."

Too taken aback to question her sudden interest in the fifteen-year-old tragedy, I heard her question mine.

"What did you expect to find in the stories? What put them in your mind?" I said nothing. She paused. "Did you decide to come here after you learned Laura Twining hadn't returned the high-school annual?"

"So you knew that, too!"

She nodded, crossed the room. Planting an elbow on the adjoining stack, she leaned there, languid and yet alert, in her way. "Are we friends or aren't we? Didn't we agree to work together, you and I? How can we, if you make a mystery out of everything?"

Incomprehensible, that woman with her calm assumption that she and I were allies. How like her to demand my confidence, when as recently as yesterday she had fobbed me off with unblushing lies! She was waiting—a reply was indicated.

I said coldly, "There's no mystery. I've heard a lot about Jane Coatesnash and I was curious."

"Which means you refuse to say why you wanted to read the papers."

"Will you say why you did?"

"I didn't want to read them," was the provoking answer. "I only wanted to see if they were here, I thought they might not be"

"Why should you think that?" I demanded irritably. "If you are sick of mysteries, so am I! How could you possibly suspect newspapers fifteen years old had disappeared?"

Annabelle shifted the elbow. "My reason wasn't logical; it was just a hunch I had. After learning yesterday about the high-school annual, I remembered the articles in the *Blade*. I thought Laura might have carried off the newspapers; so this morning I dropped by to see. I'm convinced now she took them. They're gone."

"Laura! But why?"

"She took the annual."

"Where did you find out? From Miss McCall?"

She shook her head. Again she smiled, and dropped a bombshell in my lap. "The high-school annual isn't really missing. I have it."

"You have it! Where?"

"At home."

I was amazed and silent. Also I daresay I looked skeptical. She studied my face. "You don't believe me, do you? Why don't you come to the house and see for yourself? I'll gladly show the thing."

"How does it happen to be there?"

"It's a long story. I'll explain at lunch." She glanced at her watch. "It's past twelve. Suppose you postpone your researches and lunch with me. Then we can talk."

I recalled an old saw to the effect that one should beware the Greeks bearing gifts. Annabelle Bayne was an opportunist, a born trader, a glib and talented liar. Obviously there was a joker in the invitation. In some unknown fashion, what I knew or what she suspected that I knew must be important to her. On the other hand, she knew certain things I needed to know. Facts important to me. I badly wanted an explanation of the high-school annual. Unless I went, it was evident she would not explain.

I accepted.

The Bayne home, a spacious colonial dwelling which I had viewed only from the beach, bore throughout its interior the imprint of Annabelle's personality. She lived there alone, and she had made restless and like herself a serene landmark of the past. Pine-paneled walls were hung with startling black and whites, and garish lithographs. Copies of *Spur* and *The New Yorker* spilled from a Sheraton table; a square cushion-like contraption, more comfortable to look at than to sit on, unfolded beside a Chippendale sofa; a smart portable typewriter, painted red, struck an anachronistic note on a seventeenth-century desk. Bakelite bowls of flowers, oddly shaped, mingled the deep blue of bachelor buttons with the raw disturbing orange of marigolds.

Annabelle flung off her hat, sank to the cushion-like contraption, rang for lunch. Rummaging in an open bookcase partially hidden by the cushion back, she selected a volume, tossed it to me. "Here's the annual. Are you convinced?"

"Won't you tell me where you got it?"

A stout-waisted village girl, absurd in a frilly cap and apron, entered and began to set the table. Annabelle nodded at her.

"Velva turned it up." To the girl she said, "What became of the wrappings?"

Velva produced a square of thick brown wrapping paper, creased in the shape of a book, and a length of cotton string. She gave me a dully curious look. Her mistress spoke.

"Now about your finding the book. Tell it just as you told me."

The girl assembled labored phrases. "I was dusting yesterday around ten o'clock, or maybe earlier. I took out the books. This one had been pushed behind the others, stuck against the wall. It was wrapped—I thought it was a package, a box of stockings maybe. Soon as I seen it, I gave it to you."

"You don't," said Annabelle, "dust half enough, my girl. Else you would have come upon it weeks ago."

Velva shuffled her feet. "The book wasn't hurting no one, the dust neither. They was out of sight."

Annabelle laughed. "A new definition of successful housekeeping, not a bad one either. Now run along. Tell Mary we will have sweetbreads and ham—and fresh peas, if she ordered them."

The kitchen swallowed Velva. I glanced at Annabelle. "But how came the annual to be in your bookcase?"

"'Laura Twining forgot and left it there. On top, of course, but it slipped behind. Nearly two months ago—the day she sailed. February 17th, wasn't it? That's the only time she has been here."

"She called on you?"

"Dear me, no." The brown eyes twinkled. "Laura and I are chronic enemies. She thinks I'm fast; I think she's a bore. She got out of the car with Mrs. Coatesnash for the usual polite good-byes—they were on their way to New York then."

At once the case which Jack and I had patiently evolved developed an annoying flaw. If Laura Twining had stopped at the Bayne house, she had not been murdered on the back road leading from Hilltop House to Crockford—not unless the limousine had retraced its course. There were other back roads, deserted, suited to secret purposes. But a casual farewell call hardly suggested itself as a prelude to murder. Would Mrs. Coatesnash have brought her companion here, paused to chat with a friend, if she had had murder in her mind? Annabelle stirred among her cushions. "Why are you frowning so? Have you thought of something?"

"Nothing of any consequence."

I hurriedly opened the book. Immediately, on page 33, it fell apart. From the center of the page the picture of a dark young girl gazed out with dark, young, uncomplicated eyes. Jane Coatesnash, class of '20. President of the Sorosis Club, Treasurer of the Quill Club, class historian. Her average for the four-year term was A; her ambition was social service; she was bound for Mather. Not a beautiful girl. Instead, deadly serious and a little plain.

"Oh," I said. "I imagined she would be pretty."

"Jane," said Annabelle, "was exquisite. More than pretty. Much, much more. She had the virtues that have gone out of fashion. Plus sense and spirit. Plus charm. She wasn't priggish." A caption, typical of high school wit, was printed beneath the photograph. I read it: *"This is a matter be-*

yond our ken—little Jane craves older men. " A senseless, silly, perplexing rhyme to be associated with the grave young face. I read the couplet a second time.

"What does it refer to?"

Annabelle shrugged. "Those kid things always baffle me. No doubt the lack-wit editor was lamenting the fact that Jane preferred study to callow boys." The subject was distasteful to her, and she briskly changed it. "Did you hear me say we found the annual done up in wrapping paper? This paper. It struck me as curious. Why should Laura wrap a library book?"

I felt startled. "Perhaps she intended to mail it back."

"Why mail it back? The car must have gone directly past the Square. Why didn't she plan to drop it then? Apparently she didn't. Furthermore, she must remember where she left the book; it's long overdue, and yet I haven't heard from her." Annabelle's steady gaze fastened upon me. It was my turn to shift the conversation. "Did you see Laura leave the annual?"

"Not actually. However, she was sitting in the Windsor chair beside the bookcase, and I've a hazy recollection she carried a squarish package. It lay on her lap awhile."

Lunch arrived. Perfectly cooked, perfectly served. Annabelle knew wines, herbs and sauces, as her type would, and kept her staff at its culinary best. We ate indifferently, virtually in silence, busy with our separate thoughts. At length my hostess poured coffee, handed me a Wedgwood cup. "I'm certain Laura Twining took those newspapers, stole them in honest fact. I'm equally certain she had no intention of returning the book. But there I stick. I make nothing of it."

Suddenly, like the long-sought answer to a riddle, a possible explanation occurred to me. There was a hint of the psychic in Annabelle Bayne, or perhaps she only saw my face and guessed. She straightened. Her eyes grew big and almost frightened. "Good God," she whispered, "is it possible?" She carefully laid down her spoon. "Suppose Jane were still alive. Suppose Laura Twining knew it."

This approximated my own stumbling theory. But Annabelle appeared to forget me. Her next words were uttered in the musing fashion of one who thinks aloud. "That would explain many things."

"For instance?"

"It might clear up Laura's interest in the annual, mightn't it? Also it would clarify the missing newspapers."

"Are you being entirely frank?"

The slow exasperating smile emerged. "Compared to you, I'm transparent as a pane of glass. You're a queer little person, Lola Storm. You sit at my table, stiff as a poker, wary, suspicious, expecting the worst from me. Always the worst."

I seized the opening. "You puzzle me. Miss Bayne. Enormously."

"Nonsense. I'm very simple."

"You weren't simple yesterday. Why did you say you had never met Franklyn Elliott?" Her expression did not vary, but I fancied she was embarrassed. I cast discretion to the winds. "Thursday night, about eleven o'clock, he came here. I was on the beach. I saw him."

She flushed, was confused. She recovered herself. "I won't for a minute deny you're right. But really I had to lie. Let me explain. It was the day of the inquest; Elliott didn't wish to testify; he asked me to keep quiet about his being in the village. I promised and I *do* keep my promises." She laughed ruefully. "When I can."

She annoyed me, but I almost liked her. She was one of those dangerous people who readily admit to their faults, and by doing so force you to accept them. I lighted a cigarette. "Would you mind saying what he wanted?"

"Not at all. I am probably Mrs. Coatesnash's closest friend, and she is his client. We discussed her and nothing else. It was a purely formal interview, quite short. If you had been in the room, you would have been immensely bored." She sipped stone-cold coffee. "It was my first meeting with Elliott. He's dull, but we got on fairly well. We had a common interest. I am distressed that Mrs. Coatesnash has been drawn into the Darnley case. So was he."

I stopped liking her. "Exactly. You are like everyone else in town—watching out for her and letting Jack and me watch out for ourselves."

She adopted the older-woman attitude. She sighed. "You are young, excitable and—mistaken. No one is persecuting you. Certainly I am not. You deceive yourself and refuse me when I try to help."

Her words seemed strained, pretentious, artificial. I looked her straight in the eye. "I'm not a child, Miss Bayne. You help only when it suits your own purposes. I daresay you still deny you saw the light. Just as you denied it yesterday."

"The light?"

"The light in Hilltop House last night. I can assure you there was a light."

"There was!" Her fingers—strong fingers for a woman—closed about my wrist. "Tell me how you know."

I declined to answer, and blundered seriously. As I was to discover long afterward, I told her too little or too much. I might have altered the course of our later tragedies, saved one life certainly and possibly two, had I completed the confidence or failed to make it. She shook me.

"I insist you explain about the light."

I had my small revenge "I'm awfully sorry, but I gave my information to the police. They asked me not to talk. I promised, and I keep my promises."

She dropped her hand. Her eyes were filled with unspoken questions, but she uttered no further protest. She assisted me with my wrap and accompanied me to the door. To the end she clung to the fiction that we were in friendly accord, working together toward the same objective. I didn't know what to make of Annabelle Bayne.

As I walked down the steps, I glanced back and saw her in the foyer. She picked up the telephone, rang the Tally-ho Inn and requested Franklyn Elliott. We know now the tenor of her conversation. She repeated to the New York lawyer everything which had occurred during the meeting at the library and luncheon at the house. Consequently when Franklyn Elliott was interviewed by the police later on that afternoon, the lawyer was prepared.

The luncheon, pregnant with its clouded inferences, occupied less than an hour. Through the fresh, sweet-smelling day I strolled on to Dr. Rand's offices. His home and office were combined in a large, comfortable, rambling house somewhat in need of paint. Jack, Harkway and the physician were parting on the porch as I arrived. Jack waved at me.

"Sorry to hold you up, Lola. We were longer than we expected."

"It's all right. I was sufficiently diverted."

Harkway gave me a quick look, tipped his cap, asked Dr. Rand to phone him when he finished his report, and strode off toward the station. The physician followed us down a crocus-lined sidewalk to the car.

"You folks in a hurry?"

I said we weren't.

"Can you spare me several minutes?"

We could. He took us through a waiting room, in its way as revealing of personality as Annabelle's living room had been. It had glassed-in bookcases and graceful Windsor chairs. Bound volumes of *The Stage* and copies of *Variety* were mixed with medical journals and reports, and patients could take their choice. A reproduction of Rembrandt's Consultation hung from one wall, but on the opposite wall an inscribed photograph of Lillian Russell showed a majestic bust and gleaming teeth. The actress had visited Crockford in 1901, and village gossips still reported that the physician had been her host at supper.

We entered the consultation room. Dr. Rand closed the door, sat down and looked at us. Then in a voice so impersonal I hardly recognized it, he said:

"Take chairs, you two. I think it's time we had a talk."

We sat down and waited. Swinging to his untidy desk, Dr. Rand selected a labeled envelope and shook from it a charred splinter of bone. "I perceive," he began, "that my good advice met the usual fate of good advice. I deliver a spirited lecture on the evils of curiosity and today you bring me this. Not content with ordinary prying, Mr. Storm, you indulge in housebreaking—a serious crime—run violent hazards, expose your wife to the gravest danger. You're fortunate you didn't get her killed. And for what, I ask? For this!"

There was no adequate answer to his disgust and disapproval. We made none. He replaced the bone in its envelope. He continued to glare at Jack.

"Are you without reason? Without common sense? Does your life mean nothing to you? Your wife's life? Must you satisfy your unwarranted curiosity at any cost? Haven't you learned at your age to mind your own business? I say it's time you should."

Jack valued the other man's opinion. He looked very young and taken aback as a guilty schoolboy, when he said defensively, "Probably last night's performance was foolish and dangerous. I know I wouldn't repeat it. But as things turned out, it was lucky we went up the hill."

"Lucky!" The exclamation came in quieter tones. The physician was silent a moment before he spoke again. "Hiram Darnley is dead, murdered. Someone else may also be dead. We can't bring them back to life. I grant a policeman's right to concern himself in such affairs. It's his business, just as it's mine to heal the sick, and yours to paint, and your wife's to write. It's not your business and it isn't mine, to go through the world as a Peeping Tom. You've heard of the Elwell mystery? The Hall-Mills case? Murderers, my dear young man, can go unhung and the world remain a pleasant place." He looked out his office window to the garden underneath, where early jonquils were opening to the sun. He looked back at us. "What do you two kids know about people? About human trials and tribulations? What do you know about suffering? Only the young and callous would try so hard to trap an old, half-mad woman and get her hauled up for murder."

"In other words," Jack said slowly, "you believe Mrs. Coatesnash is a murderess?"

Dr. Rand drummed thin, white fingers on his desk. "You've got detective blood. Personally, I haven't."

"That's hardly fair."

"I suppose it isn't." The physician hesitated. "I would like to find in your heart, assuming you have a heart, a little honest sympathy. I'm half inclined to bargain. If I say what I think, will you promise to go back to painting? And keep what I say in confidence? The police will find out soon enough."

Jack said gravely, "I'll do only what I am required by law to do. Unless—" he, too, hesitated "—unless I am positive that either Lola or myself is in actual danger. Of course, anything you say is between us two. Is that enough?"

After deliberation, Dr. Rand inclined his head. "Very well. Since the identification, I've believed that Mrs. Coatesnash was the moving force behind Hiram Darnley's death."

"She's three thousand miles away in Paris."

"She could leave confederates."

"And her motive?"

Dr. Rand went into a long reverie. Finally he started off on a tangent. "Bachelors," he said slowly, "often develop soft spots. Comes from no responsibilities, irregular hours and restaurant cooking. My own soft spot is families. Family life. I like seeing fathers with their sons, whooping it up at baseball games, like seeing mothers shopping with their daughters, like the vigor and noise of crowded households. Kids going off to school, rushing home to spend vacations." He paused again. "If Luella Coatesnash conspired to murder Hiram Darnley, she had the best motive a grief-crazed mother ever had. Her only child. Her daughter Jane."

I leaned forward. "Dr. Rand, has it ever occurred to you that Jane Coatesnash may be alive?"

"It never has," said the doctor brusquely, "because it isn't true. The identification was unquestionable. The girl is dead." Again I interrupted. He ignored me. A second time he said harshly, "Jane Coatesnash is dead. I know. The poor child killed herself. She killed herself for love of a worthless scoundrel. I knew she would. I couldn't stop her. She was just nineteen and the man was married."

"The man was…"

Dr. Rand took the words from Jack's mouth. "The man was Hiram Darnley."

The cheeping of robins came loudly into the quiet office, and sun splashed the faded carpet. White hair rumpled, blue eyes lacking the usual gleaming light, Dr. Rand sat and looked at us.

"Aren't you two willing to let up on the old lady? Wouldn't you say she's had her share of trouble?"

Jack stirred and sighed. "Why did Mrs. Coatesnash wait fifteen years?"

"Wait!" Dr. Rand expelled a breath. "You don't imagine she knew the situation at the time! No one knew—no one except myself. I learned only because the girl appealed to me as a physician, an old family friend. She came to this office, sat in that very chair and calmly asked for poison. She wanted a deadly poison, quick, painless, not disfiguring. Poor heartbroken youngster, she favored a pretty death." His eyes seemed to look down the corridor of the years. "We had a talk, Jane and I; she cried but I got the story out. A heartless, threadbare tale—conventional enough. Darnley was a thoroughgoing rascal, the type of man who feeds his vanity on conquest and on youth. Little Jane, just nineteen, was probably his easiest victim. I tried to talk iron into the girl, good hard sense; thought I'd succeeded, though obviously she still adored the man."

"Then you didn't tell the mother?"

"Certainly not! I didn't guess I had failed until Jane disappeared from college. I knew then. It was too late. Three weeks too late. Three weeks after coming here she killed herself."

"Then you were the only person who had an inkling of the truth?"

"Unquestionably I was. Jane was a reserved kid, no chatterbox."

"Then how," inquired Jack, "would Mrs. Coatesnash stumble on the facts after fifteen years? She trusted Hiram Darnley with the very search for Jane. Until two weeks ago he handled all her business."

Scraps of information began to fit together in my mind like pieces in a jig-saw puzzle. Laura Twining had exhibited a surprising interest in the Coatesnash girl. Suppose she had discovered not that the girl was alive, but that she was a suicide. A forgotten letter might have put her on the right track, a diary—could Jane have kept a diary?—or a phrase of idle gossip. Such an impetus might clarify her visit to the library.

I jumped into the conversation. "Perhaps Laura Twining found out and told Mrs. Coatesnash."

"Why should she?" said Jack. "She would have felt as the doctor did. That the dead past should stay dead."

Unexpectedly Dr. Rand came to my assistance. "Don't be so glib, young man. Human beings are the product of their brain cells, their hormones and their experience. They vary, they progress, they disintegrate. Experience changed Laura, or in my opinion it did. She was a good fool when first she came to Crockford, pious, eager to please, humble, meek, a collection of the drearier virtues. But she had years of a damn tough life, and worms turn; fools change their coats.

"Women in Laura's position—paid companions, living in an atmosphere of wealth without a penny to bless themselves—often go to pieces, morally, spiritually, any way you choose. They lead unnatural, servile, hemmed-in lives; they breed neuroses, envies, gnawing jealousies. For a decade Laura got kicked around, grinned and bore it. People sometimes turn the other cheek, but they seldom love the person who makes them turn it. Say Laura did learn about Jane. Would she remain a Christian? I doubt it. Would she keep her mouth shut when by breaking the news in some subtle feminine way she could do Mrs. Coatesnash a mortal injury and even the score of years?"

I saw Laura in a new and blinding light. It made me uncomfortable and—sad. Jack stared at the physician. "Sheer malice sounds rather weak. Laura needed her job. Mrs. Coatesnash would probably refuse to credit the story and Laura would be out on the street."

"Assuming Laura did find out and did tell, we can assume she had a better motive than malice. Jane Coatesnash is still a vivid conversational topic in Crockford. How's this? Laura threatened to broadcast the news unless ..." Dr. Rand shrugged. "Mrs. Coatesnash is wealthy. The companion hadn't a dime. Maybe the poor soul thought she saw a chance to secure the independent old age she often talked about. And then discovered," the doctor finished grimly, "that blackmailers sometimes have no old age to worry about." With that he stood up from his desk. "I haven't talked so much in a month. I've said things I shouldn't have said. But anyhow you've heard my facts and my opinions."

Jack rose, too. "Of course, there are a good many unanswered questions. Why, for instance, did Hiram Darnley carry that bagful of money? On what pretext did Mrs. Coatesnash lure him here? You probably know that Franklyn Elliott is in the village, has been since the day of the inquest. What's his purpose? Do you think he's implicated in his partner's murder? Could Elliott explain what happened to Laura?"

Dr. Rand would not be drawn. "I don't," he said, "propose to work out the convolutions of the mystery. I wouldn't if I could. And you'll remember, please, that you two promised to abandon any independent activities. Go home and give your brains a rest. Though," he concluded meditatively, "it might not be a bad idea to keep an eye on Silas."

CHAPTER SIXTEEN

A Telltale Piece of Glass

At three o'clock that April afternoon John Standish returned to Crockford from Osage, New York. He had seen Hiram Darnley's widow in her mountain sanitarium; he had found her a languid, willing, non-productive witness. A woman well past middle age, crippled with arthritis, Abigail Darnley had lived for so long in a world of pain that her husband's murder had little significance except as it affected her. Since the early period of an ill-starred marriage, their interests had been diverse and separate; she had concerned herself with the petty routine of the invalid and Darnley had paid the bills.

"I hadn't seen him in months, Inspector. He hated hospitals."

"Can you tell me why, on the night of March twentieth, he thought it necessary to use an alias?"

She said in querulous bitterness, "I can't imagine, unless he was planning to visit some girl. He was your careful sort." Standish was old-fashioned enough to wince. "The money your husband transported in his satchel, a hundred and eight thousand dollars, has been traced to his account. It almost wiped him out. A sizeable business transaction must have been involved to demand such an amount of cash. Wouldn't you know about his business?"

"I didn't," she said fretfully. "That was like Hiram—to keep me in the dark." Then she said in sudden alarm, "The money reverts to me, of course. When will you turn it back?"

"Very soon, madam. We would prefer, however, for you to collect the money after we arrest your husband's murderer."

This, then, was in Standish's mind as he turned into the village police station. Jack and I, weary as we were, awaited him there. We had wanted to go home to bed, but Harkway had insisted upon our presence. After Standish summarized the sparse results of his interview with Darnley's widow, we outlined the Crockford situation. We told of our expedition to Hilltop House, of the garden grave, of Laura Twining's vanished luggage. We told of the charred bone fragment, of the transformed house and grounds. Only one thing was omitted from our account, and that was the story which had been related by Dr. Rand.

But the account was telling enough. That was patent from John

Standish's shocked and sober face. For the first time Jack and I managed to shake him in his allegiance to Mrs. Coatesnash. Unwilling as he was, he could not fail to see the implications of her lengthy silence on the subject of her companion. Luella Coatesnash might be a member of an old and honorable Connecticut family, but here was proof of a continued lack of candor.

"That lawyer of hers," said Standish, "has been aiding and abetting her. He told me he went down to the *Burgoyne* to see the women off to Europe. He volunteered the statement. I didn't ask."

"He told us the same." Jack hesitated. "Did you know that Elliott was here at the Tally-ho Inn?"

"I saw him yesterday," said Standish shortly. "I wanted to find out what he was doing here, why he evaded the inquest and still saw fit to make a trip to Crockford. I didn't find out. Elliott *said* he came here to protect Mrs. Coatesnash's interests in the investigation. That's nonsense! He didn't choose to protect her interests by appearing at the inquest."

I had a vivid recollection of a hurrying figure on a moonlit beach. I said, "He called on Annabelle Bayne that very night."

"So he told me," said Standish, "though I suspect it was because he thought I'd gather the information from some other source. Elliott has a talent for anticipating questions and answering them before they're asked. So far as that goes, if he is in Crockford for the reason he says—feeble as that reason appears—it's quite plausible he'd call on Annabelle Bayne."

"Surely," I said, confused, "Elliott must have been—well—embarrassed when you asked him why he avoided the inquest." "Lawyers," said Standish, "aren't easily embarrassed. Elliott merely said he didn't consider his presence necessary at an informal hearing. Said Miss Willetts could tell us as much about the case as he could, so he delegated the job to her. Well, maybe. But it does seem queer that directly afterward he should climb in his car, drive to Crockford and settle down for a lengthy visit."

"Maybe," Jack suggested, "Elliott feels Mrs. Coatesnash needs 'protection' of a different kind than that furnished at inquests." Standish did not reply. He swung to his feet. "I propose we have a talk with Franklyn Elliott. The situation has changed since yesterday. I hope we can persuade him to be more communicative by using Laura Twining as a lever."

Together with the two policemen, Jack and I drove to the Tally-ho Inn. Bill Tevis grinned at us from the desk. Standish talked to the clerk a moment and I gathered that the lawyer was in his room. "He's almost always in," Bill said cheerfully. "Only goes out for meals. No, he's had no callers. Too busy, I suppose. He keeps the wires to his New York office busy."

Bill then telephoned our names from the lobby, and Elliott requested that we come up at once. The fat man met us in the upper hall. He was in his shirtsleeves, and was casually pulling on a velvet house coat. He welcomed Standish and Harkway cordially enough, though he did cast an odd glance at Jack and me.

"This is quite a convention," was the way he put it. "But I daresay in small towns you run your investigations differently. Come in. Sit down. Make yourselves comfortable."

I found myself watching him in a kind of angry wonder. What right had he, if half the suspicions I harbored were correct, to be looking and acting so calmly, to be suggesting with every faintly patronizing gesture that we were presuming on his time?

He ushered us into a room which indicated an indefinite stay. A portable typewriter had been set up, and various personal possessions were scattered about. On the dresser I saw and immediately recognized a photograph of Annabelle Bayne. I chalked up another lie to her score. Not four hours earlier she had told me Elliott was a stranger to her on the night he called at her home. The lawyer intercepted my gaze and I know for a minute I annoyed him. I know, for he managed to pass by the dresser, and knock the photograph face down. But he wasn't really disturbed.

And it was he who opened the interview. "Well, Mr. Standish, what can I do for you? Have you any fresh information on my partner's murder?"

Standish brushed that aside. "Mr. Elliott," he began, "you and I have talked before. Relative to your presence in Crockford, what you're doing here, what your real purpose is."

"And during our previous conversations," Elliott broke in less affably, "I've explained repeatedly that I came up here, at some personal sacrifice, to watch out for Luella Coatesnash's interests. Ordinarily I wouldn't touch a criminal case, but this situation, as you fully comprehend, is different. My own partner was murdered. For a reason which I fail to fathom my partner was responsible for leaving suspicion on an old and valued client. Under those circumstances I felt morally obligated to drop my other business, come to Crockford and see that Mrs. Coatesnash received justice."

"No lawyer is morally obligated to stand between a client and the police!"

"I don't like your tone." Elliott stood up. "I'm Mrs. Coatesnash's lawyer, and that's all I am. Certainly I'm not standing between her and the police. On the contrary! I'm more than ready to answer any civil questions."

"You're convinced in your own mind Luella Coatesnash was not responsible for Hiram Darnley's murder?"

"Utterly convinced!"

The fat man sat down again upon the bed. A slanting bar of sunshine illumined his placid face. His expression didn't vary when Standish said, "When did you last see Laura Twining?"

Elliott knit his brows. "It must have been the day the *Burgoyne* sailed. Offhand, I can't recall the date. But I recall the occasion vividly."

"Then—" said Standish, and a note of urgency crept into his voice, "you saw her off with Mrs. Coatesnash."

"No," said Elliott smoothly, "I didn't see her off. Miss Twining didn't sail." For a moment I couldn't believe my ears and then Elliott repeated in a meditative tone, "Miss Twining didn't sail." There was a moment of utter consternation. The big scene had gone awry. Jack and I looked blankly at each other. Beside us Harkway emitted a noiseless whistle. Then Standish strode into the center of the room.

"Why wasn't I told before? You deliberately gave me the impression both women were aboard the *Burgoyne.*"

"I did nothing of the kind," said Elliott, and sounded merely peevish. "I never mentioned Laura Twining, nor did you. If you got the wrong impression, it's not my fault. How could I guess you'd be interested in Laura Twining's plans? You could easily have learned she didn't sail by consulting the *Burgoyne* passenger list, by asking me at any time, by cabling Mrs. Coatesnash."

"When Mrs. Coatesnash left here," said Standish angrily, "it was generally understood Laura Twining was accompanying her to Europe. So generally understood that everyone in town believes they are both abroad. Why, within twelve hours of leaving Crockford, were Mrs. Coatesnash's plans completely changed? Why, in the weeks since then, should you, and only you, have known the plan was changed? Will you explain the secrecy?"

"There was no secrecy," said Elliott impatiently. "If Mrs. Coatesnash didn't shout the news in letters home, she was merely trying to protect her companion from ugly gossip. I regret to say the Twining woman was a thief."

"Laura Twining a thief! I don't believe it."

"You may be right at that." The plump shoulders shrugged. "Mrs. Coatesnash thought so, but I wasn't entirely convinced myself. The evidence seemed rather slight. Would you like to hear the story?"

"I would!" said Standish.

"Very well, then. Mrs. Coatesnash and the Twining woman arrived in New York some hours before sailing time and took a room at the Wickmore Hotel. Mrs. Coatesnash was tired from the drive down, and went to bed. She sent the companion out with a fifty-dollar bill to do some last-minute shopping. The bill disappeared; lost Miss Twining said, stolen Mrs. Coatesnash said. She marched her companion down to my office, and a most unpleasant scene occurred." Elliott sighed reminiscently. "Two screaming women with me between them—you can visualize it! I declined to arbitrate. They fought it out between themselves. The upshot was that the companion lost her job and Mrs. Coatesnash, mad as a hatter, sailed alone."

It was pure invention, and we knew it was. But there wasn't a scrap of evidence to disprove it, a fact of which Elliott was fully cognizant. He sat comfortably on his bed, and inwardly I felt he was equally serene.

"Where is Miss Twining now?"

"I haven't the faintest idea." The fat man made a vague, inclusive gesture. "There was a sister in the South, in North Carolina or Georgia, one of the Cracker States. She may have gone south or she may have taken another job in the city. She was far too hysterical to discuss her plans."

Elliott's plump ringed hand—he wore an unflawed solitaire—reached for a humidor which held cigars. "May I ask why you're interested in Laura Twining? Surely you aren't working on the premise she's concerned in my partner's death? I think it most unlikely."

"Miss Twining," Standish said, "has been murdered." There was a crash as the humidor struck the floor. The lid came off and cigars spilled to the carpet. Franklyn Elliott was white as chalk.

"You seem startled, Mr. Elliott."

"Good God, who wouldn't be!"

"Won't you agree," said Standish in velvet tones, "it would have been wiser for Mrs. Coatesnash to tell us frankly that her companion was not in Paris?"

"Naturally, I agree." The lawyer's color came slowly back. He took out a handkerchief and mopped his forehead. "Your news bowled me over. I didn't-I don't know what to think.

Where did the murder occur? Where did you find the body? When?"

"Please hold in mind," said Standish, "that we came to question, not enlighten you. Have you anything to add to your story about Laura Twining? Would you like to change it?"

"No," said Elliott. "No. The story stands." A peculiar quality instilled his tone. "I will say this. If you would withdraw, let affairs take their course, your mystery might solve itself."

He was quite himself again. A moment later he had the effrontery to glance at his watch and ask us to excuse him. I was furious. Maybe I wouldn't make a good policeman, but I would have liked a chance at questioning Franklyn Elliott.

The four of us left the Tally-ho Inn and drove dismally to the cottage. It was late afternoon, that twilight hour when human energies sink low. I was depressed and I know the two policemen were. We dropped into steamer chairs on the lawn. It was chilly, but neither Jack nor I had sufficient spirit to invite our guests into the house and start a fire.

"Listening to a liar," said Standish, with a sigh, "is weary work. If there's anything in this life which I detest it's a polished liar."

"Personally," said Harkway, "if we're discussing liars, I'd rather tackle an educated man than an ignorant clod. You're more likely to catch the educated man in contradictions. He talks too much. But the clod recognizes his own deficiencies and won't talk at all." He glanced instinctively in the direction of the Lodge. "Are you going to call on Silas, John?"

"I thought so." Standish rose. I believe he wanted to be alone, but on the pretext that Silas had neglected to return our keys I managed to accompany him up the hill. Silas apparently had spent the day beside the shattered cellar door. At any rate, we found him there, seated on a kitchen chair, a pitchfork across his knees. Without a word or sign of recognition, he handed me the keys to the cottage. To Standish, he said:

"I've been expecting you. I've got a complaint to make. Look at that door! Your friend Harkway kicked it in this morning, and he didn't have no warrant. I want him thrown off the force. Mrs. Storm here and her husband broke in the house last night.

I want them arrested."

Standish sidestepped the issue neatly. He said soothing, empty phrases, granted that the expedition had been illegal, promised damages and redress. He congratulated the hired man upon his devotion to his employer's interests.

Silas relaxed a little. "Then I'll buy another door tomorrow and charge it to the county."

"The county will be glad to pay."

Standish peered at the hired man. Quick to read the signs of human distress, he observed what Jack and I had observed a few days earlier. For all his bluster, Silas was distrait, worried, not himself. Obviously he was suffering some inner strain.

Standish had been acquainted with Silas since Silas's boyhood. He understood the slow, suspicious workings of the Scotchman's mind, his deathly fear of law, his determination at any cost to save himself. Convinced that the other was a moving spirit in our mystery, he adopted his own methods of establishing it. He did not storm or threaten, or, as Harkway had done, accuse Silas of destroying evidence. He set himself to woo the hired man's confidence. He piped a soft and gentle tune. In vain.

Categorically and in particular Silas denied knowledge of Laura Twining and her movements. He professed astonishment that she was not in Paris. No, he hadn't seen or heard from her. Standish was prepared for denials. But he had anticipated a tightening of tension, a show of fear, alarm. He drew a blank. A puzzling blank. Oddly, the mention of Laura Twining appeared to bring Silas an obscure relief.

"She was one of your talkers, Chief, but I never bothered to listen much. A nice lady—if Mrs. Coatesnash fired her it's news to me. They was thick as thieves the day I drove them to New York."

"What time did you leave them there? What time did you get back to Crockford? On February seventeenth?"

Silas scratched his head. "Gosh, lemme see. Traffic was pretty bad that day. I took 'em to a hotel, helped 'em settle, then turned around and started back. It's a good four-hour drive; we left here at noon. I must have got back by nine or tea o'clock."

Could Silas sit so quietly if he had blood on his hands? Would his faded eyes be tranquil if he knew Laura Twining were dead? Murdered? I looked through the broken door at the furnace, cleanly swept, cold and secret.

"Now, Silas, I want you to listen carefully. I'm told the two women quarreled after you left them. Over a fifty-dollar bill. My information is that Mrs. Coatesnash accused her companion of theft."

"Sounds funny to me. I'da said Miss Twining wouldn't steal a pin. Did you ask her about it? What does she say?"

"Laura Twining has disappeared. Vanished. Dropped from the earth." Standish's voice was purposely loud. "I'm beginning to believe she's gone for good and all."

Normal curiosity was to be expected. The hired man exhibited none. He idly dug his pitchfork in the earth. "Likely she'll turn up. A passel of her stuff is still in the house. I wouldn't worry about Miss Twining."

Standish, I knew, had hoped for a startling reaction. He looked bitterly disappointed. His lips tightened.

"So Laura Twining left things in the house? What kind of things? Baggage?"

"No, sir. She needed her bags for the trip. She packed a cardboard box with stuff that wouldn't go in. Books mostly, I guess, and magazines. She saves old magazines. Just trash, but it meant something to her. I'd swear she'd come back for it."

If Silas knew of the vanishing traveling bags, the unused passport and letter of credit, he hid his knowledge well. Standish scuffed at a heap of gravel.

"Then Laura Twining hasn't been on the place since you took her down to New York?"

"Ain't seen hide nor hair of her. She couldn't have got in if she had come. She ain't got keys; I ain't myself. Mrs. Coatesnash carried 'em with her. She always does."

Standish abandoned the unfruitful topic. He settled himself upon the doorstep. He tried another tack.

"Silas, are you acquainted with Franklyn Elliott?"

It was a random shot, but surprisingly it told. Silas woke abruptly from his lethargy. He suppressed a start. His Adam's apple fluttered in his throat.

"You mean Mrs. Coatesnash's lawyer?"

"Exactly. Do you know him?"

"Never laid eyes on him."

"Sure of that?"

"Sure I'm sure. What's Franklyn Elliott got to do with me?"

"You seemed—well—taken aback when I mentioned him."

"I been reading about him in the papers. That's all. Elliott's nothing to me. I'm nothing to him."

"Take care, Silas. Has he ever written you? Have you ever written him?"

"No." The hired man developed an irritatingly irrelevant grievance. "I ain't rich enough for New York lawyers. Folks with money can run to the law; it's no help to them without. I get into trouble. What happens? I stay in trouble. Franklyn Elliott don't pester his head with the likes of me."

The new vein had played out. Silas had said his say and we were left to face hazy, ambiguous speculations. Why had the mention of Franklyn Elliott disturbed the hired man, when the more sinister mention of Laura Twining had not? Was there a hidden link between Silas and the lawyer?

Standish shifted his bulk on the step. "Silas, it pays to tell the truth. The whole truth. Nothing is to be gained protecting others. Not in a murder case."

Silas was frightened. There was no question of it. A look of pressing worry came on his face, a look of terror, of stubborn desperation. The bones in his thin face seemed sharpened, the hollows beneath his eyes became pronounced.

"I've told the truth," he said a little wildly. "Go ahead and take me off to jail if you don't believe it. I'd be as well off in jail as I am now. Maybe I could get some sleep at nights and…" he broke off suddenly, and made an attempt to pull himself together. He went on in a different tone, "You've got nothing on me. Nothing you can prove."

"This is your chance," said Standish sternly, "to tell me what I'm convinced you know. We're going to find out who murdered Hiram Darnley; we're going to find out a lot of other things. No matter who it hurts! Someone is going to hang!"

"I hope to God," said Silas Elkins, "it happens soon."

Standish turned at once on his heel and stalked past the hired man and into the Coatesnash house. Silas meekly accepted the police chiefs statement that he was acting on his own authority, and did not object. No one bade me no. I followed. Since morning Silas's attitude had undergone a striking change. He seemed eager to assist; he made suggestions; he produced Laura Twining's string-bound, cardboard suit box. The box contained two cotton housedresses, a pair of rubbers, two books on astrology, a pamphlet on spiritualism, a dozen well-thumbed popular magazines. There were no letters, nothing personal.

Aided by his volunteer assistant, the police chief searched every cranny of the basement, first and second floor. Unobtrusively I tagged along. My presence was unofficial, and I took no part in the search. Standish himself was handicapped, slowed down because he didn't know exactly what he was hunting for. He opened drawers, chests, looked into bookcases and wastebaskets, crouched on his haunches to peer under beds and bureaus. He found mouse droppings, dust. Of Laura Twining's missing traveling bags there was not the slightest sign.

Gaining Mrs. Coatesnash's third-floor bedroom, Standish flung back rusty, velvet draperies, pushed the shutters wide and let the fast-fading sunlight in. A canopied four-poster bed, with the mattress rolled and tied, bedding folded on a chair. A flowered carpet, gray with lack of sweeping, a chaise-longue, outlines blurred beneath a wrinkled sheet, a bureau top decked in tarnished bottles. Obviously the room had not been used for weeks. Or entered.

Standish attacked the bureau drawers, the dresser drawers, plowed methodically through the contents of a painted chest. He fingered yellowed linen, patchwork quilts, smelled lavender and musk. He closed the chest, crossed to close the shutters. A gleaming metal sliver buried in the carpet caught the sunshine and his eye. He stooped. His expression grew startled, incredulous. In his hand he held a broken hypodermic needle. Silas stood very still. I hardly breathed. Standish turned.

"Do you know what this is?"

"It belongs to Mrs. Coatesnash. She said it was for medicine—medicine for her heart."

"Medicine, eh?"

"Yes, sir. I saw her use it once, stick it in her arm. She got mad at me, and made me promise not to talk about it. I never did."

Like the genii in the bottle, Luella Coatesnash seemed to materialize in her dusty bedroom. Was the old lady a drug addict? Had she filled an empty life and soothed an ancient sorrow with cocaine dreams? Did the explanation for a ten years' avoidance of society, a taste for being left alone, lie in this gleaming broken needle?

Standish was an experienced policeman. He had considerable knowledge of the psychology of the warped, drug-laden brain. He knew what drugs did to people, how they bred suspicions, sharpened dislikes into hatreds, magnified the petty slight into the unbearable injury. I watched him, and from his unhappy face could almost read the workings of his mind. If Mrs. Coatesnash were indeed a drug addict, then anything was possible. But he pocketed the tell-tale metal sliver without a word.

Silas preceded us into the storeroom. He gave me a malevolent glance, but since Standish made no objection I slid inside. The police chief worked patiently through the confusion and the clutter. He poked at chair cushions, shook the couch, opened the trunks, bringing forth ballroom dresses of the fifties and feathered hats. He had expected the evidences of wrongdoing to be vague, but here was nothing at all. Nothing except an old house, overrun with the debris of penny-pinching generations, shut up while its mistress was away.

Rubbing grime from his hands, Standish groaned and stood still. "I'm done."

"There's still the attic," said Silas.

The attic was reached by a ladder at the foot of the corridor. Standish looked at the ladder, started to mount toward the trap door at the top, suddenly changed his mind. It was past seven o'clock; he had spent three exhausting hours in the house, and he was hungry. He decided to delay further investigation until he received a report from Dr. Rand. Did I fancy it? Or did Silas look disappointed? I myself had a queer desire that Standish complete the search and enter the attic, but of course could not suggest it. As later events were to prove, my desire was well founded. The decision of a hungry, discouraged man cost at least one other life.

Standish and I returned in silence to the cottage. Jack and Harkway had settled down to cocktails, and I invited both policemen to supper. As I was starting for the kitchen, Standish stepped to the telephone, requested the long-distance operator and put in a call to Paris, France. I stopped in my tracks, and I must confess my first thought was of our telephone bill. I suppose I showed my feelings, for Standish cupped his hand over the mouthpiece to say: "This one's on the town, Mrs. Storm. I thought you young folks had earned the right to listen."

In the end, however, the call was not completed. Luella Coatesnash could not be reached. She was, according to an exasperated operator, safely in the Hotel St. Clair but in bed, sleeping under the effects of sedatives prescribed by a French physician who refused to let her answer the phone. The operator relayed the information that Mrs. Coatesnash was suffering from a heavy cold.

"A heavy cold!" said Harkway with a short laugh. "Well, maybe. But my own guess is that there are nerves on more than one side of the Atlantic."

"At that," said Standish philosophically, "it will probably be as well to talk to Mrs. Coatesnash after Dr. Rand reports on the bone. Doc should complete his analysis some time this evening. Don't look so disappointed, Mrs. Storm. You can sit in on the call when it's finally made. Let's say at the station, after we finish that meal you've promised us."

"But," I said, alarmed, "now you've warned her, Mrs. Coatesnash may awake, get up, walk out of the hotel and simply vanish."

Said Standish with a somber look at me, "No. Mrs. Coatesnash won't vanish. I haven't been so stupid and prejudiced as you've imagined, young lady, though the Lord knows I've been plenty stupid. A guard is posted at the Hotel St. Clair. Mrs. Coatesnash may not realize it, but she has been under observation some days. Since the day," he finished grimly, "I discovered Franklyn Elliott was staying here in Crockford."

On this note we sat down to supper. The sun fell in the west and outside the windows darkness gathered. I drew the shades. No one had much to say. Standish, who had admired and respected Mrs. Coatesnash, continued in his melancholy mood. Even Harkway seemed subdued. After the hectic day, the inaction, the sense of waiting, was hard to bear. At length I broke the silence.

"It isn't my place to make suggestions, but anyhow I'd like to ask a question." I looked at Standish. "Don't you believe it was Silas who filled in the hole in the rock garden, and changed the lock and swept out the furnace? Don't you believe he knows exactly who was on the hill last night?"

"I'm convinced of it."

"Then why," Jack interposed, "don't you take Silas down to jail?"

Standish smiled. "On the theory, I suppose, that jail would loosen the Scotchman's tongue?" Jack nodded. I must admit the theory seemed sound to me, and Lester Harkway I believe ,, was of the same opinion. He listened in marked dissatisfaction as the senior officer developed his own idea.

"Jail," said Standish, "might make some men talk. But it would be a man of a different type from Silas. Intimidation won't work with him. You, Mrs. Storm, saw how much he talked just now. I could trump up some charge to hold him—remember, we haven't a particle of real evidence—but I won't." Standish hesitated. "If Lester feels he wants to take the responsibility for an arrest..." The sentence was ended with a shrug.

Harkway also hesitated. "You're in charge of the case," he said at last, a shade ungraciously. "The final decision is up to you.

"Then," said Standish with vigor "we'll leave the situation as it is. Why, I believe Silas almost wants to go to jail. He practically suggested it himself."

"But..."

"There's no 'but' about it," said Standish testily. "I've had enough experience to know something about human nature. I've known Silas for years, I can read him like a book. He's scared now. You saw that, Mrs. Storm. Why make him mad, why bring out that stubborn streak in him? Once behind bars—mark my words—Silas would get and nurse a persecution complex, and rot before he'd speak. But out of jail," the policeman went on soberly, "well, that hill's a pretty lonesome place to sit, with nothing to keep you company but a guilty conscience. Let Silas's own fears and nerves and worries work on him. They're working now. Bringing him closer and closer to the breaking point—to that point when he must talk. When that time comes—and if I'm any judge, it's coming soon—we'll learn from Silas's own lips who killed Hiram Darnley and why, and the why of everything that happened last night."

"But Silas himself," I said sharply, "might have killed Hiram Darnley. In that event..."

"No," said Standish slowly. "No. It wasn't Silas who shot Hiram Darnley in the back. He has an iron-clad alibi. Ordinarily I don't put too much stock in alibis, but Silas has an alibi that can't be cracked. He *was* at band practice the night that Darnley came to Crockford, Mrs. Storm. Silas was at Fred Tompkins' barn from five o'clock until after nine. Eight members of the band swear he never left the place, and eight unimpeachable witnesses are enough for me."

"Who, then," I inquired, "do you think murdered Laura Twining?"

"When you've been a policeman as long as I have, Mrs. Storm, you'll learn it isn't wise to leap in the dark. How can I say who murdered Laura Twining? How, for that matter, can I prove she's not alive? One small fragment of bone is a good long way from the body of a specific murdered woman." He smiled at my disappointed face, and then said somberly, "Not that I've any doubt what we'll prove. And I've no doubt, none at all, that Silas is a leading member of our conspiracy."

I thought for a moment his aggravating caution—that caution of the policeman who fears to tip his hand—would bring the conversation to a close. He surprised me by saying abruptly, "I'll tell you one thing I do think—one thing I believe is safe to think. Do you remember that glass I picked up on the lawn after the attack on your husband? The glass from the broken cellar window?"

"Very well indeed. I've always wondered why you took it."

"I took it to remind myself I'd found it underneath the window on the lawn. You're a smart girl, Mrs. Storm. Doesn't that tell you anything?"

"I'm afraid it doesn't."

"That glass told me," said Standish, "that the window was broken from inside the cottage. Not from outside, as you imagined. Which is an important difference."

"Important," Harkway now said quietly, "because the broken window was only a blind. The black-faced man in the closet didn't need to break a window to enter the cottage. He had keys. He was Silas Elkins."

"That annoying alibi," said Standish, "expired at nine o'clock. You didn't encounter your 'burglar' until very late that night. So, you see, it fits."

The two policemen seemed equally triumphant. Out of a welter of impalpabilities, suspicion and conjecture they had arrived at something tangible. Jack and I exchanged a glance. I almost hated to speak, but I finally said:

"The black-faced man wasn't Silas. It isn't possible."

They stared at me.

I repeated, "It simply isn't possible. It wasn't more than a couple of minutes after I saw Jack run into the woods before I was talking to Silas on the phone. Silas couldn't have got to the Lodge from the woods, in that length of time, with wings."

"Mrs. Storm," said Standish with real dismay, "can't you be mistaken in your time? You were under a strain, you…"

I shook my head. "I thought Jack was being killed, and I moved fast. I fairly shot into the house—and when I telephoned I reached Silas very quickly. The woods must be a full mile from the Lodge."

"There," said Standish, wryly, "goes an idea I've had for days! Everything seemed to fit so nicely. That, Mrs. Storm, is what happens when a cop who ought to know better decides to leap in the dark."

He pushed back his napkin and rose disgustedly from the table. After I cleared away the supper things, refusing masculine assistance, we returned to the police station, prepared to await Dr. Rand's report. But the physician had preceded us there and was seated in the ante-room. With him was a breezy individual whom he introduced as Dr. Harvey Griggstaff, a New Haven osteologist.

"In view of my report," said Dr. Rand to Standish, "I thought you would like a second opinion. Dr. Griggstaff, at my request, has made an independent analysis."

Standish didn't notice the curious tone. "Nonsense. Your opinion is good enough for me." He opened the door to his private office. We all trooped in. The police chief turned around. "Well, let's hear that report on the bone."

Dr. Rand was silent.

"Go on," said Standish irritably. "Let's have that report. I realize the fragment was comparatively small. We don't expect too much. But could you determine the sex?"

"We determined," said the doctor very slowly, "the origin of the bone." Again he hesitated. "I'm afraid this is going to be a shock. John, that bone is not of human origin. It's a fragment broken from the femur of a good-sized dog. There's no question of it."

"None at all," said Dr. Harvey Griggstaff.

There was, in the room, a breathless, unbelieving silence. The events which had taken place in the rock garden, mysterious enough before, became incomprehensible.

Why had the unknown acted with such swift and reckless violence to prevent us from digging up the body of a dead *dog?* Why had the dog's body been burned in the furnace? It made no sense at all.

Standish began to roar. "Where's Laura Twining then? What became of her? Where's the explanation for what went on last night?"

"I couldn't say," said Dr. Rand. There was a glint of satisfaction in the glance he shot at Jack and me. "Our conversation this afternoon looks like nonsense, doesn't it? Also it looks as though you youngsters might as well have stayed in bed."

The telephone on Standish's desk started ringing. It rang on and on. Several minutes passed before the police chief snatched the receiver from its hook and spoke. The state of his emotions probably made it difficult for him to understand what was being said. We heard him shout indignant questions. And then, finally, he understood.

John Standish had experienced one tremendous shock, and apparently he wasn't temperamentally equipped to experience another. He quietly hung up the receiver, and replaced the telephone on the desk.

And in the quietest voice I've ever heard he said, "That was our Paris call. Apparently I won't talk to Luella Coatesnash after all"

"You mean she's still asleep?"

"She shot and killed herself fifteen minutes ago."

Any recital of what we thought and said, the questions we asked ourselves during the ensuing hours would be futile here. No theory which we advanced to explain the happenings on the hill or to explain the Paris suicide even touched upon the truth.

I was most mistaken of all. For I believed that Jack and I were done with tragedy. I doubted that the mystery would ever be fully solved, but of one thing I felt sure. Mrs. Coatesnash was responsible for drawing us into the affair, and with her shocking death I was convinced that Jack and I were out of it. Even now, as an exercise in logic, that thinking of mine seems passable, but of course it was wrong.

That very night, and for the second time, someone surreptitiously entered the cottage.

CHAPTER SEVENTEEN

The Short, Stout Fellow

Jack and I left the police station at eleven o'clock. There was nothing we could do, and I was too tired to stay. During the ensuing hours New York police attempted without success to discover what had happened to Laura Twining. They traced her to the Hotel Wickmore—she and Mrs. Coatesnash had registered on the afternoon of February 17th—but no one in the hotel remembered the two women, or anything of their activities.

And all the shipping company knew was that Mrs. Coatesnash had come aboard alone, limped to the purser's office—a steward recalled the gold-headed cane—and canceled Laura's passage. In Paris no further information was available. The French authorities packed Mrs. Coatesnash's effects and prepared to ship the body back to Crockford.

I woke up in the morning in such a physically exhausted state that I remained in bed. I remember suggesting to Jack that I was catching cold.

"Nonsense! You always think you're catching cold when you're overtired. You'll feel better after breakfast."

After which he gallantly served me his own idea of what the invalid might like to eat. We didn't discuss the case, or even read the papers. We were, to tell the truth, surfeited with mystery. Two dangerous criminals—the actual murderer of Hiram Darnley, and the man who had hidden in our closet—were still unnamed and still at large. We might have thought of that. But we did not. That false sense of security, that belief that we had been eliminated from the baffling drama, imbued us both. Only because of a very trivial circumstance did we discover our mistake.

Two weeks previously we had ordered coal and this coal was delivered at noon. Against express and often repeated orders, Mr. Brown drove his heavy truck into the yard. I was out of bed and stirring in the kitchen, and the noise took me indignantly outside.

The culprit greeted me cheerfully. "Where do you want your coal? In the usual place?"

I nodded sourly. "How do you expect us to grow a lawn if you persist in driving your truck across the yard? You've cut the ground to ribbons."

"It slipped my mind, ma'am. I'll do better next time."

. "Let's hope so."

I gave him the cellar keys, returned to my dishwashing. Sunlight poured in and I hummed as I stacked and scraped and splashed. Over this housewifely clatter rose the sound of the falling coal. A steady clunk, clunk, clunk. Not exactly pleasant perhaps, but normal, commonplace, and satisfying.

When Mr. Brown completed his business and came for his money, he was smiling. "I should a brung my shotgun, Mrs. Storm. There's good hunting downstairs. Your place is overrun with squirrels."

"Squirrels?"

"I saw three. Those varmints can be awful pests. If I was you, I'd mend that window."

"It's been mended."

"Then it's been broke again."

"Where? Let me see."

I followed him outside. He gleefully indicated the window through which he had dumped the coal. Broken previously, it had indeed been broken once again. Coal dust blew gently through a hole which certainly had not been there yesterday. I stared in silence at Mr. Brown. I daresay my reception of his discovery pleased him. His own enthusiasm grew.

"Funny kind of a hole, ain't it? Round as a plate. Don't recollect when I've seen a window broke like that."

The window catch was unfastened, and Mr. Brown volunteered that he had found it so. There was no glass on the lawn. I didn't need John Standish to tell me that this was an outside job.

For as I stooped to peer at the hole, I reached a conclusion which the observant Mr. Brown had missed. The window was not broken; it was cut. There was no shattering. The hole was round and neat, almost tidy. Several minute scratches rayed out from it. Such scratches as might be made by a glass-cutting instrument. Or by the diamond in a ring.

Instantly I guessed what had occurred. Someone had stepped from the cindered driveway to the window, cut the pane, thrust through a hand, unlocked the window, opened it and dropped into the cellar. The picture of myself and Jack asleep upstairs with someone moving silently about the floor below turned me a little faint. Mr. Brown was now extremely curious. "Something wrong, Mrs. Storm?"

"No, nothing."

He would have stood there talking, but I hustled him into his truck and off. Then I rushed inside and burst upon Jack who was shaving. He turned irritably at my entrance.

"This is a bathroom, darling. Can't you knock? And I wish you'd stop using my razor blades to sharpen pencils."

"Someone was in the house last night! In the cellar."

At first incredulous, Jack soon sobered sufficiently to wipe the lather from his face, pull on a bathrobe and accompany me into the yard. I showed him the window. There were no footprints in the vicinity—only smears and the coal truck's heavy tread—but leading toward the road, deep in the muddy turf which bordered the drive, we discovered at least a dozen prints. Clumsy, wide and well defined.

"A man's prints," Jack said. He bent over, looked mystified. "By George, the fellow wore rubbers. What extraordinary prudence in a house-breaker!"

At the harder surface of the road the prints disappeared. We could not fix the direction from which the intruder had come, nor could we decide whether he had arrived by car or on foot.

"I think," said Jack, "he must have walked. Wouldn't a stopping car have wakened you?"

"I was tired," I admitted.

But, tired or not, I'm usually a light sleeper, and I couldn't understand my not arousing. There were other things I couldn't understand. For one, a sensible reason for the housebreaking. A stop bolt on the door which opened from the cellar into the kitchen prevented any entrance to the cottage proper. Consequently, the intruder had remained on the basement level. But what had he wanted there?

We went to the cellar Jack turned on the light. The single electric bulb glowed dimly, and I started as a squirrel scurried past in the gloom, fled up the pile of coal and vanished through the aperture in the window. Save for the broken window there was no sign of anything unusual. The cellar presented its customary aspect—dirt and dust, ruin and decay.

I looked over the debris with which Mrs. Coatesnash had filled every available inch of space—looked and was appalled. We had never been curious enough to investigate the dismal contents of the cellar and we had no inventory. We faced then an exasperating problem. How were we to decide what had been stolen in the night when we didn't know accurately what had been there? Nevertheless, on the theory that a person retains a subconscious memory of any place where he has often been, Jack insisted upon a thorough, back-breaking search.

He flatters himself on his painter's eye, and I believe he enjoyed himself. He would arbitrarily group a collection of miscellany—a sagging arm-chair, a bird cage, a box of old light bulbs—study the group, move slowly forward and repeat the process. He touched nothing. Occasionally he would squat or step back to obtain a different perspective. With less success I imitated him. At the end of an hour my cold was getting worse, my back was breaking and I was thoroughly disgusted. Every item I specifically remembered—the painted phonograph horn, the odorous roll of carpet, the lawn mower which lacked a blade—was in its accustomed place. The disorder seemed just as bad as yesterday, no worse.

I sat down on a barrel, discarded Jack's method and tried out a method of my own. I let my imagination work, and attempted to decide what any sensible person could possibly have wanted that might have been concealed amid such worthless trash. Since the larger items were accounted for, it had to be something small. My ideas were more picturesque than practical. I recalled newspaper accounts of priceless paintings hidden beneath cheap lithographs, stories of incriminating papers left carelessly in trunks. I remembered reading of a will cunningly concealed in a plastered wall. And then, as I sat there, a strong impression overcame me.

I said, "Jack, we may as well give up. We haven't been robbed. Not a single solitary thing is missing. Nothing—I'm positive—has been disturbed."

Jack straightened. He looked as bewildered as I've ever seen him look. "Darned if that isn't what I had decided myself. But it doesn't make sense. If robbery wasn't intended last night what was intended? Why was the window broken? Why are those footprints on the lawn?"

His words were lost in the sudden roar of a motorcycle. A moment later Lester Harkway's astonished face appeared at the open cellar door.

"Good lord, what's going on?"

"An inventory," Jack called. "We have either been robbed or else something queer has happened."

"Robbed?" Hark way hurriedly joined us in the cellar. I vividly recall the surprise in his face as he surveyed in turn several broken chairs, a sagging couch, a pile of rotting books. He grinned. "I shouldn't have thought this junkman's paradise would tempt anyone. What's gone? What happened anyhow?" A little wryly Jack returned the smile. "That's it—we don't know. We know that someone broke into the cellar some time last night and that's all we do know. But you might look at the window behind you."

Harkway spun on his heel. He examined the neat round hole and the merriment left his face. "A pretty fair job of illegal entry," he said at last. "Still it's funny you wouldn't waken." Suddenly he moved across the hard packed ground, mounted the short flight of stairs which led into the kitchen, tried the door at the top. It opened.

"Was this door locked last night?"

"Locked," said Jack, "and bolted from the kitchen side."

"Your intruder may not have known that."

Harkway bent to scrutinize the lock, looking for scratches, I suppose, or signs of tampering—a far from reassuring sight. Recollections of tragedies in isolated country cottages came into my mind, and, in the damp cool basement air, I shivered.

The policeman glanced doubtfully at me. "I hate to alarm you unnecessarily, but, frankly, I don't like the look of this. You are a little far from town—or neighbors." He hesitated before he added, "Our case isn't over, you know. Mrs. Coatesnash may be dead but—" and his tone was grim "—there are others who aren't."

"Those 'others'," said Jack, "have nothing to fear from Lola and me.

Why should we have anything to fear from them?"

"The murderer of Hiram Darnley, Mr. Storm, may fear you have information which—in fact—you don't possess. The black-faced man may fear the same. That's frankly a guess. I don't need to guess that someone tried to force this door which leads upstairs to the floor where you and your wife lay sleeping. The scratches are plainly visible."

I rose with decision. "That settles it. We move to the Inn this afternoon."

Harkway was obviously pleased, but I could see Jack wasn't. We went upstairs, however, and I actually started to pack. Harkway sat on the bed while Jack paced the room.

"Has it occurred to you," Jack said at length, "that by moving into town we might be playing into the murderer's hands? Doing exactly what he planned for us to do?"

"I don't get your meaning," said Harkway, puzzled.

"Why couldn't last night's affair have been planned with the deliberate intent of driving us to town? Say someone had some—some use for the cottage. Then certainly it would be to that person's advantage to force Lola and me out of it. What better way than by frightening us until we left of our own accord?"

"But what possible use," said I, bewildered, "could anyone have for the cottage? It's just a house."

"Put your imagination to work, Lola. Do a little guessing. How's this for a guess? Something is hidden in the cottage, something quite small probably, something valuable either to the murderer or his accomplices. But the murderer (we will call last night's visitor the murderer for convenience) doesn't know the exact location of the—the object."

"If there is an object," I said tartly.

"Let him finish, Mrs. Storm," said Harkway and to my dismay I saw that he was impressed.

"I'm finished. I was only suggesting that if someone had a reason for wanting to search the cottage, a thorough search would be impossible unless it were unoccupied. It would take days to give this place a complete work-over. Lola and I hardly touched the cellar."

"But that's only a notion of yours," I wailed. "A crazy notion and I'm packed to leave."

Jack ignored my outburst, and said to Harkway, "What's your advice in the matter?"

"I hardly know what to say. Certainly you've built up a pretty convincing case for sticking around to see what will happen next." The young policeman turned to me. "Maybe we'd better leave it up to the lady."

"The lady," I said, "is going to town."

Jack gave me the look reserved for those occasions when I let him down. I went on packing. Once you weaken with him you're gone, and I was determined to spare us both another night in the cottage.

"I never thought," Jack said, "you'd turn tail and run from phantoms, Lola. My guess is that last night's visitor was only Silas."

"Now you're wrong." Harkway permitted himself a short laugh. "Silas didn't stir from the Lodge last night. Blair spent the night on the hill, caught himself a fine spring cold and nothing else. Apparently he'd have done better to put in his time down here."

"Well," Jack said philosophically, "it was just an idea I had, and the best of us can't be always right."

Again a pointed glance was directed at me. My determination to quit the cottage wavered. Was Jack's interpretation of the broken window correct? By packing my bags and preparing to flee to town was I following a cunning plan laid down for me by someone unknown?

Harkway crushed out his cigarette and rose. "If you young folks are ready I'll pilot you in to town."

Jack turned. "Are you ready. Lola?"

"Not quite," I said snappishly. "What's the hurry? We've got the afternoon."

Harkway moved toward the door. "In that case I'll run along. I'll give you a ring tonight." He looked questioningly from Jack to me. "I suppose I can reach you at the Inn?"

Neither of us replied. We trailed him to the hot sunshiny lawn where he paused to examine the footprints and to cover the clearest specimen with a handkerchief, which he weighted with four small stones. "I'll send Blair around to take a plaster-of-Paris cast."

He spoke absently and without much interest. I stared at the footprints, distinct and well defined in the soft turf bordering the drive. "I should think the prints might be valuable. They are so dear."

"That's the trouble with them, Mrs. Storm. I'm afraid they're too clear." He smiled at my surprise. "Either your marauder was incredibly bold or—and this seems more likely—those footprints were meant to be seen."

As he mounted his motorcycle a familiar automobile came up the road, turned into the drive, and Annabelle Bayne got out. She was pale beneath her rouge, and seemed very much excited. She said at once. "Have you seen the papers? Did you know that Luella Coatesnash was dead?"

"We knew," I replied.

"I can hardly believe it yet." Annabelle touched a handkerchief to her eyes, but the eyes were dry. The gesture was unpleasantly theatrical. It seemed to me that Annabelle was reacting to the death of an old dear friend with histrionics instead of honest feeling. Jack glanced at me in a puzzled way. I was puzzled, too. I felt quite sure that Annabelle hadn't come to the cottage to discuss the news which had been blazoned in the morning papers. My belief was confirmed, when she turned and said to Harkway, "I see you're leaving. Please don't let me delay you."

She spoke in the cool remote way she reserved for those she considered her inferiors. Harkway was not abnormally sensitive, but he caught on. He flushed but stood his ground. "I'd like to know, Miss Bayne. Have you a theory for the suicide?" She shook her head. Again she touched the handkerchief to her eyes. "Luella never seemed to me the type of person who would kill herself."

"Then," said Harkway baldly, "you don't consider it an admission of a guilty connection with Hiram Darnley's murder?" There was a flash of hostility in Annabelle's gaze. "Certainly not! My opinion would be that the police authorities have driven an innocent and unfortunate old woman to her death."

For a moment I was afraid Harkway intended to argue the point, but he only shrugged and started a second time to leave. Jack abruptly suggested a stirrup-cup. He went into the house, and I guided my antipathetic guests into the chairs beneath the apple tree. For several minutes I carried on a single-handed conversation; then Jack came out and handed drinks around. The liquor didn't help. More awkward minutes passed. Annabelle was patiently waiting for Harkway to depart, and he exhibited no signs of haste.

Finally, suddenly, she said, "Lola, I'd like to talk to you." Jack smiled blandly. "Why not here? We like your company." Annabelle bit her lip. She stared across the sunlit open field toward the narrow band of woods. Smoke climbed from the Olmstead chimney and made a pattern against the sky.

She looked surprised. "I hadn't heard the Olmsteads had opened their place. They seldom come so early."

"I saw Olmstead downtown this morning," Harkway said. "Buying paint."

I wasn't especially interested. I didn't dream that a New Haven architect whom I had never seen would play his own small part in our drama. I said, "Well, anyhow, it's nice having neighbors for a change."

"Curious, your saying that." Annabelle straightened in her chair. "I've been wondering. Don't you ever get—well—lonely. At nights? I should think you might."

Lonely was a mild word to describe my emotions about the cottage, but I made some vague reply.

Annabelle plucked a blade of grass and twisted it around her finger. "I thought you two might like to move in a while with me. Until—things get straightened out. I've loads of room. You could have a suite on the second floor."

Harkway set down his glass so suddenly that it overturned. Jack drew an astonished breath. As for me, I didn't know what to think. Although Annabelle treated the matter lightly, her burst of hospitality was not only unexpected; it was incredible. Our previous relations had certainly not been friendly, and now she proposed to open her house to us—to hand us a second-floor suite.

She paused. "Have I spoken out of turn—or what? Don't you want to come?"

"Your—your invitation is something of a coincidence. As it happens we were thinking of moving in to the Inn."

"Splendid. Then you'll come to me instead."

Jack looked at me. I looked back at him. I said, "It was kind of you to ask, but we can't possibly barge in on you. Anyhow, we aren't going to town. We're staying here."

"I'm sorry." Her bright eyes traveled restlessly about the silent group. "What *is* wrong? Did I crash in on an important conference? Has something happened which wasn't printed in the papers?"

"Why should you think that?"

She laughed. "So what am I supposed to think? With the air of mystery so thick you could cut it with a knife! Also, I use my eyes." She gestured toward the spot where Harkway's handkerchief lay pinned, a white square on the grass. "That helped. It's covering a footprint, isn't it? Can't I hear what it's all about?"

Jack flipped away his cigarette. "I suppose there's no harm telling. Someone broke into the house last night."

"Oh!" She sat very still. Then, "That proves it," she said passionately. "You should come into town! Please, please let me put you up."

"Sorry. We've decided to stick it out."

"You have courage," she said in a tone which implied we had more courage than sense, and on this note she departed.

A little later Harkway followed. After Annabelle's visit he changed front completely, and vigorously applauded our decision to stay.

"Your hunch was o.k., Storm. I believe a definite attempt is being made to get you out of your home. That woman's invitation was a shade too pat. By refusing to budge, you may do a lot for our case."

This was logical, if not precisely comforting. Nor was I particularly cheered when he handed Jack his own gun and insisted that it be kept on the premises.

I gloomily unpacked.

We discussed our burglar; we debated what the burglar might have wanted; we discussed Mrs. Coatesnash. Everything in the cottage belonged to the Coatesnash estate, a fact which made the situation extremely baffling. Luella Coatesnash hardly seemed the type who would leave anything of value on rented premises. Nevertheless, there appeared to be in the cottage something of interest to persons unknown. Since nothing had been taken from the cellar—we were sure now on that point—the something must still be there. Jack suggested it might be a clue to the murder.

I agreed. "A clue," I said, "might be contained in written matter. Many clues are. There are tons of letters upstairs. In the attic."

We went to the attic. It repeated the confusion downstairs. With a difference. Furniture and household debris were stored in the cellar. Boxes and trunks filled the attic. They overflowed with old clothing, books, old magazines and old correspondence.

Jack plunged into a wooden box. I selected an elegant cardboard carton which once had housed a Paris hat. I sorted out two old bathing caps, a dozen dance programs and several strings of beads. I attacked a pile of letters tied in faded ribbons. They bore ancient postmarks; they were addressed to Jane Coatesnash; they were schoolgirl efforts of the most banal kind. In 1919 Jane sailed and swam; she went shopping in New York; and though in 1920 she had met a mysterious and tragic death, I discovered nothing of interest in these letters from her friends.

I turned to Jack. "I'm simply wasting time."

"Same here. I've drawn plumbing bills and advertising circulars. Luella hung on to everything."

"Let's quit."

"Let's don't. You can't tell what might turn up."

In silence and in dust and in futile labor the afternoon faded into evening. My head began to ache. Jack looked wearily around.

"Buck up, pal. We should finish the boxes anyway."

"I think my cold is getting worse."

"Maybe you'd better go and rest."

I stubbornly stuck to the job. It was six exactly when the phone rang downstairs. Jack rushed to answer, and I gratefully abandoned work to follow. I flung myself on the couch.

"Who was it?"

"Olmstead down the road. He wants to talk to us."

"What about?"

"He didn't say. Why don't you stay here? I'll be back in a minute. Probably it's nothing important."

A moment before I would have sworn that an earthquake could not have budged me from the couch. Now I rose promptly. I didn't choose to be left alone.

From the Olmstead chimney the ascending smoke lost itself in a twilight sky. A raw wind blew from the Sound. Shrubbery surrounding the small brown house bent before it. Olmstead met us on the porch. He was a middle-aged, colorless man with mild sad eyes. He shook hands.

"I came over from New Haven yesterday," he told us, "and I've been meaning to call you since morning. Won't you come in?"

He led us into a house in the upheaval of being settled for summer habitation. He then remarked hopefully that neighbors should be better acquainted, and, without further preamble, attempted to draw us into a discussion of Hiram Darnley's murder. "Fanny—my wife—and I have been following the case in the papers, and being neighbors and all..."

Jack and I refused to be drawn.

Mr. Olmstead looked hurt. "I hope you don't think I'm curious. There was plenty of talk in the village, but I say what's the point of listening to the butcher? You have to get to the people on the inside. And it does seem the people on the inside aren't very talkative. I dropped in on Standish yesterday; I helped to appoint him, but he practically threw me out of his office. Even Silas. Silas has been our caretaker for years. He was here this afternoon helping me put up my screens. Mum as a clam, and he used to talk a blue streak. When I said something about Mrs. Coatesnash's suicide, he nearly snapped my head off. Flung down the screens and went off in a huff. That's the way it's gone. I live in Crockford five months a year, but for all I know about the Rumble-Seat Murder I might as well be living in Alaska."

His curiosity was so evident and innocent that Jack had to smile. "I'm sorry to disappoint you but…"

"It's Fanny," said Olmstead, with a sigh. "She entertains her bridge club Wednesday and…well, you're married yourself." We turned to escape. Olmstead rose hurriedly in alarm. "Wait a minute. Fanny says I'm long-winded and I guess I am. Any-how what I wanted to ask was this. Did you folks have any trouble last night?"

We stared at him. "Why," said Jack, "do you ask?"

"Because I saw someone sneaking around your place."

Jack sat down again. "Tell me about it."

"I'd better start at the beginning. It makes a funny story. Well then, last night I was sitting out on my porch. It was late—around midnight. A car drove up and parked on the other side of the road across from the porch. A man was in it—I could see the tip of his cigar. It was dark; he couldn't see me. He just sat there, and every now and again he would pop out his head and look up the road. I began to wonder what he was looking at."

I was on edge with impatience. Olmstead's unhurried voice continued. "I stepped off the porch, quietly, so as not to attract his attention. I looked up the road. There wasn't a darn thing to look at but your house. All your lights were burning. While I watched and while he watched, your lights went out. The man across the road took out his watch and looked at it. I looked at my watch. It was twenty minutes to twelve. By this time I was pretty interested. At ten minutes past twelve—we both looked to our watches again—the man climbed out of his car. He started in the road. I followed." Olmstead sighed. "And then the accident happened."

"What accident?"

"Up to then he hadn't seen me. But I stepped on a stone. It made a noise. He heard me. He had a flashlight; he turned around and flashed the light on me. There was nothing for me to do but walk on past. He stood still in the road till I went by."

"You didn't speak?"

"Not a word. I think I made him sore. He acted sore."

"What became of him?"

"I had to walk on. I walked about a hundred yards past your place, then turned around and came back. He was gone. There wasn't a sign of him. But I was suspicious. I sat down on your stone fence and waited. It was cold. I waited a long time. I got up to go. It was lucky I didn't. Because just then this fellow stepped out of your yard. He saw me again. He was mad as hell.

He gave me a look, then hurried down the yard, jumped in his car and drove off."

"Of course you didn't know the man?"

"I can't remember his name offhand, but I could find it for you. His picture has been in the papers. He's mixed up in the case. He's that short, stout fellow, that New York lawyer."

Jack's eyes and mine met in a long, steady look. Our midnight visitor had been Franklyn Elliott.

CHAPTER EIGHTEEN

Dark Red Splotches

We escaped from Olmstead. We drove straight to the Tally-ho Inn and demanded Franklyn Elliott. He wasn't there; he wasn't even in the village. Bill Tevis, the clerk, told us about it.

"Elliott made up his mind at least three hours ago. Tossed some things in his bag, called for his car and lit out for New York. Business, he said. I guess it was, too. His secretary phoned."

From the Inn we drove to Standish's home. His housekeeper was serving him dinner. She answered the door and wasn't disposed to allow us to disturb his meal, but Standish heard our voices and shouted out that we were to be admitted. The housekeeper pulled a long face, sniffed and retired to the kitchen.

Standish was so excited by our news that he pushed back the dishes and failed to eat another bite. The three of us gathered at the table, and mapped out our campaign.

"Elliott," said Standish, "could explain why he robbed a poor box if he had ten minutes to think. We've got to accuse him before he learns he's suspected. And we've got to be sure he's available." With which he went to the telephone. To my surprise the long-distance operator easily located Franklyn Elliott in New York. He was calmly dining in his Fifth Avenue Club, and willingly left the table to talk. The policeman explained that he was coming to town and wished to see a copy of Mrs. Coatesnash's will. Elliott was unsuspicious. An appointment was agreed upon for two o'clock the following afternoon. No mention naturally was made of Jack or me.

"I'll be by for you," said Standish jubilantly to us; "at six in the morning. We'll take the milk train in. Elliott will talk tomorrow or I'll know the reason why. At last we've got something definite on that lawyer!"

Franklyn Elliott, as we knew quite well, faced a far more serious charge than burglary. After we departed, Standish called in Lester Harkway. It was decided that the younger officer should go immediately to the Catskills, seek out Elliott's hunting lodge and check exhaustively on the lawyer's alibi for the night of March 20th.

"It's a long time ago," said Standish, "but let's hope you can dig something up. Elliott says he went out with his guide on the twentieth. Find the guide. Talk to the natives. Make a survey of the gas stations in the vicinity and try to find out whether Elliott bought any gasoline on the twentieth. He had his car with him. He swears he spent that day and night in the Catskills, but maybe you can establish he didn't.".

"If it can be established," drawled Harkway, "I'll establish it." He pretended to be indifferent, but he was excited. "It looks like a hot trail to me."

The two men shook hands and separated. That very night Harkway started for the Catskills.

Our alarm clock went off at five a m the following morning. The sky outside our bedroom windows was a misty slate gray, sprinkled with a few pale stars. I woke with one of my heavy colds. I had sinus, and the sinus made my head ache as though someone had hammered it. My eyes ran and my nose dripped. Jack got me a slug of brandy. I swallowed it. I felt worse. He insisted I abandon the trip. I indignantly refused, started to put on my clothes and collapsed in tears. I was beaten and I knew it.

I crawled back into bed. Jack earnestly deplored my misery and did what he could to alleviate it, though I must say he kept his eye on the clock. He made me coffee which I drank and toast which I pushed aside. At six precisely a horn tooted outside and Jack gave me a hurried kiss.

. "Stay in bed, sweetheart. I'll be back at five this afternoon. Don't be so blue. The minute there's news I'll phone."

"Will you phone when you leave Elliott's office?"

"You bet I will."

He rushed outside. A car door slammed, gears made a shrieking sound and an automobile shot past my window to the road. I went back to sleep and when I opened my eyes it was noon. I felt a little better but not much. I tottered to the bathroom, where I sprayed my nose and throat. That improved my head. It was possible for my eyes to focus.

Walking gingerly like a person who walks between eggs, I went to the kitchen. I squeezed six oranges and drank the juice. I reached for a cigarette. Jack had taken the last package; the carton was empty. There is no calamity in our house which equals a total lack of cigarettes. I searched feverishly through my pocketbook and desk, through Jack's bathrobe and suits, only to discover that there wasn't a cigarette on the place. I fished a butt from an ashtray and smoked that. It was awful.

I held out for an hour before I decided to drive to the village. When I entered the bedroom to dress, I thought I observed a man standing on the opposite side of the road. I pulled down the shades. Fifteen minutes later I locked the back door and started toward the garage.

There was a man on the opposite side of the road. It was Silas.

His attitude caught my attention. He stood in the Coatesnash pasture; he leaned on the pasture gate; he stared at the cottage. He was like a statue. While I watched he moved, opened the gate and advanced to the center of the road. Again he became immobile. Then to my surprise he turned around and retraced his steps. Once more he sank his elbows on the cross-bar and started toward the garage.

It was a peculiar performance. Because I was a little frightened my voice sounded sharp. I shouted, "Silas! What are you doing? Were you coming here?"

He jumped. Immediately he saw me, he ducked through the gate and began clambering up the hill toward the Lodge. In the face of an alarm so evident, my own fright vanished. I shouted again. Slowly Silas came back, crossed the road, stood before me.

"What do you want, ma'am?"

"The point is: what did you want? Weren't you coming here? Why did you change your mind?"

He swallowed. "I was…" He broke off, peered up at me. "Is your husband at home?"

"He's in New York. He won't be here until evening. What is it? Won't I do?"

Silas shook his head. His hair hadn't been combed for days. He looked like a very sick man. I saw desperation in his face and stark misery. He scuffed the dirt in the road, kicking it back and forth, not seeing it.

The situation had the unreality of a dream. It was one of those moments when an ordinary human being becomes possessed of an intense mental lucidity and insight, a sort of sixth sense that amounts almost to clairvoyance. I understood precisely what ailed Silas. The time Standish had predicted had at last arrived; Silas had reached his breaking point. And I didn't know what to do about it.

I said, "Come in the house. You can talk to me."

He grew suspicious. "Who said anything about talking? I want to see your husband—not you."

"But Jack won't be here until evening."

"A few hours means nothing to me. I've had weeks of hell. Did you hear me? I said weeks."

His voice was hysterical and he wasn't quite sane. Whatever part he had played in our crimes I felt then that he had paid for it. I told him—and I was honest—that I was sorry. He didn't seem to hear. I couldn't reach him in any way. He had braced himself to speak to another man, and even in wretchedness he retained his contempt for the female sex. Sullenly, monotonously, he refused to talk to me. He said only one other significant thing.

"Is it true, Mrs. Storm, that someone broke in the cottage?"

"Yes, it's true."

His already pale face lost color. He was trembling. "You can put your mind at rest from now on. This thing is going to stop. And I'm going to stop it. I'll see your husband tonight. No police—do you understand? No police. I'll talk to him alone. I've done a lot of thinking and—and—he's my pick of the lot." With that Silas went away. Sick with disappointment, I crawled weakly into the car and drove downtown. At the Tally-ho Inn I stopped for cigarettes. While I waited at the cigar counter for change, Bill Tevis spied me and sang out cheerily from the desk.

"Your old friend is back in the hotel."

I frowned, walked to the desk. "What friend do you mean?"

"Elliott, of course. He blew in about noon. He's upstairs now." Bill grinned. "Shall I tell him you're calling?"

I looked at the clock. It said twenty minutes past two. I was lost in a sort of mental fog, compounded of physical illness and total bewilderment. "Elliott can't be here," I said. "He had an appointment with Standish in New York twenty minutes ago."

"Then he broke it."

"You're joking!"

"I was never more serious in my life." Bill's voice sank. "Would you like to hear the dirt? Annabelle Bayne is with him. She's been there an hour."

I hung on to the desk. Things were happening too fast for my comprehension. I saw that Bill was alarmed by my condition—his face seemed blurred and queer—but it didn't matter. I just hung there. The stairway was behind me, and it seemed eminently natural that Annabelle Bayne should appear at the head of the stairs, walk down, catch my arm and say in a shocked tone:

"Lola, you're ill."

"I felt a little faint. I'm all right now."

Bill hopped around the desk. "You'd better lie down. I'll open a room for you."

"I'm going home."

"At least let me call Jack. You aren't fit to make the drive. What's your number?"

"Jack isn't home. I can make it all right. Let me go," I said to Annabelle.

Her grip tightened on my arm. She shook me. "Jack not home! Do you mean to say you're staying at the cottage alone? Are you crazy?"

"Please, both of you, let me alone. I've got to get home. I'm expecting a phone call. It's important."

"Then," said Annabelle, "I'll go with you. We'll take my car and leave yours here. Bill, park Mrs. Storm's car at the Inn garage. Lola, give him your keys."

She swept me before her. Her assertiveness and determination and assurance overwhelmed me. I objected feebly, but not enough. Presently, in a state of dim wonderment, I found myself in her car, headed toward the cottage. She attended strictly to driving, and didn't talk, except to ask if I were quite comfortable. She had handled me like a child and I knew it.

My head felt as though it would burst. I was exasperated beyond endurance. It was imperative that I reach Jack by phone, and Annabelle's presence was the last thing I wanted. It had been made plain that she expected to spend the afternoon as my guest. I decided to get rid of her.

I said, "You've been extraordinarily kind, but you've done enough. Too much. When we get home I can manage nicely for myself."

"You cannot remain another minute in that cottage by yourself. For one thing you're ill, and for another it's dangerous. You needn't protest. I shan't budge till your husband arrives."

I knew that she wouldn't. She turned the car off the Post Road and we started on the last lap home. A number of courses occurred to me, and I selected the course which seemed to offer the least in the way of conflict. I was too physically low to engage in a prolonged dispute, and anyhow I was doubtful of success. I decided to telephone Jack from the Olmsteads'. When we neared the brown clapboard house, I asked Annabelle if she would stop.

"I'll be only a minute. I've an errand."

She nodded. "Why don't you stay in the car? I'll hop out and do your errand for you."

"I'm sorry, but you can't."

Annabelle looked a little hesitant as she pulled up beside the road. She got out and opened the door for me, and watched as I walked up the flagged path to the dwelling. April was in the air. A few yards beyond, the woods where Jack had lain bleeding and unconscious showed a tentative, exquisite green.

Henry Olmstead arrived at his door with a paint brush in hand. I cut short his welcome.

"May I use your telephone? Is it connected yet?"

"We keep it connected the year around. It's cheaper that way. Hasn't the company told you about the difference between winter and summer rates?"

He led me inside.

"Please, please where is your telephone?"

"In the hall behind you, Mrs. Storm. But first I have something to tell you. Your husband phoned you about half an hour ago."

"Phoned me? Here! Why should he phone me here?"

My tone was probably intimidating. Henry Olmstead looked abashed. "He didn't exactly phone you here. But we're on the same line and I—I happen to know your ring—four short rings, isn't it?" He glanced at me timidly. "When I heard your ring several times, I imagined you were away and I began thinking I should answer. To take a message, you see? Well, finally I answered. It was your husband. He was surprised, but glad to give me a message. Very glad. I hope I haven't offended you." Something stirred in my mind, a recollection, a memory—vaporous, unsubstantial. I stared at Olmstead. I shook my head. It hurt.

I said sharply, "So you answered a telephone call to me in this house! You could, of course, on a party line. Funny, but I've never in my life given any thought to the peculiarities of a community telephone." I leaned against the wall. My hands were ice cold. I said, "Silas Elkins is on this line, isn't he?"

Olmstead's head bobbed rapidly. "Yes, he is. You must know that, Mrs. Storm. Three of us share the one fine—you folks, Silas and—and your humble servant."

I must have presented a forbidding picture, for hurriedly and again he apologized. I scarcely heard him. I saw suddenly and clearly that Silas had been the black-faced man in our closet. I saw how he had managed.

Olmstead's telephone provided the long missing link and such a simple link, once you had it.

Silas's alibi rested upon the slender fact that when I telephoned the Lodge he had responded promptly to my appeal—and now I perceived that he need not have been at the Lodge.

As plainly as though I had been present I realized where he had been and what he had done. He had left Jack unconscious in the woods and fled toward the Olmsteads' house. He had heard the telephone ringing in the silence of the night, identified his own signal, and guessed I was calling him for aid. There must have been then an instant of panic, of indecision. Swiftly it passed. He let himself into the untenanted house—he had keys—rushed to the telephone, answered it and allowed me to assume that he was in bed at the Lodge. It was a good trick. For two solid weeks it had deceived us all, and now at long last I saw light.

I whirled on my bewildered host. "You talked to Jack. Where is he? I must reach him at once."

"But you can't, Mrs. Storm. That was his message. He was leaving New York, taking the train here. He spoke of a broken appointment. He was angry, I think."

"I understand."

What I didn't understand was what my next move was to be. I had to talk to a person in authority, a person I could trust. Jack and Standish were quite out of reach—on their way to the train or aboard it. Harkway had started toward the Catskills, and God only knew where he was. I could imagine the type of intelligence I would find in charge at the station. But I had no choice. I decided to phone the station.

I was ill, and when I rose from the chair I discovered it. The floor also seemed to rise. My head which had been heavy now seemed to float, and the rather small room seemed enormous. It was fever, I suppose.

Coincidence had ruled the day. It had trapped Silas and was to trap him again. If I had reached the telephone one minute earlier or one minute later, I would have found a free wire and the course of a hideous afternoon would have been changed. Instead I removed the receiver when I did—at a moment when the party line was busy.

Other voices sped over the wire, and I heard them. Two men—in the heat of a violent argument. What they said didn't at first make sense, nor did the voices—which I immediately identified—make sense. One speaker was Franklyn Elliott; he was in a towering rage.

He said, "You'll see me today and you'll like it. I've taken all from you that I propose to take. You play ball now or you fry. Do you get it? You fry!"

The second voice was terrified. It stammered, protested, mumbled its words. I have forgotten the words, but the voice I shall never forget. It was the voice which had decoyed Jack and me to New Haven and I recognized it at last. It was Silas Elkins' voice.

Memory, in the final analysis, is a matter for the psychologists, and I cannot attempt to explain what I believe is commonly termed a brainstorm. Silas's voice on the previous occasion—on the two previous occasions, for he had phoned twice—had been deliberately disguised. It was not disguised now. I had talked to him many times without suspecting, but now I knew. Possibly the fact of my hearing his voice over the wire was the necessary clue; or possibly the unnatural strain and excitement in his tone struck the proper chord; or perhaps it was that my mind having reached one conclusion was peculiarly receptive to another. I don't know. I do know that I identified Silas instantly as the source of our mysterious voice.

The conversation went on.

Elliott said, "You can expect me at once."

Silas quavered, "Here at the Lodge?"

Elliott said fiercely, "At the Lodge!"

Two receivers clicked. The wire was free, and the operator was plaintively asking me what number I wanted. My brain was confused. I couldn't remember why I had gone to the phone or whom I had intended to call. It was a distracted Henry Olmstead who took the receiver from me, replaced it, put his hands on my shoulders and forced me into a chair.

He would not allow me to rise and, himself, at my urgent request, telephoned the police station. He got no answer whatever. I was frantic. Olmstead, who had got increasingly out of his depth, also became frantic.

It was thus that Annabelle found us. She instantly took charge, rushed me to a couch, demanded and got brandy. But when finally we resumed our trip to the cottage—every minute passed like an hour—I had determined to take charge myself.

Once we were in the cottage, I permitted Annabelle to make me comfortable. She was a solicitous nurse; she shoved a footstool forward, adjusted a pillow beneath my head. Then she removed her hat and gloves, and settled down to stay indefinitely. As feebly as I dared, I announced that bed was the place for me. Annabelle was gratified but suspicious. She followed me into the bedroom. She watched me kick off my shoes. I peeled off my dress.

I said faintly, "My nightgown is in the closet. Would you bring it to me?"

She stepped to the closet where Silas had hidden. I arrived there simultaneously with her. I shoved her forward. I slammed the door. There was a key in the lock. I turned it f must credit her with a certain amount of sporting blood. Aside from a gasp of surprise she made no outcry, and immediately, imperatively she rapped at the locked door.

"Are you delirious?"

"I'm as sane as you are."

"Where are you going?"

"That doesn't matter. I'll be back soon. Make yourself at home. I hope you can find the light. I'm sorry I can't leave you a magazine."

The closet exploded into protest. I paid no attention. It took me only a minute to dress. It took me several minutes to locate Harkway's gun. I didn't think I would need it, but it seemed best to go prepared. I thought I could eavesdrop on the interview at the Lodge without being seen, and I sincerely hoped so.

The afternoon was very clear. The sky showed an almost painful blue. I rapidly left the cottage, crossed the road, slipped through the gate and began a hurried ascent of the pasture path. Looking up the steeply climbing hill beyond the Lodge, I could see Hilltop House, the cupola and the elaborate porte-cochere. A yellow roadster—Franklyn Elliott's car—was parked beneath the porte-cochere.

My heart sank as I realized that my speed had not been great enough. The lawyer had preceded me. I had thought I had plenty of time. And then suddenly it was borne upon me that I had no time at all. My errand was useless. The meeting was over. Even as I glimpsed it the yellow car throbbed, moved forward, gathered momentum, sped around the house and out of sight.

Why I began to run I can't say even now, but I did run. Breathless and trembling, I gained the Lodge. The door stood ajar. Reuben was inside. He barked wildly, and then was quiet. I knocked.

"Silas! Silas!"

There was no answer. Silas had to be there, I thought. Or could he have accompanied the other man in the yellow car? I had not glimpsed its passengers. The open door decided me. Silas set too high a value upon his possessions to go away and leave an unlocked door.

I knocked, and again called. Reuben emitted another whimpering moan, subsided. The whole world seemed still. The sun shone down with a brassy brilliance, and the motionless trees and shrubs seemed cut from cardboard. Like a stage set. Silence gripped the Lodge, deep and utter. Something pulled me away from the door, and something stronger drove me toward it f pushed inside.

I entered a small living room. From the adjoining kitchen where he was imprisoned, Reuben set up a renewed clamor. I looked around. The living room was in dreadful disorder. Furniture was broken and overturned.

Smashed crockery was scattered about. Dark red splotches stained the floor and walls. I saw that the splotches were blood. I saw Silas.

He lay at the far end of the devastated room, his skull crushed, his eyes wide open, and beside him were the remnants of a broken chair.

Things began getting black. I didn't faint. I staggered to the only un-injured piece of furniture on the place—Silas's bed—lay down and closed my eyes.

CHAPTER NINETEEN

The Forgotten Purse

After a long while I got up. The sun was setting and its last red rays made everything around me sharp and mercilessly clear. The upset furniture, all those signs of dreadful sanguinary battle, the dead man. My nerves screamed violent protest, and I started backing toward escape. I trod upon something soft—a bakery cookie. Half a dozen other cookies lay scattered on the floor. I noticed them with the tense consciousness that accompanies shock, and noticed also the upended table, the coffee pot, the two smashed cups. Two cups.

I said out loud, "They had been eating before they fought."

Reuben had quieted. He heard me now, scratched at the kitchen door, and whimpered like a child. Perhaps the bravest thing I ever did was to cross the room to let him out. I walked unsteadily. I stumbled against a pail of water. A scrubbing brush floated in the pail, and sunk to the bottom was a bit of stained rag. An area of the floor was freshly scrubbed, a section of the wall was smeared where a damp cloth had been drawn over it, and I knew my arrival had interrupted a hurried attempt to clean up the place.

I opened the kitchen door. Reuben shot forth, jumped wildly up and down, licked my hands and then rushed to the spot where Silas sprawled.

I looked into the kitchen. Pans of milk were setting about, and the dog had turned one over. I saw the print of a man's foot in the spilled milk, and I saw how the killer could have fled from the Lodge and reached the yellow car, without my glimpsing him as I approached. A back door led from the kitchen to a covered porch—a sort of utility room equipped with an ice box and cream separator—and beyond the porch was a back path. Someone had run along the path. Deep footprints showed in it.

I closed the kitchen door, and then remembered that I shouldn't touch anything. Reuben crouched beside Silas's body. I called to him. He lifted his head and howled. The sound rose and kept on rising. I ran outside, and Reuben followed.

I staggered down the hill to the cottage. Jack and Standish had finally returned from the city. The police chief's car was parked in the yard. I went into the house. The men had freed Annabelle from the closet. I could hear their voices in the living room. I heard her voice. She was insisting that she didn't know where I had gone. I entered the living room. They all turned around. Jack jumped to his feet.

"Lola! Where have you been?"

"At the Lodge."

"But what"…"

I said, "Silas is dead. Franklyn Elliott killed him. Beat him to death with a chair."

Annabelle stood up. "That's preposterous. It's a lie. A cruel, wicked lie."

"It's the truth. I overheard Elliott and Silas talking on the phone; Elliott was angry; he made threats; Silas was terrified. They made an appointment. I got to the Lodge too late to do Silas any good. I wasn't too late to see Elliott's car leave."

The men rushed for me. Annabelle stood quite alone. She was the color of chalk. She turned, moved swiftly toward the door, ran outside to her car. Standish caught her as she reached it, and brought her back inside. He shoved her into a chair.

"You sit there till we get this straightened out!" He turned to me. "Is that all the story?"

"No. Silas came here this morning to talk to Jack. About Darnley's murder. He was going to tell everything he knew. I believe Elliott found it out. I believe that is why he returned from New York. I believe that is why he murdered Silas."

"That's fantastic," said Annabelle, and thereafter said nothing more whatever.

Standish tried to make her talk. He failed entirely. She ignored the simplest inquiry, and behaved as though she had lost her hearing. He gave up, stepped to the telephone, called the Tally-ho Inn. Elliott wasn't there. Standish hadn't expected him to be. In rapid succession he called a series of numbers and notified every police station in the vicinity to watch out for Elliott's car. He gave them the description; he gave them the number. The telephoning occupied some minutes. In the meantime, Blair, who had been missing from the station when I sadly needed him, rushed out from the village. He took it upon himself to guard Annabelle. He kept a gun on his lap, and pulled his chair so close to hers that his breath blew down her neck.

Jack and Standish left the three of us together and went up the hill.

I lay upon the couch. Annabelle sat straight as an arrow, lighting one cigarette on the stub of another. She didn't say a word. My head ached wretchedly, and I had not eaten since morning. Time blurred, slid by. At length I glanced at Annabelle.

"You still don't want to talk."

"I can see," she said bitterly, "you do. Very well I'll give you something to think about." She paused and then made a curious remark. "Did it ever occur to you that a hundred and eight thousand dollars splits three ways?"

"Three ways?"

"One third of a hundred and eight thousand dollars is thirty-six thousand. I believe three different people expected to share in Darnley's money and conspired to murder him for it." She studied space. "Thirty-six thousand dollars looks like a colossal sum to some people."

"It would to Silas."

She nodded. "Of course."

"But Mrs. Coatesnash..."

Again she nodded, and I fancied she was dimly pleased. "The Coatesnash estate is upward of two million dollars."

I caught the drift of her oblique defense of the missing man and though I wasn't at all convinced, I kept on playing. "Franklyn Elliott..."

"...could make thirty-six thousand dollars on a single case." Unfortunately, at this point, an interruption occurred. Dr. Rand came in and said that Jack had phoned him to stop by on his way to the Lodge. He took my pulse, pursed his lips, and ordered me to bed. Annabelle lighted another cigarette. Her hands trembled. She looked ghastly. Irresolutely the physician turned to her.

"Would you like a sedative?"

"I would prefer a drink."

I said, "There's brandy in the kitchen."

She achieved instant vehemence. "No, thank you. I have imposed sufficiently upon your hospitality."

Embarrassed, Dr. Rand offered his own flask. She accepted it, and drank neat, as a man would. A little color returned to her face. Dr. Rand helped me into bed. Annabelle and the ubiquitous Blair remained in the living room. After the physician went away I heard her turning the pages of a magazine which I knew she was not reading. Perhaps fifteen minutes later Harkway entered the cottage, paused and spoke to her. She didn't answer and I summoned him into the bedroom. His face was drawn and tired, and he explained that he had driven over 200 miles since two p.m. On his return from Elliott's mountain camp, he added wearily, he had received the shocking news of our latest tragedy. He told me he had not been to the Lodge as yet, and he seemed disposed to be bitter over the whole affair.

"If I had been in complete charge of the case, Silas would have been alive. In jail—and alive."

A similar thought had occurred to me, and a shade uncomfortably I changed the subject. "Did you discover anything at Elliott's camp?"

"I talked to his guide—a dumb Canuck. Spoke French mostly and I had a hell of a time making him understand me. I finally penetrated. Elliott lied to us."

"About his alibi?"

"He has no alibi for the twentieth, Mrs. Storm. Maybe he hunted that day," said Harkway with a certain gallows humor, "but he wasn't hunting rabbits. He went out with the guide on the nineteenth, but not on the twentieth. The Canuck remembered perfectly. His sister's child was christened that day, and he knocked off work and stood up with it."

"Then Elliott could have been in Crockford at the time Darnley was shot?"

"He could have been," said Harkway, "and I believe he was."

The door into the living room was open. The rustle of the magazine ceased. There was no sound. Annabelle had heard everything we said, as I believe Harkway intended she should. He stepped into the other room and shot rapid questions at her. He met the same blank wall. Silence.

The useless interrogation continued until Jack and Standish returned from the Lodge, and then the police escorted Annabelle home. She bade me a contained goodbye, but she wasn't as composed as she seemed, for although she carefully adjusted her hat and pulled on her gloves she neglected to take her purse. I remember her as she looked that night, a taut, pale, contemptuous woman with a policeman on either side. I remember her scornful smile as she glanced from one to the other.

"My bodyguard," she said.

The door slammed. They drove off. When they reached the Bayne home I believe Annabelle roused her maid and ordered coffee. "Since it appears you gentlemen plan to stay." They stayed on and on, drank quarts of coffee, spilled ashes on her carpets and bombarded her with questions which she answered with a shake of the head.

"I am sorry. I do not know where Franklyn Elliott is, why he went or when he will return. If I did know I would not say."

They pointed out that Elliott's flight and her silence indicated his guilt. At this, Standish told us later, she whitened. "I won't be drawn into any discussion of the matter. I have nothing to tell you. Elliott will return and explain the things which I cannot explain."

Her resolution was inflexible, and in the end she wore them out. When dawn streaked the windows they permitted her to go to bed.

Contiguous with this futile questioning the relentless search for Franklyn Elliott and the yellow car moved along the Atlantic seaboard. Town by town the search advanced as the midnight hours wore away. Roads were patrolled, hotels were notified, and many a policeman missed his rest. To no purpose. Car and driver seemingly had dropped into a void.

The morning newspapers raged and raved and demanded action. The Darnley case revived with a bang. One of the more sensational papers editorially linked up the disappearance of Laura Twining with that of Franklyn Elliott and asked its readers if the two might not be in hiding together. A love nest was hinted at. Which was as far north as any of the suggestions went.

I spent the morning in bed. My cold was in the handkerchief stage. I used them by the dozens, but admitted I would survive. Jack and I read the papers and awaited news. The police were busy elsewhere.

We guessed their activities at the Lodge, and since there was a clear view up the hill from the bedroom windows we shamelessly drew back the curtains and watched. Men strode purposefully in and out the building. Various bulky objects—the distance prevented identification—were removed, and Jack hazarded that some of the damaged furniture was being conveyed to the station. Blair trotted about the pasture, rounded up Mrs. Coatesnash's three blooded cows and drove them off. An ambulance arrived, lumbered almost to the door and carried away a sheeted, silent figure. Reuben was lying on my lap. He stirred and whined, and I've always half imagined that he knew.

Toward four o'clock Harkway came down from the Lodge, caught us at the window, smiled and dropped into a chair. He said at once, "Tell me, Mrs. Storm. How long was it after you heard Silas and Elliott quarreling over the phone before you went to the Lodge?"

"About half an hour."

"No longer?"

"Hardly as long."

"You are sure they were angry?"

"Elliott was in a towering rage."

"Then," said Harkway, "I cannot understand why immediately he arrived the two men sat down together to drink coffee and eat cake. As the broken crockery indicates they did. You saw the two smashed cups on the floor, the two plates, the two overturned chairs. And they are an important part of the pattern we have built up."

"What is that pattern?"

In brief, terse sentences he sketched out the bloody crime as the police recapitulated it. Silas had been on the verge of confessing to the truth about Hiram Darnley's murder. Elliott knew it. He phoned Silas, and by appointment proceeded to the Lodge. The two men seated themselves, and the lawyer attempted to dissuade the other from his purpose. After failing by argument, he resorted to violence. Thus, if the recapitulation were correct, the interview which had ended in an appalling battle had begun on an amicable note.

I had been too shocked during those frightful minutes at the Lodge to draw logical conclusions. But now the picture struck, me wrong. In the first place, when I had heard Elliott talking on the telephone he had been in no coffee-drinking, conciliatory humor. In the second place, it seemed to me the lawyer had barely time enough to rush to the Lodge, wreck the room and kill Silas before I got there. Add the hurried attempt at order—the pail of water, the partially scrubbed floor—and he had no time left.

"Let's drop the crockery," said Jack impatiently. "Maybe Elliott did arrive in a rage. Maybe Silas prepared the food in advance and laid the table in the hope of creating a friendly atmosphere. I saw those cups last night—or the fragments of them. You couldn't tell they had both been used."

"Both had been filled," said Harkway quietly. "It seems unlikely Silas would *pour* in advance of his guest."

However, the coffee cups seemed a small mystery in the maze of mysteries, and since no one, offered any better explanation, I concluded Jack was probably right. Harkway reached restlessly for another cigarette and then said there was another facet of the case which he regarded as still more puzzling. It was the flight itself.

"An ordinary citizen—you, for instance, Storm—might kill a man and run off out of sheer funk. But Elliott isn't an ordinary citizen. He is a lawyer. If he had stuck around he could have put up a damn good defense for himself. There were no witnesses to the battle. And the scrap was not one-sided. So far as any physical evidence goes, Elliott could have claimed that Silas struck the first blow."

I said promptly, "But he had made threats. I heard him on the phone."

"A thing which Elliott couldn't know. And even though he made threats I honestly doubt he went to the Lodge with murder in his mind."

"How can you say that?"

"So clumsy a murder could not have been premeditated. Think it over, Mrs. Storm, and you will agree. A murderer goes prepared. He carries a weapon. A gun, a knife, a dirk. He doesn't count on using a kitchen chair! Silas died of a fractured skull. In addition, he had a broken collar bone, a broken wrist, three fractured ribs and nineteen separate bruises and contusions The seat of the chair was cracked, one leg was loose and a rung was out at the back. You remember the blood-splashed room and the upset furniture. It all points to fury, and again fury seldom accompanies a premeditated murder."

I envisioned a Franklyn Elliott gone berserk, swinging a bloody kitchen chair. I suppose I went a little pale. Jack noticed, but Harkway did not. He eyed the glowing tip of his cigarette. "Which brings us up to Elliott's suit."

"His suit?"

"The light-gray suit he wore yesterday."

At this moment Standish walked down the hill and into the cottage. He had missed his lunch, and gratefully accepted coffee and a heaping plate of cinnamon toast. While the newcomer munched and drank, the conversation was resumed. It appeared that when Elliott quit the Tally-ho Inn to go to the Lodge he had worn a light-gray suit. Bill Tevis remembered because he had thought the lawyer was "rushing the season."

Harkway glanced at me. "It's unpleasant to think about, but after the fight Elliott would have had to get rid of his suit. Immediately. He must have been spattered with blood from head to foot. I can understand how he might contrive a temporary escape except for that. I don't see how he could manage a change of clothes."

"A bag perhaps in his car?"

"The car was empty. The garage attendant took it around to the Inn and is certain."

"In some ways," Standish said, "strong as it is, I don't like this case. We've got almost too much on Elliott. His threats, his presence at the Lodge, that stupid flight." He added wearily, "We've got too much in one sense, and not enough in another. We haven't been able, for instance, to establish that there was friction of any sort between Elliott and Hiram Darnley, and the Lord knows we've tried! So far as we've been able to discover, Elliott had no real reason for wishing his partner dead. The fact that Mrs. Coatesnash had a motive for wanting Darnley murdered would hardly seem sufficient to weigh with Elliott. And yet it appears he beat Silas to death to prevent his uncovering the original conspiracy."

"There might be some hidden motive."

"No doubt there is." The policeman moodily sipped his coffee. "But even so the problem isn't solved. How does Laura Twining fit into the picture? What's become of her?"

"Don't you believe that Laura's dead?"

"I do indeed. I think," said Standish slowly "that the unfortunate woman was murdered. I don't know why; I don't know how. It may be barely possible that her body *was* buried in the rock garden."

"But the bone…"

"The best of specialists can make mistakes. I'm not concerned at present over a three-inch splinter of bone. I have other worries."

"Our worry at the moment," said Harkway, "is catching Franklyn Elliott. The details will have to wait."

Standish nodded. "I daresay you're right. Certainly the time for guessing has passed. We can only hope that with Elliott's arrest we can tie up the loose ends in our case."

But he sounded strangely doubtful. Jack and I were much perplexed. Neither policeman had any more to say.

Presently Standish glanced at his watch. Reuben was seldom agreeable to company, and Jack had previously bundled him off to the kitchen. I heard him scratching at the door. A plaintive signal that he was ready for supper. Jack excused himself and went to feed the dog. When he returned, the policemen were putting on their coats.

I spoke then of the dog. "Shall we keep him?"

Standish smiled. "As you choose. You needn't worry about other claimants. If the dog is a nuisance, we can drop him off at the pound." Jack and I had grown fond of Reuben, and in this informal manner gladly took possession of him. Standish glanced toward the window. It was dark now, and the Lodge was lost in shadows. He sighed. "Things up the hill are in an awful mess. You can picture it. No one in charge. Mrs. Coatesnash dead, one of her lawyers dead, the other missing. We simply boarded up the Lodge and left it. I daresay the court will name other executors soon. Mrs. Coatesnash named Darnley and Elliott."

Standish and Harkway were at the door before Jack remembered Anna-belle's purse. He ran for it. "Here's something you can drop off. It belongs to Annabelle Bayne. She forgot to take it home with her last night."

We had been curious, but we had not touched the purse. Standish opened it at once. Two five-dollar bills, a smart enamel compact, a match-ing lipstick, an initialed cigarette case in white and yellow gold, a ten-cent tintype of Annabelle and Elliott, linked arm in arm, photographed in New York. The lovely familiar arch of Washington Square showed behind them, and both were laughing. Jack and I had once had tintypes made at Washing-ton Square. On such a day. In such a mood.

Jack said rather quickly, "You will leave the purse with her." Standish thrust the purse into his pocket, abruptly changed his mind. "No. I'll leave it here. You're friendly with the woman. Or friendlier than I am. The purse will give you an excuse to call. Maybe you can get her talking. That's more than I can do!" I distrusted the experiment, and, with circumstances as they stood, had little taste for prying into Annabelle's secrets. I felt sorry for her.

Standish left the purse.

CHAPTER TWENTY

The Burglar Alarm

After supper Jack was restless as a cat. He prowled up and down the living room until I became almost as restless as he. He turned on the radio. The news broadcast reported the unceasing search for Franklyn Elliott. He had vanished twenty-four hours earlier. He had not been found. Nor had the yellow car. Jack snapped off the radio, went into the dining room and closed the door.

I heard him shifting furniture and wondered what he was doing. I went to see. What he was doing—in view of past events—seemed normal and familiar. He had rolled up the rug and was looking under it. He had taken down the pictures from the wall.

I said patiently, "I should think there had been sufficient investigation of this house. Or have you got the habit?"

"I—I had an idea, Lola."

"Would you mind explaining it?"

Jack hesitated. "I don't like to make you nervous."

"Your air of mystery is not a tonic."

"All right then. I believe Elliott wanted something that was hidden in the house when he broke in last Wednesday night. I believe he went off without it. I mean to find it."

The notion had previously flickered through my mind, and I had hurriedly banished it. It now occurred to me that if Elliott had wanted something in the cottage as recently as Wednesday he probably would still like to lay his hands on it. I had a dismaying vision of the lawyer, clad in a stained gray suit, creeping noiselessly through a dark spring night upon the cottage.

I said faintly, "You mean he might come back for it?"

"Of course not, goop! He's getting away from Crockford as fast as his plump legs—or rather his yellow car—will carry him. He's in too deep to bother us again or show his face in Crockford. However—" Jack paused on the word "—however, I agree with Standish that there are missing links in the case. Lots of them. I'm not sure Elliott's arrest will clear everything up. If I could find something in the cottage—some clue—if T could figure out why he came here three nights ago I'd feel better satisfied."

"Jack!" He turned guiltily. My suspicion was confirmed. "Do you think someone else—not Elliott—but someone else might break in? Is that why you're hunting?"

Jack's explosive denial was neither convincing nor reassuring, and I retired that night in an uneasy frame of mind. I had hoped that Elliott would be under arrest when I awoke in the morning. It was a vain hope. The newspapers reported nothing. Jack telephoned the police station before we breakfasted, but Standish apparently had removed the receiver from the hook, for a continuous busy signal was reported. There was nothing to do but wait. After breakfast Jack resumed his self-appointed researches, tapping the walls, examining the moldings and baseboards, rapping at the fireplaces, until I was distracted. The wallpaper in the cottage was casually applied. He loosened it further. He got plaster in the rugs. He made a wreck of the house. He found nothing.

By mid-afternoon I was thoroughly on edge, and Jack himself was discouraged. It was in that mood that he suggested we return Annabelle's purse. I didn't want to go there unless Standish accompanied us and Jack agreed with me.

"God knows," he said, "we've done our share of snooping. Our share and then some! I have my own opinion of Annabelle, but she's suffering. Suffering like hell. Maybe she'll talk with Standish present; maybe she won't. Anyhow it isn't up to us to trap her."

We proceeded to the police station. The anteroom buzzed with action, and for one wild moment I thought that Elliott had been captured. Loud voices came from behind the closed door of Standish's office. Many unfamiliar men—neighboring police judging from their appearance—bustled in and out. A telephone rang steadily and no one answered it. Jack tried to find out what was going on, but no one seemed to know. Eventually a small boy escorted by his mother emerged from the office. He wore a boy-scout uniform with an eagle badge and he clung tightly to his mother's hand. There was a mixture of embarrassment and pride on his face.

When we went in, Standish was alone. He explained the excitement. Elliott was still at large, but the yellow roadster had been located. It had been abandoned in a thickly wooded section some ten miles beyond Crockford.

"It was well concealed," said Standish. "Four miles off the road, driven straight across the tree stumps, and a bumpy ride it must have been. Three flat tires and a busted headlight to say nothing of ruined springs. We had a lot of luck in finding it. A boy-scout picnic. Those boy scouts have sharp eyes. I've been talking to the kid who spotted it." He smiled. "To the kid and also to his mother. She was pretty anxious I should commit the township to a medal."

"There was no sign of Elliott?"

"The car was empty."

"Could he be hiding in the woods?"

"Fifty men say he isn't. They've been hunting since nine this morning, and those woods have been covered inch by inch. No. Elliott isn't there." Standish made his fingers into a church steeple. "That roadster was conspicuous, and Elliott was smart enough to know it. My hunch is he drove immediately from the Lodge to that isolated spot, got rid of the car and then lit out on foot."

"Walking four miles at night through unfamiliar woods to the road?"

"A man can walk when he has to. But where did he walk? He didn't walk to the railroad station and buy a ticket; he didn't walk to the bus station; and he isn't the type hitchhiker a car owner would be likely to forget. His picture has been in all the papers. He was wearing a light-gray, blood-stained suit. We know that. The steering wheel of the car is bloody. And there is blood upon the seat."

"Elliott stayed in Crockford some days," Jack said at length. "Maybe he made previous arrangements in the event of an—an emergency."

"Maybe," said Standish noncommittally.

With that he rose and suggested that we descend upon Annabelle. It was a sparkling day. The Sound was a bland deceptive blue, and motes of sunshine twinkled on the water. Summer cottages were opening. We saw workmen hanging awnings and gardeners planting tulip bulbs. Forsythia bushes bravely bloomed.

We drove along the beach where Jack and I had seen Franklyn Elliott walking. The beach was deserted, but it promised life. You could picture striped umbrellas, and boys and girls in bathing suits, and children digging in the sand. Two enthusiastic youths in a motor boat to wed a life raft from the shore. They shouted advice at each other.

The Bayne garden looked cheerless and unkempt. Unraked leaves skittered in the sharp breeze, and Silas had never appeared to clip the privet hedges. A policeman lurked at the gates. He was not in uniform. He wore his hat pulled down and his coat collar up, and he was about as inconspicuous as a cigar-store Indian.

We mounted the steps of the stone house, rang the bell. The same dull-eyed Velva whom I remembered from my previous visit showed us into the spacious living room where Annabelle and I had lunched, discussed Jane Coatesnash and traded questions and evasions. It was as neglected as the gardens. Flowers wilted in the bakelite bowls; newspapers littered the Sheraton table and collapsed upon the floor; dust gathered on the trig little typewriter.

Velva said her mistress was lying down, and went off to call her. Presently Annabelle came in. She wore a rumpled negligee; she looked white and tired, and I knew from her eyes that she had been crying. She smiled wanly and then saw Standish. The smile faded.

"Oh! I see! This is an official visit."

I said quickly, "We've brought your purse. You left it at the house."

She thanked me, and drifted to a chair. No one spoke. Standish, who had expected I would lead the interview, sent me a reproachful look. The awkward silence lengthened. Annabelle opened her purse. She looked up.

"My cigarette case is not here," she said curtly.

"Your cigarette case?"

"A small gold case—initialed. I'm sure I had it in the purse. I always carry it."

I daresay I looked confused. "If it isn't there, then it must be at the house. I will send it down tomorrow."

"So you opened the purse!" She glanced scornfully around the circle of faces. "I might have known you wouldn't pass up such a chance." Her tone became brittle and defiant. "I would like the case back. It happens to mean a lot to me. Frank gave it to me."

Standish leaned forward. "We found his car this morning."

Incredibly, hope leaped into her eyes. It died as Standish told the story. She linked her hands about her knees. She said in a small, gray voice, "I had hoped you would find him, too."

"Then why don't you help us?"

"I assure you I cannot."

"You have not been in communication with him since his flight from the Lodge?"

"I haven't had a word from him since he *left* the Lodge," she replied, emphasizing the word. Her face sketched brief contempt. "As you are well aware. Every piece of mail which enters this house is examined before I see it; my telephone wire is tapped so you can keep up with what I'm ordering for lunch; and as for Frank's coming here in person—" she gestured toward the lawns "—certainly your myrmidon at the gates would seize and arrest him."

Standish persisted. "You do not know his whereabouts?"

"God knows, I wish I did."

"You insist he did not murder Elkins?"

"I do."

"Can you give us any other reason for his disappearance? Do you know of any other reason?"

"I can guess another reason." She stood up in a frenzy of nerves, despair and—I thought—incertitude. Her trailing gown swished from one end of the long room to the other. She paused at the window and faced us. One white ringless hand grasped the monkscloth draperies. "I don't know why I should defend Franklyn Elliott to you, but I will. He came here three weeks ago—not in his own interests—but in the interests of Mrs. Coatesnash, his client and my—my friend. As he saw it, she was in for some pretty important trouble. He hoped to protect her from accusations he imagined might be made—in the investigation of his partner's murder."

"Then he suspected her from the first?"

"He knew she was not guilty. It was impossible."

"Then why did Mrs. Coatesnash kill herself?"

"I couldn't say." The harassed and desperate expression deepened on her face. "I can say this. Frank had a second reason for coming to Crockford. He wanted, indeed he was determined, to discover who had murdered Hiram Darnley. The lead he was following—and I assure you he had a lead—was one which he could not divulge for reasons which I cannot go into now. He suspected Silas. And that is why he went to the Lodge. I was with him at the Tally-ho Inn earlier that very afternoon. Before I left, he told me that he was going to telephone Silas and make an appointment at the Lodge." She shot a feverish glance at me. "That is the conversation you overheard and misinterpreted so dreadfully. I do not know what happened after Frank reached the Lodge. I can guess. I believe Frank found Silas dead and, from the body, the room, or perhaps from something else, made deductions which he thought would carry him to the person who murdered Darnley and then murdered Silas to cover up the crime."

It might have been merely the defense of a loyal, frightened woman. But her air of desperate sincerity moved me. She so obviously believed in Elliott's innocence that I myself was shaken. What lead could the missing man be following which would necessitate flight, concealment of his information from police officials? Annabelle knew something more. Why wouldn't she speak it out?

Standish was provoked and skeptical. "You suggest Elliott is in pursuit of the murderer now?"

"I do."

Standish said ironically, "He has been missing forty-eight hours. How long a time would you say should elapse before he reports progress?"

She burst into tears. It was amazing coming from her. Also it was pitiful. She turned her back and fought for control. Again she faced us. "You must excuse me. I have been troubled and unstrung." Her eyes were now quite dry and remarkably steady. "Forty-eight hours isn't a test. If and when Franklyn Elliott has been missing a week—and there is still no word—I will tell you the little I know. You may then decide what to do. Now, please, will you leave?"

Under the circumstances there was nothing else to do. The interview had distressed and unsettled me. I had been much more certain in my opinions before I entered the house than when I left it. Standish, too, seemed disturbed.

"Women," he growled, "always upset a case. And a woman in love is pure poison. It's foolish to put any stock in Annabelle Bayne. After all she is engaged to marry Elliott."

"Engaged!"

"She is indeed," he said soberly. "So her defense of the man means nothing. But damned if I can understand what she's so close-mouthed about. She has a theory of her own. Why should she stipulate a week before she's ready to talk?"

He lapsed into moody silence. Then suddenly he said, "Hark-way tells me she tried to persuade you two to move out of the cottage."

"She invited us to stay a while with her."

"Jack believes," I said, "that something is hidden in the cottage. Something that Elliott wanted and couldn't find. He's been hunting for it. He hasn't found it. Maybe Annabelle knows what it is. It wouldn't hurt to ask her."

"It wouldn't help. She refuses to admit that Elliott broke into the place." Again the police chief was silent. He roused from his thoughts. "It occurs to me that you might like someone out there at night. My force is pretty small, but Harkway could probably shift his things from his boarding house. He mentioned it this morning."

"Thanks, but it isn't necessary," said Jack, before I could leap at the offer. He grinned. "Personally I anticipate no trouble, but if there's trouble I'll be prepared to take care of it."

I sent him a questioning glance. Standish looked curious, but Jack volunteered no information. Shortly afterward we separated. Standish went back to the station, and we started home. Jack stopped the car at the village electrical shop.

I watched him through the plate-glass windows. He talked earnestly to the town's electrician. Shortly he returned to the car with a large, bulky bundle which he conspicuously failed to explain. We arrived at the cottage and I started sorting the groceries. I kept my eye on Jack. He hunted up a hammer and a box of staples, took the package and retired to the bedroom. I heard pounding.

When my curiosity became unbearable some five minutes later, I casually entered the bedroom. Affixed to the wall beside the bed was a small new electric bell. Dropping from the bell to the floor was a long ribbon of wire. Jack was busily leading this wire along the baseboard, securing it with staples. He looked up at me and grinned.

"I really expected you sooner."

"What is that thing?"

"It's a burglar alarm. Next time—if there is a next time—anyone breaks into the cellar I'll know it." Jack's grin vanished to leave an expression almost terrifyingly serious. "There's been too much talking in this case. Lola. Talk always means leaks. I want this—this trap of mine kept strictly between us two. Then there'll be no leaks. Particularly," he said, "I don't want Annabelle Bayne to find out."

I agreed with him. Many times since I have wondered whether the coming events would have been changed in their course if I hadn't been so scrupulously careful not to mention our burglar alarm.

Jack carried his operations on into the cellar, and summoned me to hold a flashlight. Moving along in the semi-gloom he awkwardly nailed the length of wire to the overhead beams. He cut it off at the cellar door. I have no clear comprehension of electrical appliances, but I realized that the small oval copper plate which Jack fastened over the raw ends of the wire must be the contact. A tiny, loosely joined copper crossbar was then screwed to the door frame in such a position that the parallel arm of the cross tilted to touch the copper plate when it met resistance. The opening of the door, of course, would furnish the resistance.

Slicing into the main stem of the wire, Jack grafted on an offshoot and carried it to the cellar window, where he arranged a second electrical device. We were now, in his opinion, adequately protected against unannounced and unwelcome visitors. With a contented sigh he turned to me. "Let's try it out. You run up to the bedroom while I go outside and shove up the window and open the door. It should work."

It did work. Hardly had I taken my position before the entire cottage exploded into sound. High, shrill, ear-splitting—like the scream of a locomotive in the night. Jack came rushing up. "My God, that would wake the dead." An hour's tinkering and a dozen tests eventually reduced the bell to a volume sufficient to wake us and insufficient to alarm a possible intruder.

Jack firmly twisted the final screw. "Not bad—if I do say so myself. From now on, Lola, I sleep at my post like a fireman." He then produced and examined the gun which Harkway had lent to him. He smiled grimly. He has had experience on clay-pigeon ranges at Coney Island and fancies himself as quite a shot. He slipped the gun and flashlight beneath his pillow.

Our protection failed signally to improve my slumbers that night. Half a dozen times, certain that the bell was ringing and that hordes of intruders were congregated in the cellar, I started bolt upright only to sink back with the realization that I had been dreaming. It was a dark moonless night, very quiet. Not a leaf stirred outside, not a blade of grass.

Reuben was curled on an old coat near the bed. Occasionally in the darkness I would hear him whimper. Once he frightened me badly by leaping to the bed and attempting to crawl beneath the covers. I suppose that must have been his habit with Silas.

The slow hours wore away. I dreamed and roused and dreamed again. In the morning I looked thirty. "Tonight we leave a light burning," I announced at breakfast.

"And spoil everything?"

"You slept like a log. I didn't close my eyes."

"You'll sleep tonight."

I daresay no one can maintain a state of consistent terror. On the second night after the installation of our burglar alarm I retired at ten o'clock and didn't wake until eight a.m.

I was relieved and inclined to be a little caustic at Jack's expense. I know that he was disappointed. He had felt so sure that another attempt would be made to enter the cellar. Curiously enough it was at this point, and with the conclusion of our tragedies so close at hand, that he declared his belief that the mystery would never be solved.

"That suits me," I said. "I'm fed up with gumshoe work. I'm sick of the country and of theories and of policemen bobbing in and out of my life. I want to go back to New York." Jack said slowly, "I know how you feel. You've been a good sport, Lola. And it won't be long now. We're leaving soon."

"How soon?" I demanded suspiciously.

"Next week if you want to. I saw Standish this morning when I went down for the papers. He said we could get out of Crockford on Monday. Regardless of whether Elliott turns up."

I gave a cry of joy. "Why not now? I'd love to pack and go in tomorrow."

"Try to contain yourself until Monday."

It was a gray, misty, sunless day calculated to increase my restlessness. The idea of New York took hold of me so that I couldn't concentrate on anything. I made biscuits for lunch and left out the baking powder. I didn't get my dusting done, and the carpetsweeper sat in the living room until nearly two o'clock. I did straighten the papers in my office, but any mental work was out of the question.

In the early afternoon I heard Dr. Rand's ancient car passing on the road, and recognized at once the distinctive engine noises—a weird combination of a hiss and a chortle. I ran to the window and rapped on the pane. The physician alighted and came in.

"You young folks look too healthy to need my services."

I gleefully imparted our news. "We're going back to town next week. Jack just got word this morning. On Monday we'll be free as the air."

"Lola!" Jack looked annoyed. "I was asked not to mention our going."

The physician smiled. "I'm tight-mouthed as a clam. Why the secrecy anyhow? I wonder."

Jack shrugged. "I suppose it's a matter of pride. Once we leave, the whole village knows the investigation has blown sky-high. Until then we're the only ones who know that Standish is completely stymied."

"Don't deceive yourself," Dr. Rand said sharply. "Standish is slow and maybe a little stupid, but my guess is he's got something up his sleeve. I've thought so for some time." He yawned. "I'm not in his confidence any more. He's still miffed at me for holding back the Jane Coatesnash story—he called me an antisocial menace, said I was morally responsible for the Paris suicide. I daresay he's partially right, but it's a burden I'm glad to carry. Standish seems to feel that Mrs. Coatesnash would be better off coming home in chains, standing trial, facing imprisonment and maybe worse—better off that way than lying peacefully dead. I can't say I agree."

Pleading a long list of patients, the physician soon departed. Our boredom closed down again. We started a laggard game of double canfield. At four o'clock we had a surprise.

Annabelle Bayne made a call at the cottage.

She was dressed in black, that dead, dusty black which looks like mourning. She didn't wear a trace of rouge, and her white face with its pronounced lines and angles was stark as a primitive. I had neglected to send down her cigarette case, and she brusquely announced that she had come for it. I was too surprised that she had been permitted to come to be very tactful. I simply gaped at her.

"I can see," said Annabelle, "you're wondering how I broke out of prison. You Storms have transparent faces."

"Please—"

"The police force is probably in a dither now." She gave a mirthless little laugh. "At least I cost the county a little gas. I was followed from homeland it took me sixty miles to outwit a thick-skulled constable who had a faster car than mine. Now are you feeling easier?"

I said nothing. Jack said nothing. Annabelle sank to the lounge. "You can phone and report me if you like. I've had my fun."

She didn't look as though she were having fun. She stared hard into the fire and I knew it was to conceal the tears in her eyes. She was as remote, as rude, as deliberately mysterious as ever, but I pitied her. She turned.

"Well, where's my cigarette case? I mustn't neglect to remember my excuse for calling."

"It's in the bedroom."

She rose and started there. It was Annabelle's habit always to make herself at home wherever she happened to be. Jack managed to stop her at the door. Sharp as her eyes were, she had not, I am certain, glimpsed our makeshift burglar alarm. Jack brought out the cigarette case.

"Why did you come?"

She glanced from him to me. "I meant to tell you how much I hated you, but now I'm here I'm softening." Her lips twisted. "Some day you will learn the harm your meddling's done. Some day very soon."

Her manner invited no questioning; it was impossible to enter a defense to an accusation so oblique. She was referring somehow to Franklyn Elliott, but I couldn't say I hoped their affairs would straighten out when I felt quite sure they never would. Outside, a light breeze suddenly became a stiff wind. A shutter banged against the window. Jack started the radio.

Annabelle listened tensely. "Is that a short-wave set? Can you get police calls?"

Jack shook his head.

"It doesn't matter." She forced herself to shrug. "I know they are still broadcasting Frank's description." She ended almost like a person speaking to himself: "Frank has been gone four days now. It seems much longer."

"You—" Jack hesitated "—you could help if you would. Are you quite determined to wait out the week?"

"If the little—the very little—I have to say would help the police find Franklyn Elliott," she replied fiercely, "I would have said it. Why should I speak prematurely—perhaps endanger his life—merely to satisfy your curiosity?"

Her hostility stood between us like a stone wall. Outside, the breeze was freshening and clouds were scudding along the sky. We sat in slowly growing tension. Annabelle smoked many cigarettes. She was in a crackling state of nerves. She talked rapidly, pointlessly, and her sentences ran together. At length, abruptly, she rose.

"I have some news that might interest you self-appointed sleuths," she said in parting. "Luella's body arrives in Crockford some time next week. I thought you'd want to know."

The callousness with which she spoke echoed an earlier manner, the manner in which she had referred to the suicide. Yet where Franklyn Elliott's safety was concerned she showed the deepest feeling. Once she had shown feeling for Luella Coatesnash. I remembered the day of the inquest when, in court, she had defended her old friend ardently, violently and to her own great danger. Annabelle dropped the cigarette case into her bag.

"Bromley is preparing now to receive the body. The funeral will probably be the biggest this town has ever seen." She wound up in a curious way, "That funeral, if nothing else does, may clear the air."

On this elusive note she left. She refused to permit Jack to escort her to her car. She declined to stay for supper, although we urged her strongly.

"I must get home. I'm terrified of thunderstorms and this one is going to be a lulu."

Her prediction was correct. She had hardly stepped outside before the storm crashed down. Wind howled in the trees; a loose shutter whirled from the roof and struck in the yard. There was the sharp imminent smell of rain in the air. Jack started hurriedly closing doors and windows. With Reuben at my heels I rushed out to call Annabelle back. Her car was already gone from the drive.

I was returning to the house when Reuben seized the opportunity to run across the road. I shouted at him, but he ignored my command, slipped under the pasture gate and made a beeline up the hill toward the Lodge. Poor dog, he, too, was terrified of thunderstorms and the dreary little dwelling still meant home to him. I shouted again, then started in pursuit. The rain was just beginning. A few heavy liquid drops struck upon my bare head, but I thought absurdly that I had time to capture Reuben and regain the cottage. My mistake was brought home to me an instant later. Suddenly the wind increased to gale velocity; there was a deafening clap of thunder; lightning jumped across the sky, and as if by signal the rain poured down. Yards ahead Reuben gave a terrified yelp, scudded off the path and took refuge on the open back porch of the Lodge. Angry and annoyed, drenched to the skin, I joined him there.

A part of the porch, equipped as the dairy room, was partially sheltered by a lattice to which clung dead morning-glory vines. Whimpering, Reuben crawled behind a pile of milk cans and pressed himself against the wall. I squeezed between a cream separator and an electric ice box—oversize because Silas had stored there Mrs. Coatesnash's milk and cream—and began to wring out my soaked clothing.

The dead vines like frantic castanets beat against the lattice, and the whole place was damp, dark, unutterably dreary. Water seeped across the plank flooring and blew in streamers through the crevices. Like Reuben, I pressed farther back against the wall. My eyes were fixed upon the world outside. A world of blackness, wind and rain. Something—I don't know what—made me turn. There was a window just beside me, a window which looked into the kitchen of the deserted Lodge. I glanced through it.

I went cold all over.

Inside in the darkness someone struck a match. A brief flare which flickered and then went out.

I screamed.

Someone called, but my vocal cords were too paralyzed to permit of any answer. I couldn't move or speak or think. I don't know who I thought was moving inside the Lodge. Silas perhaps looking, just as he once had looked—or Silas's murderer wearing a blood-stained suit, smiling a sleepy, murderous smile. The door leading from the kitchen to the porch opened, and John Standish stood blinking bewilderedly about. He had a flashlight in his hand. Another man peered over his shoulder.

My paralysis of fright evaporated into weak and stupefied relief. But still I couldn't speak. Eventually Standish's flashlight picked me out.

"Mrs. Storm! You—what are you doing here?"

Then at once he came to me, took my arm and pulled me into the dry, dark kitchen. He set his flashlight on the table so that it served as a sort of lamp. He jerked a blanket from a bed in the other room and wrapped it around my shoulders, clucking at the foolishness of young people who don't know enough to come in out of the rain. He introduced his companion as William Hardisty, a local lawyer who had been designated to take charge of Mrs. Coatesnash's scrambled affairs. Mr. Hardisty, a methodical, fussy little man, was plainly astounded at my appearance and seemed more than half inclined to make something faintly illegal of it. Standish kept up a flow of bantering talk until, eventually, I smiled. He, too, smiled.

"I'm sorry we gave you such a turn. We were caught here ourselves. Maybe you'd like a cigarette?"

I gratefully accepted. Mr. Hardisty continued standoffish. While Standish and I enjoyed a companionable cigarette and while I began to laugh at my late fears, the little lawyer pottered about, listing the furnishings of the Lodge for the purposes of an eventual tax assessment. I believe he termed his activities "protecting the interests of Mrs. Coatesnash's heirs." Under the circumstances and with the storm roaring outside, his neat busyness struck me as ridiculous, and I daresay he read my thoughts, for he gave me an occasional cold, suspicious glance. Finally Standish said:

"What did bring you up the hill, Mrs. Storm?"

It was only then that I remembered Reuben, and somewhat conscience-stricken went to the door to summon him. A gust of wind and rain blew inside. Despite my urgent calls, Reuben refused to stir, and Standish plowed out after him. Mr. Hardisty followed. Reuben stuck stubbornly behind the milk cans until Standish's impatient hand hauled him forth.

The little dog huddled on the floor before the ice box. The hairs on his neck bristled. Through the sound of wind and rain came the ominous growl in his throat. A growl which rose and kept on rising.

Standish frowned. "What's got into the dog anyway?"

"It's the ice box," said Hardisty. "It's something about the ice box."

Standish was staring at the great white refrigerator. His flashlight shone on its polished surface.

He said in a queer voice, "I hadn't noticed that refrigerator before. I wonder what the trays are doing on the floor?"

I saw the trays then. The refrigerator was an electric model—one of Mrs. Coatesnash's real extravagances. The metal trays made to hold squares of ice and the wire fittings fashioned to cut off the interior into separate compartments lay in a scrambled heap under the cream separator.

"We never touched that ice box," Standish said.

He spoke like a man in a dream. He took a slow step, grasped the handle of the heavy metal door before him, and then said in a voice that changed swiftly, hideously:

"Don't look, Mrs. Storm!"

But I had looked. As the catch of the door was unloosed, pressure from behind forced it forward and Franklyn Elliott's body sagged outward and to the floor.

The lawyer had been shot four days earlier. He had been shot through the back and had died instantly.

CHAPTER TWENTY-ONE

The Triple Murderer

The car in which Standish and Hardisty had driven to the Coatesnash estate was parked beneath the porte-cochere of Hilltop House. Battling the storm, Standish carried me there. Hardisty, terrified at his precipitation into tragedy, remained in charge of Franklyn Elliott's body. I can still recall his frightened protestations, the last glimpse of his pale face peering after us. Of the wild ride down the hill I recall nothing whatever.

Jack met us at the door of the cottage, took one look at me and without a word or question lifted me into his arms and bundled me off to bed. Standish saw me safely settled, and then left at once.

I remember and cherish his parting pat on my arm, his admonition that I wasn't in any way to blame myself. There was no reference to my account of having seen Franklyn Elliott flee from the Lodge, no suggestion that a wiser, less prejudiced witness might have realized that a glimpse of a man's car is not a glimpse of the man himself. The truth—the truth I hadn't grasped four days before—at least in part was clear. Franklyn Elliott, his motives still obscured in mystery, had gone to the Lodge and had there surprised, red-handed, the murderer of Silas Elkins.

No other conclusion was possible. Elliott's movements on that sunlit afternoon were at last apparent. As was customary with all of us, the lawyer had left his car in the driveway up the hill and walked down to the Lodge on foot. He had telephoned Silas. He was expected; he doubtless knocked at the door and then pushed in. He must have seen—in that first, appalled moment of entrance—far too much. He must have seen a murderer stooping over a blood-filmed pail of water, swabbing with a wet towel at crimson stains. Probably he cried out, probably he turned to run. At any rate he paid for his arrival there with his life.

Whatever disposition the killer had intended to make of Elliott's body—we believe now that he planned that the lawyer's body would be found in his abandoned car—was upset by my advent on the scene. There was no time for anything then. No time to finish washing the walls and floors of the incarnadined living room, no time to sweep up the broken crockery, barely time in which to lift Elliott's body and start with it through the kitchen toward the back path which led to safety and the yellow car.

The murderer's situation was desperate. To the original murder of Hiram Darnley there had been added two others—the murder of Silas, who was on the point of disclosing the whole murky dark conspiracy, and then, swiftly following, the murder of the New York lawyer who had opened a door, and in so doing had signed his own death warrant.

When the killer set foot on the back porch I must have been very close to the Lodge. My approach on the front path could be clearly seen from that porch. And Franklyn Elliott was a heavy man. The whole murderous structure was about to collapse. Burdened with Elliott's body, the killer could never reach the car or make good an escape. The ice box, swept free of its trays, offered a solution. Here again chance entered into the case, and played into the killer's hands. Elliott's absence, coupled with the accident that no one had happened to investigate that open back porch, had deceived us utterly. We had believed, all of us except Annabelle Bayne, that Franklyn Elliott himself was our murderer.

There were blank spots in the picture—questions which even the finding of Elliott's body did not answer for us. Elliott's own behavior remained inexplicable. We did not know why he had broken into the cottage, what he had discovered which had sent him to his death at the Lodge, or why he had failed to share his information with the police. Least of all did we understand Annabelle Bayne. She had been terrified for her lover's safety; during those four days of his disappearance she must have envisioned just such an end as he had met, yet she, too, had refused to talk with the police.

I lay on my bed as I thought of these things. I drank the hot milk which Jack brought me, obediently swallowing the sedative he produced from the medicine chest.

"Try not to think, dear," he said to me once. "Try to sleep."

In my condition sleep was an impossibility. Outside, the storm had taken on renewed life, as if further to banish sleep. A whirlwind was loose in the world that night. Everything that could blow or rattle or shriek was in motion. The noise of the thunder was deafening and each clap was followed by a flash of lightning which turned the bedroom a fierce and vivid blue. Jack stayed close beside me.

At exactly nine o'clock every light in the house went out. A bad storm almost always resulted in an abrupt and prolonged cessation of our electric power. I knew by previous experiences that there would be no more electricity until morning, and I began to weep. Jack tried to comfort me, then handed me the flashlight and went off to search for candles. The bedroom floor slanted as floors slant in most old houses, and I can recall now the moment when the highboy rolled majestically from one corner to the other. That was just as Jack returned with the candles, and I responded with a fit of violent hysterics.

Eventually Jack quieted me, and for a long time sat beside the bed, saying an occasional soothing word, holding my hand in his. After a while the sedative commenced to work. I was drowsy when the telephone rang, and Jack gently disengaged his hand to step into the other room. When he came back a few minutes later, I was already half asleep, my brain almost wholly stupefied. I didn't at once take in the information that Annabelle Bayne was missing.

"She must be home," I said stupidly. "She started there hours ago-

"She didn't go home. That was Standish calling." Jack stepped closer to the bed. "I hate like hell to bother you, Lola, but she's got to be found. Immediately. She—she may be in deadly danger. You went after her when the storm broke. Did you notice which direction her car was headed?"

"I didn't see the car at all." I roused to a vague, drug-laden surprise. "And I remember looking toward the road. She made a fast getaway."

Jack was regarding me oddly. "I believe," he said slowly, "that Annabelle came here on foot. I let her in this afternoon, and I'm almost sure her car wasn't in the drive then. She couldn't have walked from far; she must have left her car parked somewhere close. If we know where she left the car, and why she left it.

I was beyond the point of mental activity, beyond the point of anxiety or wonder. I was indeed only fretfully conscious that Jack had again quit the room to telephone to Standish. Of the long worried conversation which took place between them I had no knowledge. I slept the heavy, unrefreshing sleep of the drugged...

I woke suddenly. The bedside candle was flickering, and the room was filled with a kind of noiseless bustle. Everything seemed strangely still. The tumult outside had lessened, although the rain poured steadily, softly down and dripped through a window Jack had been unable to force entirely shut. Reuben was curled beside me, his nose cold on my shoulder. I was sleepily pushing him away when I became aware of the sound which had aroused me.

A low, monotonous buzzing which ceased even as I identified it. The burglar alarm!

"Jack," I whispered I reached for his hand, sat up. I knew then that he had gone. He had taken with him the revolver he kept beneath the pillow.

The night stands forth in my memory as a phantasmagoria of confusion and ascending horror. I remember chiefly the small, agonizing details. I recall that I seized the candle, dropped it and in anguish saw the light plunge out. I groped for matches, found none, stumbled over Reuben on my way toward the door.

In the living room I discovered a box of matches, but before I had lighted the candle an uproar commenced in the cellar. Something went over with a terrific crash. I heard three shots fired in rapid succession, heard the shatter of glass, the thud of a heavier object. It sounded exactly as though a man had run amuck; but I knew there were at least two persons in the cellar and that one of them was Jack.

How I got down the stairs I can't explain, any more than I can explain why I didn't fall headlong in my haste. Somewhere en route I lighted the candle, and its yellow, unsteady rays illumined the devastated cellar. The window over the coal had been jimmied, and lumps of coal were strewn wildly about. A dresser lay on its side; the ash can was overturned, and beside it lay a man's dark felt hat. The signs of furious combat were present, but there was no one in the place. Where Jack had gone was plain enough. The cellar door stood open and rain dashed in.

I rushed outside. Instantly my candle was doused and with it my sense of direction vanished. I was lost utterly in my own back yard. The wind whipped my night clothes and drowned out the sound of my voice. I rushed blindly toward what I thought was the road. I stumbled; someone seized me, and I screamed like a maniac.

Jack's voice said, "Lola! That you?"

He was kneeling in the yard, and as I remember it he rose, shook me savagely and said, "Stop screaming! Stop it, I say. You've got to help me get her inside."

"Her? Who?"

"Annabelle Bayne. I'm afraid she's badly hurt."

I was only then aware of the crumpled figure lying in the sodden grass. Jack again stooped. "She's coming around, I think. Let's get going." He lifted the unconscious woman into his arms, bade me hang on to him, and through the pouring rain guided us back into the cellar. I was moving like an automaton. I had no idea what had happened, and even after Jack had picked up from the floor a fallen flashlight and directed it on Annabelle Bayne's pale face and the ugly stain on her shoulder, I supposed she had attempted to murder him.

I said, "Are you all right? I heard her shooting at you."

"Shooting at me!" Jack swept a litter of objects from a broken couch and laid Annabelle there. "She wasn't shooting at me, Lola. As it happens, she saved my life. Here, you chafe her hands—I'll go upstairs for whisky."

Hardly breathing, Annabelle Bayne lay white and motionless, more defenseless than I had ever seen her. I removed the small black hat which still clung tightly to her head, straightened out her clothing, unloosed her soaked and blood-stained blouse. She had been shot through the shoulder, and the wound was slowly bleeding. I tried to staunch it.

Jack returned with whisky and a pile of blankets. "How's she doing now? Hold up the flashlight, will you? I want to see that shoulder." He leaned over the couch. "By God, it doesn't look serious. I believe she's only fainted."

As if to verify his quick, intense relief, Annabelle stirred, shuddered, opened her eyes. She looked blankly at us—at me with the flashlight in my hand, at Jack who held out a glass of whisky to her.

Jack said, "Get that down."

She accepted the glass obediently, drank, shuddered again, half rose only to sink back again. She whispered. "I remember now. I had the killer trapped when you came crashing down the stairs. What happened? Did he get away?"

"Clean," Jack said. "I don't know yet who he was. Do you?"

She said, "No."

Her dark, questing eyes moved involuntarily to the jimmied window and the heap of coal beneath it. I turned the flashlight. I saw then what I had not seen before. Someone had shoveled deep into the coal, tossed aside a great pile, and a spade stood upright in a hole which tunneled the dirt floor beneath.

"I suppose," said Annabelle, "the bag went with him."

"What bag?" I asked.

No one answered. Jack had darted past the heaped up coal and seized the spade. Like a woman in a dream, I watched him begin to dig. Dirt flew helter-skelter. The hole deepened with a swiftness which announced that the hard-packed earth had been previously disturbed. Suddenly the spade met resistance, thudded, stuck. Jack dropped to his knees and commenced clawing with his hands.

"It's here!" he cried to Annabelle Bayne.

From the excavation he hauled forth a leather Gladstone traveling bag, its handle moist and clamp, but its hardware bright, unrusted, almost new. The Gladstone bag was initialed, the gilt was only slightly discolored and the letters showed plainly. *F. E.* I repeated the letters to myself a second time before I comprehended their significance. *F. E.*

I said bewilderedly, "That's Franklyn Elliott's bag."

"Of course," Jack said. "Elliott buried it in the cellar a week ago. Don't you understand, Lola? That's why he broke into the cottage. To leave the bag." Jack glanced at Annabelle. "Did he tell you? Was he instructed to bury it in our cellar?"

She said, "Yes."

Those two—Jack and Annabelle Bayne—shared a comprehension in which I had no part. I stared at them and waited. Jack slowly unfastened the catches of the Gladstone bag and pulled back the lid. Money cascaded to the floor. Ten, twenty, fifty-dollar bills—$108,000 in bills—the identical amount which Hiram Darnley had carried and concealed in a similar bag. Jack kicked at the fluttering currency.

He said in a tired way, "The only thing that's left to do at this point is to call the police. And—" he tried to smile at Annabelle—"you'll need Dr. Rand's attentions."

"The doctor," said Annabelle, "can wait. I'm not in pain. As for the police, what can they do now?"

I said loudly, "You two—both of you—know something I don't know. I think I'm going crazy. What's the money for? Why did Elliott hide it here?"

"The money," Jack said, "was raised for ransom. First Hiram Darnley raised and attempted to pay it over. The conspiracy went haywire and he was murdered. Then Elliott was contacted and he too…"

Jack broke off.

"Go on," said Annabelle in a hard, contained voice. Her eyes were dry, direct, steady. "I know Frank's dead. I've known it all along, really, but I wouldn't—I couldn't believe it until—until this afternoon." Tears welled up in the brilliant eyes, but she stubbornly restrained their fall. "I've been down here since afternoon. I didn't leave your place at all. I hoped—never mind what I hoped. Anyhow I heard what went on upstairs."

She said nothing of the terrible vigil spent crouched in the jelly closet while the storm raged outside, nothing of the thoughts and sensations which crowded in her mind and heart when she learned that her lover had been brutally done to death. Nor did we.

"Let's move upstairs," Jack said at last. "Lola and I can carry you." He sighed. "It's such a ghastly mess. Why, in God's name, didn't Elliott go to the police?"

"Because he was afraid they'd kill her. After Darnley's murder, he couldn't take the risk. He was determined to get her back alive."

"Get who back alive?" I said.

"Luella Coatesnash."

I gasped. "But Mrs. Coatesnash *is* dead. She killed herself in Paris."

"She may be dead," said Annabelle, "but she didn't kill herself in Paris. She never went there."

Jack interrupted. "Mrs. Coatesnash was kidnapped, Lola, kidnapped on the night the *Burgoyne* sailed. Another woman who resembled her in coloring and build sailed instead, used Mrs. Coatesnash's passport, went to a grimy little hotel where the old lady wasn't known…"

"Laura Twining!"

"Who else? Laura impersonated Mrs. Coatesnash till the going got too thick, then killed herself. Silas, who was also implicated, tried to confess his own part in the conspiracy and was murdered for his pains. Only the killer—the third person in the plot and the one real criminal—gets off scot-free."

Annabelle beat one clenched hand upon her knee. "It's too late now," she said. "We've muffed it. I'm tough, but I hate to think of that poor old woman, if she isn't dead already. Can't you see her? Waiting, watching, hoping… That's where the killer's gone, of course. To finish off Luella. There'll be no third attempt to collect a ransom."

A chair crashed to the cellar floor. Jack knocked it over in his wild rush toward the door. "I know where Mrs. Coatesnash is! Where she's been held since February!"

He ran into the yard. I reached him as he leaped into the car, managed to climb in with him. The rain was over, but the driveway was like a miniature ocean. Splashing water in torrents, we raced to the road, turned, sped around the hill and roared into the circular drive before Hilltop House.

"She's inside!" Jack cried. "She's got to be! It all fits—the lights, Silas, Laura's baggage—everything!" He jumped from the car. "You stay here. Lola."

I alighted at once, and so great was his nervous tension that he didn't notice. When I said, "Have you got your gun?" he snapped at me, "Naturally."

A dozen steps carried us to the house. The porch was pitch black, carpeted with dead, soaked leaves, unpleasant underfoot. Jack preceded me lightly, soundlessly to the great front door. Just how he planned to force an entrance I don't know. I remember my own hysterical suggestion that we should have brought an ax.

"For God's sake, be quiet!"

Jack struck a match and in the flickering illumination, with a spurt of renewed terror, I saw that the front door was wide open. What was left of it. The set-in oval glass was cracked, and a splintered panel and shattered lock showed evidences of violent assault. A pool of rain water glistened from the foyer. I knew then that the kidnapper was in the house or had been there, and it seemed impossible that Luella Coatesnash should be alive.

Jack was already inside, and starting up the stairs. I went after him. The vaulted hallway was inky black, and quiet as the grave. It was not until we gained the second floor that someone moved on the floor above. Simultaneously I smelled smoke.

Jack caught my wrist in a vise-like grip. "He's set fire to the house."

At that moment a shot was fired down the stair well. An invisible mirror broke with a tinkle of glass. A second bullet whizzed by and plaster showered upon us. The kidnapper stood at the head of the stairs, and considering the total darkness his aim was excellent. I screamed. Jack knocked me to the floor, and I slid five steps to the second landing. A third shot was fired, this time from Jack's gun. He vaulted up the stairs.

Abruptly the shooting stopped. Overhead, on the third floor, I heard the impact of two bodies, a savage yell, then the confused, muffled sounds of close-in fighting. A gun angled through the air and hit in the foyer. Whether Jack's gun or the killer's gun, I had no way of knowing.

The smoke was thicker; it was pouring down the stair well and far off and above me, someone—a woman—was shrieking. Muffled, hideous, horror-stricken shrieks. I crawled to my feet and staggered toward the third floor, only to be knocked down again as Jack and his murderous adversary crashed past me to the second landing.

Coughing, weaving, I clung to the third-floor balustrade. I was conscious of brilliant, dancing light some time before I identified the source of it. A bonfire—wastepaper, rags and the like—blazed in the open hall at the foot of the ladder which led to the attic. The fire was small, but the ladder had started to char. Clouds of stifling smoke beat against the locked trap door from behind which came those hideous screams.

Tears streaming from my eyes, I tore up the hallway carpet and choked out the fire. The gesture was purely automatic. I neither saw nor felt my blistered hands.

My next move was similarly automatic. A flashlight which had fallen during the previous melee lay upon the scorched floor, throwing a beam of light across my feet. I snatched it, and ran to the second-floor landing. The fight still raged there—two men, struggling fiercely, locked in desperate embrace. I made out Jack's blond head, and brought the flashlight—my only weapon—down upon the other darker head. The dark head sagged. But Jack hadn't seen me. The unexpected flank attack caused him to release his hold. His victim slipped his grasp and rolled down the stairs. Jack shouted:

"Duck, Lola. He's got the gun."

He had the gun, indeed.

A second later he used it—upon himself. A single shot, followed by a hiccoughing sigh, followed then by silence. Our triple murderer was dead before we reached him.

"Hand me the flashlight, Lola," Jack said.

With a faint surprise I realized that I still held the flashlight. I gave it over. Jack turned the narrow finger of light upon the dead man, and I looked into Lester Harkway's face.

CHAPTER TWENTY-TWO

Homeward Bound

The rest, to coin a phrase, is history.

Standish gives us credit for the solution of the mystery, and personally I feel that we deserve it even though I must confess that I didn't anticipate the astounding denouement. Until the moment when I looked into Lester Harkway's still and strangely peaceful face, it had never once occurred to me that he might be our killer. The signs were there to read—his presence on the Post Road the night we delivered Hiram Darnley from New Haven, his interest in the "burglary" of the cellar, his professed anxiety and subtle, insistent suggestion that we abandon the cottage, even the strange way he had eyed that coal which had been dumped squarely upon the spot where, as he knew, Franklyn Elliott had buried the second ransom money.

The gun which he lent to Jack as a "protective" measure was a final bit of insolence. That gun was loaded with blanks, as Jack would have discovered, had he examined it carefully. At every turn Harkway took advantage of our trusting credulity.

In a sense, even now, I feel we were hardly to blame for the many things we didn't see. As Standish said later on. "A conspiracy is the hardest crime in the world to uncover." He smiled soberly and added, "Also it is the most difficult crime to maintain."

To this our own experience testifies.

The conspiracy to kidnap Luella Coatesnash had hardly been set into motion by our three plotters—Silas, Laura, and Harkway—before it fell to pieces. It fell to pieces when Lester Harkway—at the cost of one murder—attempted to cut out his confederates and seize for himself the $108,000 which Hiram Darnley carried in our car. Unfortunately for him, the double-crosser got possession of the wrong bag.

I sometimes try to visualize that moment when Harkway opened the bag, bought so dearly, and saw its worthless contents. He had risked everything and come off with another man's laundry. I cannot visualize and will never understand his cool and ruthless nerve. By prearranged plan—or so we believe—the policeman followed our car from New Haven, watching the passenger who rode upright and defenseless in the rumble seat. Hiram Darnley was bound for our cottage, where Silas awaited him, prepared to take over the ransom money. But that meant a three-way split--and a three-way split was something which Lester Harkway had decided to prevent.

He saw his chance when Jack began to speed the car. He stopped us, engaged in the three-cornered dispute, and then, immediately we got under way again, he shot Darnley and seized the bag in the seat beside him. It was a terrible gamble, but it worked. Our windows were closed, and the sound of our motor combined with the pop-pop of the policeman's motorcycle prevented our hearing the shot. We drove into Crockford with a dead man as our passenger.

Even then we might have guessed. But, on Main Street, Blair picked up the exploded automatic shell which fixed the murder in Crockford and removed from our minds any suspicion of the true facts. The presence of that shell when examined closely, and Standish did examine it closely, proved relatively simple. After the discovery of his hideous blunder, after he had discarded the worthless bag, Harkway returned to the spot where the murder had occurred and recovered the shell. When Standish telephoned for him, he carried the tell-tale bit of metal into the village, and casually dropped it for Blair to find.

Lest this recapitulation sound too sure, I hasten to add that we have positive evidence on the point. In the first place, markings on the shell matched precisely markings on other shells fired from Harkway's service gun. This use of the service gun is curious in itself and another instance of Harkway's almost fanatic indifference to his own safety, for Standish informs me that police officials must report the disposition of every bullet fired. Just what sort of report Harkway would have made of the bullet fired into Franklyn Elliott's back I'm not prepared to say, but his official record for March 20th shows that he killed "a brown rat" in his own back yard.

Standish, characteristically thorough, wasn't satisfied with the knowledge that the bullet which killed Hiram Darnley was fired from Harkway's gun. He inserted in local papers appeals for interviews with people who had driven to New Haven on the night of March 20th. Here he had a piece of luck.

A Mr. and Mrs. Abramson came forward. March 20th was Mrs. Abramson's birthday, and the couple had driven to New Haven to celebrate the anniversary. On the trip there both of them had observed a policeman with a flashlight—they identified Harkway from photographs—searching the road at the point where the tragedy occurred. Mrs. Abramson had actually seen Harkway pick up and pocket something which she was ready to swear was an exploded automatic shell. Since the Abramson car didn't stop, her testimony would seem to be on the positive side, although Standish, who immediately tested her eyesight, found it very good.

At any rate, Mrs. Abramson satisfied us all as to Harkway's means of shifting the scene of the crime from the place where it occurred to a public street in Crockford.

The first crime, then—the murder of Hiram Darnley—in every detail is clear to us. Method, motive, opportunity—we can reconstruct them all. A blank period follows, a period we can never hope to fathom, since every actor in it is dead. We can only guess at Laura's frantic thoughts when she learned that Darnley had been murdered, that the plot had gone awry, that instead of the security she longed for she was faced with the electric chair. Our only testimony is the affidavit of a French chambermaid to the effect that "the lady seemed low in her mind."

Silas and his thoughts during that same interval are similarly obscure. He had grabbed a tiger by the tail—on the one hand was Lester Harkway, of whom he was in mortal terror; on the other was Mrs. Coatesnash, held prisoner in the attic of her own home and in his custody. If he freed the old lady she would instantly expose him, for it was Silas who had forcibly brought her back from New York City to Hilltop House. During those days when he lost weight visibly and jumped at shadows, Silas guarded Luella Coatesnash, fed her, kept her heavily drugged, and slowly approached his own breaking point. I am sure on the afternoon Standish and I made our futile tour of Hilltop House, he was close to a complete confession. He was close to it when Standish picked up the broken hypodermic needle and drew the wrong conclusions; and, when the policeman decided against a search of the attic, I believe the hired man was more disappointed than relieved. He wanted, I am convinced, to have the decision removed from his own hands.

It seems certain that neither he nor Laura ever contemplated murder. Darnley's death struck terror in them, and brought with it the bitter knowledge that they were merely pawns in Harkway's larger game. They must have comprehended perfectly the motive which caused Harkway to upset the original scheme, for thereafter, all the evidence goes to show, they acted in unison with him only to save their own necks. Thus, before panic and desperation drove her to suicide, Laura continued to send the cables signed with Mrs. Coatesnash's name; and Silas worked both with and against the man he hated. He was playing Harkway's game—and God knows with what aversion and reluctance—when he obliterated the traces left after Jack's and my midnight foray into the Coatesnash grounds.

It was Lester Harkway, of course, with whom I struggled in the storeroom. I often wonder, with a shudder of reminiscent fear, that he didn't kill me on the spot. I daresay he felt too secure to think it necessary, and the chilling memory of his low soft chuckle in the darkness would seem to confirm the belief.

He outwitted us at every turn that night. He spirited Laura's baggage from the storeroom, confident that we would guess—not impersonation— but that Laura herself had been murdered. More important, he prevented any examination of that sunken plot in the rock garden. Ivan, the mastiff, was buried there, Ivan who had been returned from New York with his mistress and promptly killed. Had either Jack or I glimpsed the dog's body, I am sure we would have guessed the truth. For Ivan supposedly was in Paris with Mrs. Coatesnash!

But we didn't see the mastiff's body; it was cremated in the furnace, and the fragment of bone we found there merely bewildered us. A bit of canine bone didn't suggest Ivan to us, and I remember that I even wondered whether Dr. Rand might not have distorted the analysis for some reason of his own. After all, he had withheld other vital information from the police.

I admitted this to the physician on our last day in Crockford, and he responded with a roar of laughter which subsided as he said:

"That makes us even, young lady, for I certainly thought your husband was a suspicious character. He looked it; he acted it; he had a dead man in his car; the dead man carried a pile of money, and your husband—" he paused and added with a straight lace "—your husband was a needy artist. All in all, that's a pretty telling case."

"I can see it is," I said stiffly.

Everyone laughed at me. It was a soft and tender April day; the doors and windows of the cottage stood open to receive the spring; and, as I remember it, our packed, strapped luggage was awaiting removal to the car. It was the last time our little group was to gather there. Standish had come to escort us to the hospital where Luella Coatesnash was recovering from her terrible experiences, and he had brought with him Annabelle Bayne. Annabelle's shoulder was bandaged, and her eyes were shadowed, but she looked better than I had seen her look in many weeks. The worst had happened to her; the terrible suspense was over; if she had nothing more to hope, she also had nothing more to fear.

I said uncomfortably, "I know, Annabelle, that you thought Jack and I were guilty."

"I thought," said Annabelle, "you were guilty of kidnapping, after I learned there had been a kidnapping."

I was surprised. "You didn't know all along that Mrs. Coatesnash had been kidnapped?"

"Not at first. I played stupid like everyone else. It seems absurd now but I imagined that the old story—Jane's story—had reached Luella and that she had got together with Silas to kill Hiram Darnley. I saw Luella yesterday. As it happens, she doesn't know that miserable story yet—and I hope she never learns it—but that was my bird-brain reasoning at the time. Frank himself, in the beginning, thought that Luella had engineered Darnley's murder, after hieing herself to Paris."

"Those letters that came from Paris…" I ventured.

"The letters deceived me too," said Annabelle, "although they shouldn't have. Luella wrote the letters, all right, but she wrote them from the attic of Hilltop House. Then they were posted to Paris and Laura mailed them back here. It was a smart enough trick, but I should have seen through it. Luella was always a wretched correspondent, and I remember my amazement at receiving a half dozen letters. And their tone somehow struck me wrong. I suppose because they were dictated to her, and she simply put down what she was told."

"Then Darnley," said Jack curiously, "didn't tell Elliott what was going on?"

"No. Not a word. Frank was out of the city at the time Darnley came here, but I doubt he'd have spoken anyway. Judging from the various precautions he took, his alias and all the rest of it, he'd been thoroughly impressed with the fact that his trip must be kept absolutely secret." Annabelle paused, and a cloud crossed her face. "I know Frank was threatened with what would happen to Luella if he let out any hint of his efforts to ransom her. It was on the day of the inquest," she said slowly, "that Frank was contacted by the kidnappers."

"Contacted by Harkway!" said Standish in harsh interruption. "I talked to Mrs. Coatesnash yesterday, and although she was drugged and hazy a good deal of the time she remembers Silas arguing that point with Harkway, pleading with him."

"It hardly matters now," said Annabelle, with a flash of bitterness, "who was responsible." Very quietly she resumed her narrative. "Anyhow, Frank got this note signed by Luella—she even fingerprinted it—advising him that she was a prisoner and in deadly danger. The note ordered him to bring a hundred and eight thousand dollars to the Tally-ho Inn, and to wait there for a telephone call which would tell him what to do with it." The speaker smiled wanly. "Frank came; we talked the situation over—not too sanely you may imagine—and eventually we decided that Frank should stay here, await his second instructions, and try to catch the kidnappers if he could."

"At which point" said Jack dryly "you started in on me and Lola."

She colored faintly. "In a way, I suppose that's true. We suspected you and Lola. But it was only suspicion. Two other people we had cold to rights. One of them was Laura Twining. She *had* to be the woman in Paris. The second was Silas."

"Why Silas?"

"For a curious reason. Frank did go down to see the *Burgoyne* off, and reached the dock after the gangplank was up. He glimpsed the Coatesnash car, saw Silas at the wheel, and was astonished to see a woman huddled in the rear seat. He hopped out of his taxi, shouted, but the woman pulled down her veil and the car shot off."

I gasped. "Do you mean that Mrs. Coatesnash permitted the impersonation? It sounds like that."

Standish cleared his throat, "I can explain that. The poor old soul did authorize Laura's sailing in her place, and unwittingly made her abduction as easy as rolling off a log. She was hoodwinked by forged letters into believing that she was being taken to her daughter Jane. I've seen those letters—and I believe Laura forged them, copying from notes she probably found in Hilltop House. They were mailed from a small New Hampshire town, signed with Jane's name, and each one—there were only three—begged Mrs. Coatesnash to come secretly to this town to be reunited with her loving daughter." The policeman sighed. "No explanation was given for the need of secrecy, although some kind of disgrace was hinted at. But Mrs. Coatesnash wasn't the type of woman who would require an explanation. She thoroughly believed—and the three plotters knew that she believed—her daughter was alive."

The last fragment of our puzzle slipped into its proper place. I saw at last the explanation for Laura Twining's interest in the newspapers and in everything that had pertained to Jane Coatesnash. If she were to forge letters which would deceive even a credulous mother, she would need to possess an intimate knowledge of the girl.

Annabelle caught my eye and evidently read my thoughts, for she gave me a wanly reminiscent smile. "It all fits, doesn't it? You have an orderly mind, Lola, and should go far with it." But her tone removed any possible sting from her words, and told me that she had forgiven Jack and me our interference in what she had so valiantly considered her own affairs. Her own and Franklyn Elliott's.

When I reached for her hand, she mutely returned the pressure. Standish beamed at us in a benign and fatherly fashion, then stretched and rose. "It we're going to the hospital," he said regretfully, "we'd best be getting started. Mrs. Coatesnash isn't too spry yet and she turns in early. She'll want to see you folks before you leave."

I would willingly have avoided contact with Mrs. Coatesnash, since any expression of gratitude usually embarrasses me, and in my innocence I feared that the grim old woman might prove effusive. I might have spared myself anxiety.

Mrs. Coatesnash was still suffering from shock and undernourishment, but she had the type of personality which triumphs over bodily ills. She occupied her narrow hospital bed as though it were a throne, and the familiar dirty diamonds sparkled on her emaciated wrists and fingers. She greeted us with a regal wave of the hand, and a rather detailed complaint of the hospital service. Her room, she said and glared, was far too noisy. I felt at once relieved, amused and—so accusing was her glance—guilty.

Standish was flushed and confused. "The Storms came to tell you good-bye, Mrs. Coatesnash. They're leaving Crockford tomorrow."

"So I understand," said the lady.

Jack gave me a wicked grin, and said softly, "We felt we couldn't go until we had told you how much we had enjoyed our stay."

She took him with the utmost seriousness—she was never remarkable for humor—and said something vague about the cottage being a pleasant place to live.

Standish, who had pictured quite a different sort of meeting, by now was intensely irritated. "Mrs. Coatesnash," he said sternly, "have you forgotten my telling you that these young people saved your life? Risked their own to do it?"

"Forgotten!" she echoed, indignantly. "Certainly I had not forgotten. I was just about to say it was most kind of them. Most kind."

She extended one jeweled hand to me, another hand to Jack and gave us her belated and beneficent blessing. After a visible mental struggle, she even promised to mention us in her will.

"There now, Lola," Jack said a few minutes later, when we were safely in the hall and walking down the stairs, "you should be a very, very happy girl. Our future is so well provided for we can both quit working. Generous I call it. Most generous!"

We both burst out laughing. Standish emitted a few disgusted snorts, and then reluctantly joined in.

We reached our car. It was only four o'clock, and one of those magical afternoons in early spring when cold and darkness seem impossible. The sun was warm and beat down strongly.

Jack said suddenly, "How would you like to dine in New York tonight, Lola? I would. Let's do."

"Tonight?" I was startled. "But, Jack, I haven't paid the light and phone bills yet; I haven't…"

"Get in. We'll mail checks. Let's go now—this minute—right away."

"Our bags," I wailed, "are back in the cottage."

"We'll send for them."

"I'll send them to you," offered Standish, catching Jack's excitement and my own. "Be glad to. I'll get them off tomorrow."

I still hesitated, and Jack lifted me bodily into his arms and dropped me into the car. He pressed on the starter; the car shot forward and I had a confused glimpse of Standish's half smiling, half bewildered face. He waved.

We turned sharply, and I saw him no longer. The road ahead was wide and straight and filled with many other hurrying cars. I hardly noticed them. I was looking for a roadside sign. I found one.

It read: "New York—102 Miles."

Jack also had seen the sign. Simultaneously we smiled, and when Jack said, "The country is a nice place to visit," I chanted "but I wouldn't live there it you gave it to me!"